Singular Amours

Singular Amours

by
Edmond Thiaudière

Translated, annotated and introduced by
Brian Stableford

A Black Coat Press Book

ISBN 978-1-61227-730-1. First Printing. March 2018. Published by Black Coat Press, an imprint of Hollywood Comics.com, LLC, P.O. Box 17270, Encino, CA 91416.
Printed in the United States of America.

TABLE OF CONTENTS

Introduction

The collection of novellas *Trois amours singulières* by Edmond Thiaudière was originally published in Paris by La Librairie Illustrée in 1886; I cannot find any evidence of prior publication of any of the novellas contained therein, although the internal evidence of the texts suggests that one of them was written in the 1870s. The additional story added to the contents of the collection herein, "Le Statuaire américain," was presumably published in another periodical before being reprinted in *Semaine Littéraire* volume 168 no. 1 (1867) as a supplement to that collection's edition of Paul Féval's *Annette Laïs*. It was subsequently reprinted in the author's collection *Les Contes d'un éleveur de chimères* [Tales of a Breeder of Chimeras] (1902), an exceedingly scarce text, which, according to a review in the 5 December issue of *La Presse*, also contains three other closely-related "scientific fantasies," entitled "L'Enlaidisseur" [The Uglifier], "Changement de Corps" [A Change of Body]—indicated in another review in *Le Penseur* as a head-transplant story—and "L'Évaporé" [The Evaporated].

Edmond Thiaudière (1837-1930) is not one of the better-known contributors to the tradition of *roman scientifique* that developed rapidly in France in the latter part of the nineteenth century, but he made two other significant contributions to it in addition to *Trois amours singulières*. In the wake of the disastrous Franco-Prussian War of 1870-71, he wrote the longest and most flamboyantly imaginative of several swift French responses to that conflict imitating the narrative strategy of George T. Chesney's *The Battle of Dorking* (1871) in taking the form of a satirical account of future warfare. *La Dernière bataille, épopée prophétique de l'an 1909* [The Last Battle: A Prophetic Epic of the Year 1909] (1873), which pretended to be a translation from the German of *Die Letzte*

Schlacht by "Friedrich Stampf" (and is listed by some bibliographers under that fictitious name).

The author adopts a more radical satirical strategy than the other chroniclers of imaginary future wars of the early 1870s, as well as a more ambitious chronological reach. The story looks forward to the early twentieth century, when Europe is under the joint rule of Tsar Nicolas of Russia and the German Emperor Wilhelm III; the plot describes how war is precipitated when the daughter of the French king, Louis-Philippe III, refuses an offer of marriage from the Tsarevitch, and millions of people are killed before the slaughter prompts a general socialist revolution. It makes the author's pacifist political philosophy very clear—a philosophy that only intensified with time, especially in the wake of the Great War of 1914-18, and he was still campaigning vigorously on its behalf when he died, in his nineties.

Thiaudière followed up his pioneering future war story with the pamphlet *Voyages de Lord Humour: En Bubaterbro ou pays des jolis boeufs* [The Voyages of Lord Humour: In Bubaterbro; or, The Land of Lovely Cattle] (1874), which was in turn followed by the full-length novel *Voyages de Lord Humour; le pays des retrogrades: île de Servat-Abus* [The Voyages of Lord Humor: The Land of the Retrogades, the Island of Servat-Abus] (1876), featuring a narrator who is declared to be a direct descendent, via his mother, of the great voyager Lemuel Gulliver. Both stories are political satires, the latter including a scathing depiction of the history of France from the pre-Revolutionary Era to the fall of the Second Empire, as mirrored in the land of the worthy but none-too-bright cynocephali—dog-headed humans—whose empire is covertly manipulated by the wily fox-headed vulpiminois, a minority whose members are over-represented in politics, finance and the Church. A further report of Lord Humour's adventures in the isles of Foederia was promised but never materialized.

Edmond Thiaudière's father was a physician, as his grandfather great-grandfather and great-great-grandfather had been in the past, but he elected to break with family tradition in order to study law at the University of Poitiers. After qualifying for his licenciate in 1858, however, he opted instead for a career as a man of letters, contributing to numerous periodicals and publishing his first novel, *Un Prêtre en famille* [A Priest in the Family] in 1864. His mordant humor and radical views were already evident in such works as *L'Apprentissage de la vie, avec un dédicace à la Mort* [The Apprenticeship of Life, with a Dedication to Death] (1861 as by Edmond Thy), the poetry collection *Sauvagerie* [Savagery] and *Le Désaveu du Christ, poème* [The Disavowal of Christ, a Poem] (1869), before the war of 1870-71 sharpened his satirical wit even further.

Thiaudière would presumably have continued the adventures of Lord Humour had the first novel had more success in the marketplace, but his interests were also deflected in 1876, when he was a co-founder, and became the editor-in-chief, of the *Revue des idées nouvelles: Bulletin du progrès dans la philosophie, les sciences, les lettres, les arts, l'industrie, le commerce et l'agriculture* [Review of New Ideas: A Bulletin of Progress in Philosophy. the Sciences, Letters, the Arts, Industry, Commerce and Industry] which was one of several periodicals whose advent was occasioned by a boom in the popularization of knowledge that had begun in the previous decade, and which had already boosted the careers of such writers as Camille Flammarion, Henri de Parville and Jules Verne, while allowing the pioneering S. Henry Berthoud a late renewal of celebrity.

The *Revue des idées nouvelles,* as its subtitle indicated, cast its net very wide during the three years that it continued publication, but while he was its editor Thiaudière developed his particular interest in psychology, which was to become a central prop of much of his subsequent fiction, and he carefully nurtured a philosophy of pessimism akin to that of Arthur Schopenhauer, which he subsequently developed in a long series of essays published as pamphlets, under the general tile *Notes d'un pessimiste* [Notes of a Pessimist], beginning with

La Proie du Néant [The Prey of Nothingness] (1886) and eventually concluding with *La Vanité de Tout* [The Vanity of Everything] (1928)—advertised, somewhat optimistically, as the first of a new subseries.

Trois amours singulières is the most substantial fruit of the author's interest in psychological science, and represents a significant contribution to the evolving subgenre of "case study" fiction, in which such English-language writers as William Gilbert and Oliver Wendell Holmes produced important pioneering examples, the former in *Shirley Hall Asylum* (1863) and *Doctor Austin's Guests* (1866) and the later in *Elsie Venner* (1859) and *The Guardian Angel* (1867). The Alsatian writer who was then signing himself Jules Hosch—he later changed the spelling of his surname to Jules Hoche in order to stress his allegiance to France—produced one of the most remarkable French contributions in *Folles amours* [Crazy Amours] (1878; three stories tr. in *The Maker of Men and His Formula*)[1], and another notable French contributor to it was the neurophysiologist Charles Richet, writing as Charles Ephèyre, in *Soeur Marthe* (1889; expanded 1890; short version tr. as "Sister Marthe" in *On the Brink of the World's End and Other French Scientific Romances*).[2]

It is perhaps not surprising that the French contributions to the subgenre tend to concentrate, to a far greater extent that the English-language examples, on the psychology of amour, and Thiaudière's contributions are no exception. Nor is it surprising that the French examples take a particular interest in what Thiaudière calls "singular amours," exploring unusual instances of passion, in the hope that the peculiarities of the fundamental phenomenon might be brought out more clearly by the contemplation of its extremes. The three examples offered in the collection provide an interesting spectrum. "Le Docteur Melanski" ("Doctor Melanski") offers a fascinating account of a psychological haunting; "La Muette des Champs-

---

[1] Black Coat Press, ISBN 978-1-61227-426-3.
[2] Black Coat Press, ISBN 978-1-61227-474-4.

Élysées" (The Mute Woman of the Champs-Élysées") is a study of obsessions couched as a mystery story; and "Mistress Little" ("Mrs. Little") is a remarkable narrative of psychological dependency. The last-named story is also affiliated to another rich subgenre of *roman scientifique*, which it is perhaps better not to specify in advance, although its eventual revelation within the narrative will certainly not surprise the reader, in the way that it does the extraordinarily slow-witted teller of the story-within-the-story.

In all three novellas the author functions as a primary narrative voice, albeit only briefly in the third, and is sufficiently active within the stories to make his philosophical pessimism evident as a significant mordant aspect of his commentary. The second and third stories also have a subsidiary narrative voice, possessed of its own quirks, which adds a further layer of filtration to the stories they have to tell. That results in a particularly complex layering in "La Muette des Champs-Élysées," where the dialogues between the primary and secondary narrators bracket a third first-person narrative, which explains the mystery but also adds another psychological viewpoint in sharp contrast to its observers. Although the resultant narrative is inevitably tangled, it is also commendably enterprising, and although the subject-matter of the story has to be reckoned modest by comparison with that of the more exotic fantasies that bracket it, it represents an interesting narrative experiment in its own right.

By comparison with the three novellas, "Le Statuaire américain" ("The American Sculptor") is undoubtedly trivial, and readily admits the fact in its throwaway last line as well as its blithe tone, but beneath the surface of frivolous comedy it does raise some interesting questions as to what people might and ought to want if they it were possible to remodel their bodies and personalities, and those of others. It is little wonder that the author was led to extrapolate its central fancy further, and it is a great pity that no copy of *Contes d'un éleveur de chimères* is currently available in order to permit examination of those further explorations.

The translations of the three stories from *Trois amours singulières* were made from the copy of the 1886 edition re-produce on the Bibliothèque Nationale's *gallica* website. The translation of "Le Statuaire américain" was made from the copy of *Semaine Littéraire* volume 168 no. 1 reproduced on the Internet Archive Digital Library at *archive.org*.

Brian Stableford

THE AMERICAN SCULPTOR

Paris is a singular city. False miracles make an enormous racket there, while true miracles remain absolutely unknown.

Thus, the Davenports' cupboard, Talrich's talking head and the torpedo-child occupied public attention for months, but no one at all thinks of recounting the marvels accomplished by Mr. Bread.[3]

In truth, the latter avoids renown with as much care as others seek it, which is rare in a compatriot of Barnum.

Personally, I owe my acquaintance with Mr. Bread and his corrections of nature to the greatest of hazards.

The other day, I was going up the Rue Blanche at about one o'clock. The ascent of the Rue Blanche is a very difficult thing, but it becomes a little less so when one has ahead of one a well-dressed young woman walking with grace. That sometimes happens.

This time I had before me a young woman with a very advantageous figure and beautiful blonde hair, the latter flowing over the former and seemingly authentic, and desirable

---

[3] The Davenport brothers, Erastus and William, were fake spiritualist mediums active from the 1850s to the 1870s whose most famous trick involved their being tied up inside a large box containing musical instruments, which would begin to play when the box was sealed. Jules Talrich (1826-1904) was an anatomical sculptor famous for making lifelike heads. He opened a wax museum In Paris in 1867. The "torpedo-child"—torpedo presumably referring to the fish also known as an electric ray—may be one of the "electric boys" exhibited in the latter part of the 19th century capable of inducing electric shocks when charged with static electricity, but the easily-discoverable references postdate the story.

legs. From what I could see, only the shoulders left something to be desired As elevated in their attachment to the arm as in their attachment to the neck, they did not have an appropriate curve, and I said to myself: *It's a pity that it isn't in the power of any human to give them the slope that the sovereign artist has adopted in designing human shoulders. Oh, if they were only in stone, I believe that, with the aid of a chisel, even though I'm not a sculptor, I'd be able to lift them as much as they need to be lifted; but even the author of the Venus of the Capitol could do nothing. He couldn't displace those bones or those muscles.*

I was carrying out that petty reasoning internally when I was overtaken by a strange tall gentleman who approached the lady in the gravest and most polite fashion, and asked her whether she would like to rearrange her shoulders.

The lady looked at him with a fearful expression and begged him to go on his way.

He persisted: "You're mistaken, Madam; you are a beautiful person; it is only your shoulders that spoil you. A brief session would suffice to lower them for you."

In the meantime, the lady shrugged them and went into number 78.

"Do you understand that?" he asked, turning to me. "I offer that lady something that she ought to accept with enthusiasm…of course, she imagines that I'm making fun of her."

"I fear so," I said.

"That's the only excuse for treating me like that.," he went on, "but a man who has straightened up women who were entirely hunchbacked, his own wife among others, can incline with all the more reason two or three lines of the shoulders of a woman who has a very good figure otherwise."

"You're an orthopedist?" I said, examining the bizarre individual, whose poorly-fitted wig allowed the skin of his scalp to show in places and whose long side-whiskers resembled the bristles of a wild boar, while his broken nose and little colorless eyes, mobile and distorted, gave him the appearance of a caricature.

"Orthopedist! Not at all—not, at least, as it is usually understood. I'm a sculptor, but for a long time I haven't worked in clay, stone or marble. I model human bodies themselves, or rather, remodel them, when Nature has modeled them poorly."

"Oh! Really?" *He's a poor lunatic*, I thought. *He doesn't seem malevolent. It's necessary not to offend him.* "And what instrument do you use?" I added.

"No instrument! I only have to move my hands over someone's body, with a premeditated design; it immediately takes on the forms that it pleases me to imprint on it. It's a very personal gift, for until now, I haven't been able to take any pupils."

"So," I replied, striving to remain as serious as possible, "when it pleases you to change a man into a woman, and *vice versa*, that's the easiest thing in the world for you?"

"Oh, that, no," he said. "My power doesn't go that far. It's limited to refashioning the skeletal system and the carnal fabric over the bones, the sex, age and animal quantity remain the same. I can't make an individual pass from one sex to the other, rejuvenate him or take away any of the constituent molecules, but if someone gives me a Don Quixote and a Sancho Panza, I'll undertake to extract two well-proportioned men by the development of one in breadth and the other in height. Do you grasp my meaning?"

"Perfectly, Monsieur," I said, astounded to see a madman reasoning with such precision.

"You, for example," Mr. Bread continued, "have a face that's a trifle long..."

"Alas, Monsieur, I agree."

"Well, I'd only require a few seconds to shorten it...here, like this..."

And at the same time, before I could react, he put one of his hands to my chin and the other to my forehead, and pressed rapidly—without, moreover, causing me the slightest pain.

In the movement, my hat had fallen off; he hastened to pick it up and hand it to me, with exquisite politeness.

I was furious, however, that the lunatic had manhandled my face like that, and I thought that the expression of his folly had surpassed the limit.

"I beg you to stop," I exclaimed.

"I certainly don't want to leave you in that state," he replied, very calmly. "It's necessary for me to finish what I started. You only have the sketch as yet of the new face I intend for you, and when I say sketch, I'm very honest, for in struggling, you caused my hands to slip in such a fashion that, involuntarily, I've compressed your face too much between the forehead and the chin."

"No matter," I said, with a pitying smile; I'm content with the sketch, imperfect as it may be. Adieu, Monsieur."

He held me back by the sleeve.

"It's impossible," he protested, "for me to leave you with a face like that. You're horrible."

"That's fine by me...."

"I see; you're reluctant to look at it. Would you like me to accompany you home?"

Who is this animal? I thought. *Is he mad? Is he a crook? Is he something else?*

"I want you to leave me alone this instant," I said, energetically.

"So much the worse for you," he said, "but here's my name and address. I'm convinced that you won't take long to come to see me."

I took his card mechanically, and went home as fast as possible.

My concierge, who was near the stairway, in the process of waxing my boots, stopped me in the corridor by saying: "Who do you want, Monsieur?"

"Ah! So, Père Sauvage, you're mocking people? You don't know me now?"

"I know your voice, your hazelnut-colored overcoat, your silver ring with a black stone, your thick yellow cane and the boots you have on your feet, which I waxed yesterday, but never in my life have I seen you with such a head."

"It's certain, Père Sauvage, that my features must be a trifle upset. I encountered a madman just now who took all the trouble in the world to knead me."

"What? Features a trifle upset? That's to say that they're no longer your own—that you have someone else's face."

"Get away, you old joker!" I said to my concierge. And I went upstairs at a run.

I went into my apartment, whistling a tune from *Thérèsa* cheerfully. As was my habit, I put my hat down on the writing-desk, my cane in the corner of the fireplace and my overcoat on the bed. Then I darted a glance at the mirror.

Immediately, I uttered a cry of horror. Unless I was also seeing things, like my concierge, unless I had gone mad, like the corrector of Nature, it appeared to me that I definitely no longer had my habitual face.

Whereas before, it had measured about ten inches high by about five wide, it must presently have measured the opposite: five high by ten wide: one of those ridiculous and odious faces that certain distorting mirrors show you.

Although I had also proved a hundred times over that that one was accurate, I looked sideways at the one on my dressing-table, and then yet another.

Always the same head!

Then I tried to squeeze it with both hands on the sides, in order to make it resume its original shape.

Vain efforts!

I had an equal desire to laugh and to weep: to laugh because my present head was reminiscent of that of a notary of my acquaintance; to weep because I thought that it was even worse than his.

With that, there were three curt raps on my door.

Great God! I knew those three little raps. And when I heard them, my heart ordinary skipped a beat. But where was I going to hide my head, for I no longer dared show it to the lady of my dreams, as people used to say—or the lady of my expenses, as one says nowadays?

Well, yes!

I would show it to her, in order to judge as a last resort whether I had or had not been metamorphosed.

I opened my door and my arms.

She gazed, nonplussed.

"Pardon me, Monsieur, I've made a mistake..."

"Alas, no, you're not mistaken, angel of my life! It's really me, your friend. Don't you recognize my voice? Enter without fear. Nothing has changed here apart from my head; and then, believe me, it's only a transitory head that I have here...I can give myself any head you like; you only have to choose. Look, here's the card of the animal who will render me a handsome fellow."

MR. JOHN BREAD
American Sculptor
124 Rue de Vaugirard

She remained petrified. Then, suddenly: "No, it's not possible that that's you. Adieu, Monsieur!"

And there she goes, descending the stairs four at a time. I shout over the banister: "Rose, Rosa! What would you like my new head to look like? Reply to me, I implore you...it won't cost Mr. Bread any more. Would you like me to have a turned-up nose or a cleft chin? Do you like that sort of thing? Would you like my wayward little beard to be reassembled into a moustache, and an imposing imperiale? Rosa...!"

But Rosa was already far away.

I began to rage against Mr. Bread, who was the cause of the fact that I was about to spend a detestable evening, when I could have promised myself a charming one.

It was too late to go in search of the accursed American sculptor, who was probably not at home anyway. Sufficiently edified as to the reality of the change that had been operated in me, I did not judge it appropriate to show my horrible head to anyone else. So I deprived myself of dining, as I had the habit of doing, with a few of my friends, and I went to dine on my own in a restaurant where no one knew me, and then I went home to bed.

The next morning, at nine o'clock, I climbed into a cab and had myself taken to the Rue de Vaugirard.

As I went into the concierge's lodge to ask for Mr. Bread, I was amazed to find two pairs of living Greek statues there dressed in the French style—which is to say, Monsieur the Concierge père, Madame la Concierge, Monsieur le Concierge fils, and Mademoiselle la Concierge; in a word. Agamemnon, Clytemnestra, Orestes and Electra., all cast from the same mold, all very beautiful…too beautiful.

"Monsieur," Clytemnestra said to me, "has doubtless come to have his face arranged by Mr. Beard. Oh, he's a clever man Mr. Bread! To prove it, the tenant on the third was even uglier than Monsieur, if that's possible, and now he's as handsome as us."

"And the other tenants?" I said

"The other tenants? The same thing," replied Clytemnestra.

"You're all similar in the house, then?" I said.

"Oh, my God yes! Isn't that so, Monsieur Pipelet?" she said to Agamemnon.

There, I thought. *In that, this Monsieur Bread, who is no longer only a man, for sure, shows that he isn't entirely a God, for a God varies is creations infinitely, and he doesn't appear to emerge from the Greek type. Well, I don't want his Greek. I have no desire for him to make a Menelaus of me."*

And in thinking that, I ran at Mr. Bread's door. A young woman came to open it, brunette, pale skinned, of medium height, with very pure and noble features...

"Is Mr. Bread here, Madame?"

"Yes, Monsieur." And she added, with a malicious smile: "You're probably the person he encountered yesterday in the Rue Blanche."

19

"I am that person, unfortunately, Madame."

"It's certain," she said, bursting into laughter, "that your present face…but you'll see; it will be the simplest thing for my husband to make you another."

Madame Bread showed me into the studio; then I heard her say to husband, in a neighboring room: "John, the man you encountered yesterday in the Rue Blanche is here."

"Aha!" said Mr. Bread. "I'll be there in a moment!"

Mr. Bread's studio was no different from others, except that the art that was exercised there was very strange. One saw a few plaster casts of celebrated statues that antiquity has transmitted to us, including Praxiteles' Faun, the Apollo of the Belvedere, the Venus of the Capitol, the Callipygian Venus of the Museum of Naples, the Antinous, the Discobolos of the Braccia Nuovo at the Vatican, and a few moderns after Canova.

I was admiring those masterpieces, which I had already admired in Italy, when Mr. Bread came in, dressed in the simplest manner, like an honest fellow; you would never have taken him for a magician. You might have thought that he was an old notary coming to cast a glance over his junior clerks.

"Well," he said, with a mocking expression, "was I right to give you my name and address? What would you have done without that, capricious youth? You would have kept an impossible head for your entire life."

"It wasn't necessary," I replied, "to commence by rendering it impossible, for, before being manipulated by you, it was still presentable."

"Then you hold it against me? Think, then, that I'll make you one that will cause all those of women to turn around."

"A Greek head, no?"

"Yes, everything that there is of the most Greek, and I'll arrange you a body to match."

"No, thank you," I said, "I prefer to remain as Nature intended me to be. If I become as handsome as you desire, I'll no longer recognize myself. But explain to me why you, who have this extraordinary power to embellish people, retain your own ugliness?"

"Alas, it's because I can embellish everyone except myself."

That dolorous exclamation of Mr. Bread's motivated certain philosophical reflections on my part that would take too long to report here, which I shall leave it to the perspicacious reader to make in his turn—who will feel very sorry for Mr. Beard, because I divine that he is particularly sympathetic.

He said to me: "Look, there's no man in the world to whom it would be more agreeable for me to give what I cannot give myself: beauty. Let yourself go. I'll warm the stove sufficiently for you to undress, and you can stand on that red velvet cushion. If, at the end of half an hour—I'm only asking you for half a hour—you don't resemble Praxiteles' Faun, which you see here...then my name's not John Bread!"

"No, no," I said, "only put my face back the way it was, I beg you."

"That's a very simple thing; I only have pulled it a little lengthwise. Let's stand in front of that mirror, and you can stop me when it returns to its former shape, because I no longer remember the exact length."

In less time that it takes the most expeditious dentist to pull out a tooth, Mr. Beard reestablished my face.

I thanked him effusively; I told him that he was the most astonishing man I had ever encountered, that I was perfectly convinced of his extraordinary power, and that I would even experience a real pleasure in watching him operate.

"You can certainly do that," he said. "You'll have that spectacle, and perhaps then you'll decide on your own account. Oh, if there were a means for me to become beautiful myself, I can guarantee that I wouldn't have to be begged!"

Then, opening the studio door, he called: "Jenny! Jenny!"

The exceedingly beautiful person who had come to open the door to me, and who was none other than Madame Bread, as you know, appeared then, and said to me with a entirely

Parisian ease: "Well, Monsieur, you're already much better, but you still have a margin to cross in order to became a handsome man, and I hope that you're not going to leave it there."

I bowed without making any reply, preoccupied with the motive for which Mr. Bread had summoned his wife into the studio.

There was a brief dialogue between them in English, of which, in my quality as an ignorant Frenchman, I did not understand anything. Then Madame Bread went to the stove, but a few logs in it, took off her ankle-boots and stockings, stood on the red cushion and unfastened her dress in the simplest and most natural fashion.

I opened my eyes wide, and could not believe them.

"My wife," Mr. Bread said to me, has given her consent for me to repeat on her, before you, a double experiment that I have carried out several times before, for the edification of the incredulous. I told you yesterday, I believe, that Nature had afflicted Mrs. Bread with a rather grave deformity, and that it is to me that she owes being a very beautiful woman today—beautiful enough that she can stand comparison, as you can convince yourself, with the Venus of the Capitol. Well, in a first experiment I am going to restore her former deformity, and then, in a second, return her present beauty."

And Mr. Bread extended his hand toward his wife, who, deprived of her final garment, with her arms directed like those of the Venus of the Capitol and her gaze placid, delivered her exquisite form to my admiration.

Then he moved the Venus of the Capitol next to Madame Bread and said to me: "Now, compare and judge!"

It was marvelous!

The plaster appeared to have been modeled on Madame Bread herself. And I wondered by what privilege I, a poor poet, was seeing united in a living form those perfections, which the greatest sculptors in antiquity, in order to bring them together in their work had borrowed from twenty women.

I reported to Mr. Bread the impression that I felt.

Madame Bread smiled.

"Alas," she said, "my coquetry is about to be submitted to a rude proof, for the magnificence that you are admiring, Monsieur, I shall shortly loose, and I shall become quite frightful."

"Are you ready?" her husband asked.

"Whenever you please, John," she replied, tenderly.

Then Mr. Bread, placing one hand on her right shoulder and the other on the left, caused the vertebral column to deviate; then he staved in the rib-cage in such a way that a hump was manifest in the left shoulder—a hump that increased considerably to the prejudice of the arms and the inferior limbs, which he stripped of their harmonious amplitude and reduced to a state of rickety thinness.

The polished, seemingly marmoreal surfaces of that beautiful body were distended and creased.

It was pitiful to see.

There remained the face.

Mr. Bread caused it to swell by grasping its undulating fabric at the neck; he changed the curvature of the jaw; he magnified and deformed the nose and the ears; he altered the eyes in a singular manner; finally, he kneaded the forehead and cranium in such a manner as to give them an entirely new aspect.

Poor Madame Bread!

His task complete, Mr. Bread said to me: "You see what Madame Bread was before I took it into my head to transform her."

"My love," said Madame Bread, in an entirely new voice, "Don't weary Monsieur too much with such a disagreeable spectacle."

"I confess, Madame," I said, "that the preceding one was much more to my taste, especially when I think that if Monsieur Bread, by a fatality that it is necessary to anticipate, were to die suddenly, you would remain thus deformed. I shudder at the thought."

"But that's true, what you're saying!" cried Madame Bread. "And I never thought of that! You hear me John—it's necessary not to do this experiment again."

"Good, good...," said Mr. Bread. "Turn toward me." He added: "You've seen enough. I can operate in the contrary direction."

"I beg you to do so," I said. "It's necessary not to let Madame languish."

And immediately, he set to work to model his wife after the Venus of the Capitol, with a marvelous surety of hand and promptitude.

During that second operation, which lasted for a quarter of an hour at the most, and in which Madame Bread's beautiful forms reappeared one by one, the sculptor, the elaborated work and I chatted in a tone of the most perfect intimacy.

"Oh, Madame," I said to the elaborated work, "if I were your husband and I had Mr. Bread's talent, I would want all the world to see you hunchbacked, but when we were alone and our door was securely bolted, then I would render you splendidly beautiful. That's not an advice I'm giving Mr. Bread, for I'd lose too much if he were to follow it."

"Truly? How egotistical you men are; you would like a woman only to please you, and you would find it quite natural if she were to disgust others...much obliged!"

We discussed jealousy.

Mr. Bread smiled. One might have thought that he was a complete stranger to the passions of the human heart, who only envisaged amour from the point of view of plastic sensation. He possessed at his discretion an admirably beautiful woman, who owed her beauty to him. That was sufficient for him. As for questions of knowing whether she was faithful to him, whether she loved him exclusively, whether she dissimulated with him, he saw them romantically and did not even ask them. In any case, he was of the opinion that a well-equilibrated beauty produced as natural fruits a moderate temperament and good instincts.

In that regard, I remember that he said to me: "Have you noticed the radical difference that exists between the voice of my deformed wife and the voice of my beautiful wife? Yes, you have, haven't you? Well, in the same way, and with more reason, the structure of the cranium varying from one state to the other in the most notable fashion, the appetites must necessarily change. They are no longer the same. They are much better when my wife is beautiful than they are when she is deformed."

"You believe in Gall's theory?"[4]

"Do I believe it? Every day, I apply it and I verify it."

"How is that?"

Mr. Bread winked at me, and made a little signal with his finger indicating that he did not want to talk about that in front of his wife, and then he changed the subject.

At that moment, Madame Bread, having recovered her beauty from head to toe, was in the process of getting dressed.

As soon as she had fastened the last clasp, her husband said: Now, my dear Jenny, Monsieur and I thank you. You can return to your chores."

"Monsieur," she said to me, making a gracious curtsey, "I hope that you will take my place on the red cushion, and that you will leave here as handsome as Endymion."

"My word, no, Madame! That's evidently an absurd idea; I'll remain as I am; otherwise, no one would recognize me any longer."

She withdrew.

"How do you apply and verify Gall's theory every day?" I asked the American sculptor.

"My wife's gone; I can tell you. You know that Gall divides the fundamental drives, penchants and sentiments into twenty-seven categories, all palpable on a human cranium?"

"Yes," I said, a little presumptuously.

---

[4] The anatomist Franz Josef Gall (1758-1828) remains famous as the pioneer of what is now usually known as phrenology.

"Well," he continued, "Since I can mold the human cranium to my whim, you'll understand that it's very easy for me to develop or depress the prominences corresponding to those categories. I can just as easily enable you to show them sooner or later. There's one prominence that I modify almost daily in my wife without her knowledge: it's the first in Gall's classification—you know, the one situated behind the neck...[5] Sometimes I depress it, sometimes I develop it, When I leave for a journey, as you'll understand, I never fail to nullify it..."

"I'd very much like to know your secret, Mr. Bread," I said, laughing, "But you're not, it seems to me, as much a stranger to the passions of the soul as I had supposed, and I observe that jealousy bites you exactly like anyone else."

"Bah!" said Mr. Bread. "Let's not talk about jealousy."

"Listen," I said. "I know a little woman who isn't pretty, but who is charming. Until now her imperfections have pleased me. Thus, she has a tooth in the front of her mouth a tooth slightly corroded by a white spot of decay, which is for me a focal point, an attraction. She has slight freckles on her face which I would be very sorry to see disappear. She has one overly slender hand of which I'm madly fond. All that is not in the least Greek, and yet all that delights me. If l bring you that little woman, I don't want you won't change anything about her—except, without her suspecting the why and the how, you might palpate her cranium, and if you find there, as I dread, regrettable bumps, you could destroy them; if it lacks desirable ones, you could bring them out."

"Very gladly," said Mr. Bread. "But let's see…give me a summary of her character; you'll make my work much easier, for I'll be able to go straight to the bumps to remake. Do you think she's devoted?"

"I rather think she's egotistical."

---

[5] On 19th century phrenological charts, area 1 is generally labeled "amativeness," allegedly corresponding to the mental faculty of physical amour.

Good! That's because the bump of amity, classified by Gall as number three, is depressed. I'll raise it, and henceforth, your little woman will be take devotion to the sublime. Has she the instinct of self-defense?

"Alas! I'm afraid that she has none and that she yields too quickly to certain attacks."

"We'll give her that instinct. That's another bump to produce, number four. Is she frank?"

"That's what I've never known. She might well be dissimulating, hypocritical and deceptive."

"Marvelous! I'll seek out the bump labeled number six by Gall, and if I encounter it, I'll efface it completely. Is she docile?"

"Not very."

"Then we'll attenuate bump number twenty-seven slightly: firmness, perseverance and stubbornness."

"I'll be very obliged to you, Mr. Bread…but above all, don't alert the person in question, for she's capable of not wanting to have her faults corrected."

"Don't worry. You have nothing else for which to reproach her?"

"She does have one mania that is presently leading me to despair, because my resources can't keep up with it…a mania for traveling, but what can you do about that?"

"I can do a great deal," Mr. Bread replied, "And I assure you that I can take it away by flattening bump number twelve, that of voyages."[6]

"Decidedly, Mr. Bread," I exclaimed, "You're an admirable man, and you deserve to have your praises sung in the five continents of the world; in the meantime, they'll be sung by me, I promise you, in the capital of the world's five continents."

---

[6] This is slightly misleading; Gall's area twelve corresponds to "locality"—i.e., the perception of the location of surrounding objects, not to a desire to travel.

"I beg you not to do anything of the sort," Mr. Bread said to me; I'm afraid that my clientele might be augmented enormously, for there are few people who, like you, would prefer to remain as nature has made them, when they have the opportunity to be more beautiful."

"And what are your prices?" I asked him. "How much do you charge to transform your man or your woman?"

"It's according to the sex, the subject and the subject's fortune. For a man I charge double what I charge for a woman, because the work is less attractive; and if the subject is very deformed, naturally, my difficulty being greater, my salary must also be greater; finally, I try to apply the principle of the gospel that the breath of the wind should be proportionate to the fleece of the ewe, and my prices always vary from that point of view, between twenty thousand francs and a hundred francs. I've already earned veritable wealth from my métier as a corrector of Nature in America and England, but as I have no children, as I have a horror of luxury and as I am, thank God, endowed with sufficient good sense not to find any pleasure in hoarding money, I haven't kept that wealth. And I don't repent of the manner in which I've employed it. With the money that some give me in order to become beautiful, I render others happy."

With that, I took my leave of Mr. Bread respectfully, fixing with him the following Thursday for the reconstruction of Rosa's skull.

"Until Thursday, then."

"Until Thursday, Mr. Bread."

And then I woke up.

DOCTOR MELANSKI

I

About five years ago, one day in July—I no longer remember which—near the bandstand in the Tuileries, at about half past five, I met one of my old schoolmates, named Mauplaisant, who insisted on taking me to dinner at the Brasserie Andier.

Celebrity is always so relative and so limited that for half a league around the Rue Hautefeuille perhaps no one, except for a few artists, suspects the existence of that establishment. And yet, it is illustrious for its Alsatian cuisine and its clientele of young men, great beer-drinkers but also remarkable under other titles, and the paternal amenity of its chef, Monsieur Andier.

As he opened the door of the Brasserie, Mauplaisant said to me: "I'm going to introduce you to a fellow who will please you, I'm sure of it. He's melancholy, like you; you can commiserate over the poverties of human nature and proclaim happiness impossible."

He was talking as we advanced into the brasserie, with the consequence that the man to whom he wanted to introduce me, who was at the far end of the room with his elbows on a table, his eyes watchful and a cigarette in his hand, only hearing the word "impossible," said to him: "What's impossible, Mauplaisant?"

"It's impossible," Mauplaisant replied, "that you won't become the friend of this eccentric here." To me, he added: "I introduce to you Monsieur Gabriel Melanski, the son of a Polish refugee, student in medicine, and one of the best souls I know in the black variety."

With that I held out my hand to Monsieur Melanski, who welcomed with a visible good grace that spontaneous gesture on my part, while Mauplaisant tried to describe humorously what kind of man I am.

Certainly, nothing external advertised any possible resemblance between the character of Monsieur Melanski and mine, for at first sight we were as different as can be: he was very neatly clad, his physiognomy was cold and bronzed, his attitude very proud; I was dressed a trifle carelessly, my gaze is blue and lukewarm, my manners tender. Fundamentally, though, Mauplaisant was not mistaken in introducing us to one another as future friends; and I even think that the intimacy that issued from that almost fortuitous introduction at the Brasserie Andier far exceeded his expectations.

After a conversation in charcoal that lasted a good two hours and was a kind of portrait of our meager terrestrial destiny, I was Melanski's friend and Melanski was my friend, to a closer degree than Mauplaisant was himself. That is because intellectual camaraderie always prevails over the frivolous camaraderie of past times.

After that, we saw one another frequently and, like two old invalids discussing Waterloo and commiserating with one another reciprocally and the leg that they left there, we talked about our disastrous campaign through society, but we complained far less about what we had suffered than what still remained to us to suffer. Meanwhile, we did not yield to the illusion so common among veterans that consists of pretending that if it had depended on us, the battle would have been won. We believed, on the contrary, that we would have been the first to compromise the success of the human combat against evil by virtue of our blunders or our weakness, and that was what enraged us the most.

All of our self-esteem, by virtue of a singular reversal of vulgar self-esteem, was in seeking mutually what we called our "little serpents"—which is to say, the shameful, paltry or ridiculous underlying motives of our actions, instead of allowing us to lend them titular motives that appear so honorable, generous and noble.

Each of us became the second conscience of the other. Our two prides only any longer formed one, and they shared the benefits of our respective observations. Understandably, at that point, amity is all the more solid because it is founded on a species of egotism.

I have only wanted to indicate to the reader what the basis was of my liaison with Melanski; I shall not go on.

Three days before he sustained his thesis at the Faculté de Médecine I was obliged to go precipitately to Poitou for family affairs. I stayed there much longer than I had anticipated. Melanski had promised to write to me, but he did not, and I, piqued by seeing him so negligent, or perhaps by virtue of a negligence equal to his, I did not write to him either.

When I returned to Paris six months later and I went to ask for him at the place where I knew he lived, the concierge said to me: "Monsieur Melanski? He left Paris a long time ago, Monsieur."

"Impossible! Where is he, then?"

"He's a physician in Montivilliers."

"And where is this Montivilliers?"

"Here," the concierge said. "This is his exact address." Then he showed me a little strip of paper on which Melanski had written in his own hand: *Monsieur Gabriel Melanski, doctor in medicine at Montivilliers (Seine-Inférieure).*

"Why on earth has he gone to bury himself out there?" I exclaimed. "He always expressed to me the firmest intention of staying in Paris. And how is it that he didn't inform me?"

Under the impression of a great surprise, I went to see Mauplaisant, and for fear that he might imagine—which was, in fact, true—that I had come less to see him than to seek information about Melanski, I pretended to be unaware of the latter's departure.

"And our friend Melanski," I said to him, "how is he? Is it a long time since you've seen him?"

"I perceive," said Mauplaisant, "that Melanski has acted no better in your regard than in mine."

"Bah! What has he done, then?"

"He's quite Paris definitively, without informing us, without bidding us farewell. He's an odd fellow. One can be unsociable, but frankly, that's no reason to act in that fashion. You, for example..."

"Oh, me! Let's not say anything about me. I'm no better than Melanski, I assure you. Melanski is full of heart. You've told me so yourself twenty times over, but he's rendered strange, odd and capricious by his hypochondria."

"You make me laugh, all of you, with your hypochondria," exclaimed Mauplaisant. "There's no hypochondria involved. I ask you what we've done to deserve that Melanski..."

"In sum, where is he?" I interrupted.

Mauplaisant repeated what I had already found out.

"And how do you know his address?"

"Oh like this: I had had a slight indisposition that kept me away from the brasserie for a week. One evening, I returned, Monsieur Andier was wandering around with a napkin over his arm,. 'So, Monsieur Melanski has left for Montivilliers, then?' he said to me. 'For Montivilliers,' I replied. 'What's that?' I confess to you that I thought that Melanski had used with the worthy Monsieur Andier a procedure very familiar to those who want to withdraw from an old supplier. I went to his house the same evening to make sure that he was there. It was necessary to yield to the evidence. Melanski is presently practicing medicine in Montivilliers, in the département of the Seine-Inférieure, and has been for five months."

"Since we know his address," I said to Mauplaisant, "It's necessary to write to him to find out what insect has stung him."

"Write to him if you want," replied Mauplaisant, curtly. "As for me, I give up on him, because I think it stupid to give marks of attention to a fellow who cares so little for me."

That specious and oft-repeated argument did not convince me. I had for Melanski one of those sympathies that no offended self-esteem can compromise. I wrote to him.

My letter, so far as I can recall its terms, expressed, not as a reproach but as a psychological verity of universal application, the idea that our most vivacious affections, by a fatal law of nature, always come to be resorbed into the soul and foment other affections. I told him, more or less, that my relationship with him, although apparently terminated, had nevertheless left me with an ineffaceable memory, doubtless because its cessation constituted for me a moral loss, and was genuinely harmful to me. I added that our synnoëty—that was what we called our faculty of thinking in perfect accord—might deteriorate under the influences of opposed habits, and that if we met again someday, it was a good bet that we'd be in the heart of the tower of Babel. Finally, according to our cherished custom, I juggled, so to speak, with the most terribly cutting remarks, convinced that I was not wounding him or myself, and full of the sang-froid that distinguishes the juggler of daggers.

Alas, when one has a somewhat philosophical mind, one likes to stick a finger into the depths of things, no matter how muddy they might be; one finds a certain provocative savor in reasoned scorn for oneself and others; one etches disappointment as one had etched confidence; one puts glory into diagnosing that which might exist beneath the best semblances.

II

A month went by; of Melanski, no news. I knew him too well to attribute that prolongation of his silence to the offense that my letter might have caused him. I had given proof therein of a frankness that ought rather to have awakened his own, always ready, and as if in the forefront of his heart.

Was he ashamed of having fled far away from me without extending a hand to me, and did he not know how to apologize for that? No. That shame and embarrassment would have been appropriate to a common man; they were far beneath Melanski. The silence in which he preserved himself indicated, in my opinion, the indefinite prolongation of a state of mind that I had experienced many times, and which we had baptized pantophobia—which is to say, sovereign, tyrannical, universal disgust, as invasive as the waters of the Deluge, capable of submerging even the holy ark of duty, amour and pity.

One morning, however, I received the following letter:

My dear Synnoëte,

You are, then, even more skeptical than I am. You have a serene desolation in thought, a terrible mildness in expression, and a scornful esteem for human relationships that would frighten me if I had not caressed it twenty times over and domesticated it in my way of thinking.

Do you know what all that is? It is the unmasked enigma of the eternal sphinx, a sphinx more redoubtable than that of Oedipus, for we have divined it, and him, and have fallen nonetheless into its disenchantment, while he pursues his route skirting the disenchanted generations. Well, we still retain the superiority over the naïve victims that we can analyze our fall and support it coolly as a necessary thing. Oh, my poor friend, nothing demonstrates to me the essential concordance of our souls—or rather their definitive and irrevocable fusion—more clearly than your judicious suspicion of the banal humanity of which we have our part.

That banal humanity, which is humanity, properly speaking, will give to our amity the destiny it wishes; perhaps it will leave no trace of it; perhaps it will induce you, as it has already induced me with regard to you, to make little of me; but we possess in addition a little of the transcendent humanity that, overlooking proceedings from a great height, careless of what they are, has linked us forever by the summit of intelligence.

Blurred by one of those stupidities that ruin superficial amities on a daily basis, it would be impossible for our ideal amity to be damaged by it. Our thoughts, if not our hands, will incessantly encounter one another in the same speculation, alone but face to face, and will embrace passionately, like twin sisters held in slavery by barbarians.

You might have conserve some resentment against me for not having bade you farewell—in terms of the flesh, for in terms of the spirit, not having quit you but taken you with me, I had no adieu to bid you—but your rancor could not have rendered us strangers to one another. Fortunately, you do not even hold it against me.

It seems that with the perfect knowledge that you have of me, you have sniffed, around my abrupt departure, a bizarre, extra-personal, imperious motive: one of those motives that are only appropriate to the height of our chimeras, and that no one except us could have.

What, then, is that motive?

Frankly, my dear Synnoëte, I prefer to hide it from you, not only because it is too subtle, too unexpected and too insensate to be comprehended right away, even by you, but also because the shame that I would have in confessing it to you would be beyond my strength. Don't interrogate me. In any case, if I replied to you, you would have the pain of observing that I am going mad, and I would have the hurtful pleasure of establishing my madness once and for all. Oh, my friend, that reason, whose deceptive amplitude you would admire, is like the frog in the fable...it would burst. And an absurd mirage has sufficed to operate a lesion that will always expand.

Why were you not in Paris when that terrible mirage was about to take possession of me? You would have defended me against it; you would have shown me that I was being ridiculous; you would have opened my eyes; you would have taken out of my hands the deadly plaything that hazard or fatality had put into them, as one takes away from a child the pistol that he had imprudently picked up. There was time then to save me from the abyss into which my imagination, overstimulated by voluntary solitude, has dragged me since.

35

But no, you were absent, and if I do not have the courage, now that my madness has developed monstrously, to reveal it to you, I would have feared even more to show it at its commencement, innocent as it was, to anyone but you. Keeping it to myself, I left, but not in the hope of fleeing the object of a demoralizing preoccupation; on contrary, I left—would you believe it?—in order to find myself more absorbed by that object, scarcely suspecting that it would bring me to where I am. But I don't want give any greater proportions to something that must remain an enigma for you.

Suppose that I had an amour beyond all plausibility, the scenes of which have no analogue except in nightmare. I am presently subject to the effects of that amour for, thank God, the cause has disappeared. I am far from having returned to my anterior state, however. My mind and body are entirely disturbed, although I defy anyone to perceive it, so much do I stiffen myself. The struggle that I sustain against myself in public renders the evil worse. The relaxation is more complete in proportion to the tension, and relaxation here might be more fatal for me, for it is the free return of my abominable fantasies.

If your friendship for me has not become entirely ideal and can perhaps be rendered practical, I implore you, my dear Synnoëte, to come and spend some time with me, in order to treat me. You alone might find the means to heal the poor physician by distracting him, as soon as he has satisfied his clientele, which is already numerous and captivating—yes, I said "captivating." My God, yes; that is why I shall not willingly return to Paris, which mysterious fatality caused me to quit. Furthermore, I think of you as I think about the French flag; wherever it is, that is France; wherever you come, my Paris will come—which is to say that you will bring it to me in Montivilliers.

"Come on, a good deed! Take the train to Le Havre, and in Le Havre you will find an omnibus that will bring you to my home in three-quarters on an hour, via a road frayed long a valley with multiple crop-fields, between two delightful hills.

Having arrived in Montivilliers, you have only to ask for the new doctor, or "the Pole," and anyone will show you my door. The country is very pretty, the sea is close by. You, who like walking, reverie and labor towed gently by nonchalance, will be very comfortable here. I don't despair of keeping you for a few months—the time, for example, for you to wrote a novel from the first word to the last. We have a public library, if you please, and in the church there is a Simon's Feast that merits being seen.

Then again, to tempt you further, we shall leave the nest together, as you put it, and feed the bats. You'll see. Although I'm not entirely in my right mind, I can still chat; I can reason; my ideas hold together quite well, with the consequence that you, who are unaware of the special object of my madness, might think that it consists precisely of thinking that I'm mad.

You appear to be curious as to what led me to choose Montivilliers as an abode rather than somewhere else. It's quite simple.

After the Polish emigration of 1832 my poor father was brought here by a Parisian friend, pampered fêted and, better than that, aided. He always talked to me about Montivilliers with emotion; and I thought that in curing, "at the right price," the sons of those who has welcomed my father so liberally, I would be repaying a part of his debt.

Another trick of my imagination! The sons know nothing and the fathers have almost forgotten—which was their right. My name awakens none of the particular sympathy on which I was counting. The fault must be in my unfortunately slightly haughty manner. I have refrained, as you will understand, from reminding those who do not remember or pretend not to remember, for they would inevitably suppose the opposite of the truth—which is to say that I am thanking them on my father's behalf for having attracted their support to myself too.

I therefore keep myself apart, and I am all the more sought after as a physician because of it; but I am considered *to be a very odd man who is inordinately fond of solitude and might be a poor sleeper.*

Although you only admit it to me covertly, I observe, as I had already foreseen, that Mauplaisant is holding a grudge against me for having left without bidding him farewell. He is not wrong. Nevertheless, please soothe his rancor against me. Make that sage observer of social conventions understand, if you can, that he ought not to be too severe on the unfortunates who have a nature apart, and even more, those who are mad. Madness is not malevolence.

Persuade him, I beg you, of two things. The first is that at the time when I left Paris my soul was full of impressions so indecently romantic that I would have feared, in going to see him, involuntarily showing myself to him naked and offending his intellectual modesty—the amusing modesty that those who do not understand them always have toward slightly subtle sentiments. The second is that in the fashion of Protestants who have no need, in order to render worship to an invisible God, to kneel before an image, it is not necessary for me to shake Mauplaisant's hand in order to like in him the eternal good fellow who made me a gift of you.

P.S. Ask Allan Kardec or some other spiritist whether he does not believe that Pygmalion could communicate to his Galatea, solely by means of the amorous intensity of his gaze, sufficient magnetic fluid for the statue to walk into his arms. Personally, I find such a thing no more extraordinary than the comprehension and spontaneous movement of the simple feet of a table. And perhaps one would have even less cause for astonishment if Galatea, instead of being a single block of marble, had been composed of some substance that had partaken of organic life, and if the artist had equipped it with the articulations appropriate to a human body.

III

Melanski's letter agitated me in several ways: penetrated by weaknesses that he judged himself to be madness, but astonishing nevertheless in that it said things to me that were apparently sane, at least as far as its postscript. Curious to know the secret of all that, and piqued that he had not confessed it to me, I was even more flattered that he felt a need for me, and even happier that I might revive a little with him, so I decided enthusiastically to leave for Montivilliers.

I arrived there at six o'clock the following evening. When I emerged from the omnibus, as I paid the conductor, I said: "Do you happen to know where the new doctor lives?"

"The Pole?" he replied, placing one hand on my arm and extending the other. "You have only to take that street there, which is the Rue aux Juifs, and follow the subsequent street, which is the Rue Assiquet, and you'll arrive at a square where ten chestnut trees are planted in a circle, which is the Place Assiquet. Monsieur Melanski's house is on the square. But you'll need a man to carry your trunk..."

Spotting one of his comrades who as stationed there, he planted my trunk on his shoulders, recommending him to take "the monsieur" to Monsieur Melanski's house.

The face of the old woman attracted by our ringing the doorbell seemed petrified by the sight of me. The hour cried out that I might expect dinner, the trunk that I expected accommodation. And who was I, great God? Why was I troubling that peaceful household? It was not concealed from me very well that my importunity was keenly felt.

"Monsieur Melanski is out," I was told. "He's gone to visit a patient two leagues way. He won't be back before seven or eight o'clock, His dinner is meager and there's no other bed in the house than his."

Thus informed, I was scarcely content. Nevertheless, I spurred myself in order to laugh a little.

"Oh, the rogue!" I exclaimed. "He begs me to come and see him as soon as possible; I come running, and he has neither a mattress nor a soup-bowl at my disposal. What did I do to be given a friend like that?"

The old woman, learning that her master was not a stranger to my arrival, began to sing her psalm, that she might perhaps be able to find some cutlets, and that nothing prevented her from making a big omelet preceded by sorrel soup, and with regard to the important question of a bed, strictly speaking, the divan that Monsieur had in his study could take the place of a wooden bed.

I would have embraced her if she had not gone out to execute her culinary program.

While I repeated, as I walked swiftly into the kitchen: "God, how hungry I am! Oh, my poor devil of a stomach! etc.," although lentils are a detestable thing, I could understand the conduct of Esau. And while I was discovering with a feverish impatience the honest casserole in which were cooking, over a low heat, the two nice *ris de veau* in red wine sauce destined for Melanski, I heard a carriage stop dead and then a well-known voice cry out: "Pélagie, the big doors!"

I ran straight there, and opened them without groping, as if it had been my métier for a long time. I leave you to imagine the impression that Melanski experienced when he entered the courtyard and saw me beside his cabriolet.

"I'm replacing Pélagie," I shouted, cheerfully. "Pélagie has better things to do, I assure you, than opening the big doors. Can you imagine, my dear, that I have an appetite—and what an appetite!—and it's necessary that Pélagie reckon with it. She's at the butchers, seeing whether he has any cutlets. What a fine invention, cutlets, eh, Melanski? And omelets. We'll have one. I'm enraged, you see, enraged."

Melanski's physiognomy had visibly softened, immediately; there were no demonstrative words, though. Far from exaggerating the pleasure he felt, it was easy to see that he was seeking instead to contain it.

I had gone to the horse and I was holding the reins at the level of the bit. Melanski jumped down; then, embracing me for the first time in his life, he murmured: "Oh, my friend, how much good you're doing me."

Nothing more. At the same time, he enveloped me with a gaze moistened by tears; in addition, his hands, in which he was pressing the one that I still had free, was trembling in a strange manner.

That troubled me.

"Come on, my poor friend," I said to him, with an emotion born of his own, you ought to have been counting on me and expecting to see me face to face. You begged me to come, I came. And that's not for your benefit, if you please...you know...the little serpents...I've come because I find a genuine pleasure in your company.

He repeated, with a slight variation, the only sentence he had spoken to me: "You can't imagine how much good you're doing me." And he added: "At last there'll be a living being under my roof, for you're alive."

"Oh, my word yes, too alive, even," I replied, while occupying myself with suppressing an unruly movement of the horse. Perhaps if I were less so, hunger wouldn't be clawing me as much as it is—and that Pélagie, who hasn't come back."

I redirected my gaze at him. He was weeping copiously.

"Oh, you're scarcely being reasonable now, my friend. You're weeping for me as if I were going to die. Wait, damn it! *Nunc est bibendum...*[7] I agree with Horace... Yes, now it's necessary to drink, and at, especially eat, because what is dangerous is depriving ourselves of it."

"I'm a child," said Melanski. "Forgive me, it's involuntary. For six months, you see, I've been living in funereal isolation...seeking amour where it can no longer be, colliding with the inevitable, and I find you, and I sense life palpitating in someone I love, and you take me back to the time before my madness. You're not a nightmare, my dear friend, you're not even a dream; you're a reality. You have flesh on your bones."

Oh, the poor fellow, I thought. *He really is dotty. What is he saying to me? And how, in such a mental state, can he exercise his profession of physician?* But on that point, I reflect-

---

[7] "Now is the time for drinking," from one of Horace's *Odes*.

ed that many monomaniacs have a marvelous tact for uncovering or hiding their monomania at will.

I did not know how to respond to Melanski when, right on time, Pélagie came to break the embarrassment. I helped Melanski to unharness the horse, in order to give Pélagie time to make the soup, for I really was dying of hunger.

At table, he became again as I had known him in Paris. Having me in front of him, is born interlocutor, the man mot imprinted with his ideas and best qualified to draw the out, he made fun of himself loudly, and spoke ill of human society with his habitual profound sarcasm. He was cheerful, with the heart-ending merriment that signifies: *after all, that ridiculous dance of infamies is as hilarious as an Opéra ball*. He had the same bursts of laughter, like the cawing of a crow.

That was my true Melanski.

When dinner was over, we went to smoke a cigar in the garden, which was rather large, and whipped self-esteem even harder in chatting philosophically at the expense of anything at all.

Soon, Pélagie appeared.

"Monsieur," she said to Melanski, "you have someone there who can make you talk as I have never seen you do before, but do you know where your friend is going to sleep?"

That kind of admonition suited Pélagie's broad face very well. There was no means of taking offense at it, and Melanski could no longer be astonished by it.

"Yes, that's true," he replied. "Well, put clean sheets in my bed and tidy my room a little. I'll sleep on the divan in my study."

"That can't be," I protested. "It's me who'll sleep on the divan in your study." I addressed myself to Pélagie. "You hear, Madame? Anyway, we agreed on that before Monsieur arrived, didn't we?"

Nonplussed, Pélagie ventured the opinion that it was better not to disturb her master's habits, since I didn't seem to be a monsieur who would stand on ceremony, that the divan had a perfectly good mattress and that I'd sleep marvelously there.

For my part, I supported Pélagie so well that we ended up prevailing.

Being only the housekeeper, she had returned to her own hearth some hours before, after having arranged everything in Melanski's house, when the latter escorted me to where I was to sleep.

"I rented this house," he told me, "because of its garden, but, although it's quite large, there are no rooms in a fit state except for mine, the dining room and this one, which I use for my consultations. I'm waiting before furnishing the other rooms, for the proprietor, who is in no hurry, to render them habitable."

I assured him that I lacked nothing essential, and took from his bookshelf for myself Nicole's essay "On the Means of Maintaining Peace Between Men,"[8] of which there had been some discussion over dinner and which I had not yet read. After placing a chair equipped with some paper, a pen and ink next to my bed, in order that I could make notes, he shook my hand affectionately and left.

I was harassed by fatigue. Nevertheless, I commenced reading, so ardent was I to possess that capital work by one of our greatest thinkers. The impassioned attention that such reading requires produced the customary effect on my nerves; it agitated them to the point that repose became impossible; and when I ceased reading and blew out my candle at about half past one, it was more to spare my eyes than in the hope of sleeping.

IV

It had probably been five minutes since I had stuck my head to my pillow, my limbs extended and my gaze plunged into darkness, when the study door opened quietly. I saw Melanski appear, a candle in his hand. He was in a nightshirt,

---

[8] The Jansenist Pierre Nicole (1625-1695); the essay cited is the most famous in *Essais de morale* (1671).

walking barefoot, and he had a fixed gaze. I sat up. I moved my lips as if to ask him why he was there; I was about to speak, but fortunately, although I had never seen a sleepwalker, I recognized by the strange attitude of his entire person, that he must be one; and, very emotional, I contented myself with observing him.

He placed his candle on the mantelpiece and advanced in my direction, his hands forward, his gaze still fixed, and, it seemed, heading straight toward me. Almost frightened, I held my breath. However, he veered to the right, stopped in front of an eccentrically-shaped item of furniture of which I had taken no more notice than the others because of the ardor with which I was reading, and appeared to meditate momentarily.

He opened the cupboard, made the gesture of unhooking something, and closed it again without having taken anything out, but affecting the inconvenienced stance of a man carrying something heavy—which is to say, crouching down somewhat and trying to keep his tensed left thigh, as much as possible, in the same plane as his crooked right arm, while using his left arm, which he had just disengaged in his imagination, to close the cupboard. Then he straightened up, after taking care to pass the left arm along the corresponding thigh in order to regrasp its portion of the imaginary burden that he was supporting. Finally, with both arms bent in a semicircular fashion, except that the left remained a fraction lower than the right, he went to pick up his candle with his fingertips, without disturbing the flexion of his right arm, cleared his path by using his foot to move the study door, which he had left ajar, closed it from outside, probably in the same fashion in which I had seen him close the cupboard…and I found myself alone.

The first thing that I did was to breathe out noisily in order to relieve a long containment; the second was to light my candle, for, apart from the fact that the darkness was then causing me a vague infantile fear, I wanted to see what the devil that item of furniture was, and what was inside it.

Imagine a cherry-wood box about two meters high and about seventy-five centimeters wide, mounted on a small entablature set on four legs, the door of which, glazed in its upper half, opened from the summit to the base by means of a long rod. One might have thought it the case of one of those monumental pendulum clocks that one sometimes sees in the country.

The glass was covered inside by a small curtain of blue silk. I opened the door; the singular box was absolutely empty. All that I remarked was a peg fixed to the ceiling, from which Melanski thought he was unhooking the nothing that he carried with such astonishing precaution.

I went back to bed, my mind tormented, seeking vainly to guess what the destination of the box might be. In brief, I did not sleep a wink all night.

Since it was impossible for me to deduce anything, ought I to ask Melanski for an explanation of the mystery?

No.

To interrogate him regarding his nocturnal pilgrimage would be to run the risk of frightening him, with regard to habits that he did not know he had, or, if he knew them, the risk of humiliating him by revealing that I had witnessed them—for it was obvious that shortly before, close as he was to me, he had not seen me and was scarcely conscious that I had arrived the day before.

Furthermore, that phenomenon of somnambulism had to be connected in a very narrow manner with the object of his madness, of which he preferred not to inform me; and it was an obligatory delicacy on my part not to force my friend's secret out of him, as it were.

Sleep only arriving with the morning, I got up late. Melanski had been up for a long time and had gone out.

I chatted with Pélagie, and when she went to the study to draw the curtains of the divan and tidy the covers, making everything neat, I followed her.

"Why," I said, negligently, as if I had only just perceived it, "What the devil is this box that resembles a clock-case?"

Pélagie burst out laughing. "Of, that's like me," she said, "just like me." Laughing more loudly, she added: "Yes, yes, a clock-case, one would swear it."

"But after all," I said, "what the devil does Melanski use it for?"

"Nothing, I believe. I've occasionally seen him put his umbrella and his walking-sticks in it. He's a little eccentric; he must have bought it on a whim..."

"Good! But that peg, Madame, isn't made to suspend Monsieur Melanki's umbrellas and canes, I imagine."

Pélagie, who was only able to conjecture, like me, made me an ingenious but inconclusive response that scarcely seemed to have any connection with Melanski's nocturnal gestures, of which she had no knowledge, and which, in consequence, could not give her food for thought. She suggested that the peg might, in principle, be adapted for a small mobile portmanteau that Melanski had probably relegated to the attic because he found it more convenient simply to throw his change of clothes on to a chair than take so many precautions.

At lunch, poor Melanski, increasingly relaxed by my presence, manifested a talkative and expansive, almost cheerful amity. And yet, as I contemplated him in broad daylight, I shivered at the changes that had taken place in his features in a few months. His face had aged, his cheekbones were sticking out in a noticeable fashion, and his gaze still retained a little of the strange fixity that had distressed me the previous evening.

"Well," Melanski suddenly exclaimed, "What have you to reply to Monsieur Allan Kardec? Wasn't I right? In any case, I've assured myself of the fact, and there's nothing as convincing as experience. What one has seen, one has seen. In sum, what have you to reply to Allan Kardec?"

"My friend," I said, I left Paris so precipitately that I didn't have the time to go and consult Monsieur Kardec for you; but I confess that I'm not sorry about that, because as far as I understand, your case of spiritism is unworthy to occupy and intelligence like yours. Is it possible that you, who have made a special study of the laws of life, find anything but an admirable fable in the story of Galatea, and that you believe a statue capable of willing and executing what it wills—capable of saying to itself 'I'll go there,' and going; capable of animating itself with the magnetic fluid of a superabundant soul? Oh, how many men endowed with such a soul, if that were the case, would replace their mistresses of flesh and bone with mistresses of marble, women in moments of amour but statues apart from that? Yes, statues," I added, laughing, as soon as they threaten to become embarrassing!"

"I don't claim," Melanski replied, very seriously, "that life can be transmitted or restituted in its integrity and in its permanence by the operation of the mind. Don't get confused. I'm only saying that certain amours, at their apogee, determine a kind of reflection of their flame, like a reciprocal desire and a propulsion, for as long as it lasts, on the part of objects that are ordinarily devoid of life, but that one wants to vivify."

Although that opinion appeared to me to be too absurd for discussion, I solicited Melanski, so far as I could, to defend it, because I hope that he would be obliged to cite me his own example and lay bare is madness. He avoided the trap.

I said to him forthrightly: "When you have shown me such an extraordinary spectacle, I'll declare myself convinced.

He responded, dryly: "I won't show it to you. I wouldn't want to see it again myself. That's what rendered me mad. Anyway, let's leave it there, I beg you, my dear friend."

In the afternoon we went for a walk together as far as Bléville, which is a league and a half from Montivilliers, and we sat on the shingle on the sea-shore.

God preserved us from repeating the pretentious banalities that the Ocean has inspired in its admirers for a long time. We did not exchange many words. We restricted ourselves to feeling, and I believe that the variable colors of the waves, their regular splashing on the shore, and their perfume, gently carried to us by the breeze, gave us the same sensitive wellbeing, which I call velvet calm.

Nevertheless, I remember that Melanski, seeing a porpoise leaping over a sunlit wave, exclaimed: "Look! It's bizarre, isn't it? I have here"—he pointed at his heart—a horrible porpoise that bounds and pirouettes like that one, an eater of joys...oh, petty joys, for I've never had any great ones."

V

You will easily divine what demon kept me wake the second night of my residence in Montivilliers.

Would Melanski come again to accomplish in his study, at the strange box, the mysterious ritual that I had witnessed? Or was that only a temporary whim that would not be renewed?

Alas, the confession he had made me himself of his madness and the slow precision of his various movements indicated all too clearly a special and habitual somnambulism—which is to say that Melanski ought to repeat it every night.

There are three species of sleepwalkers: those who are acting out their dreams, like roof-walkers; those who, very preoccupied on going to bed with the following day's work, get up to do it a little in advance; and finally, those who are obsessed by a fixed idea, like Lady Macbeth.

Melanski belonged to the last species of sleepwalkers.

I had, therefore, gone to bed and had resumed my reading of the previous night with the resolution not to stop before hearing the door-knob turn. From time to time I looked at my watch, anxiously. I listened for sounds coming from the door, curiously, desiring that Melanski would come, even though I feared it, because of the distress it would cause me, and above all because of my affection for him.

He arrived. As he came in I blew out my candle, and then stiffened myself, propped up on my elbow.

Without omitting anything, he played the same pantomime that I have already described. It even appeared to me that he added something, to wit, that as he turned round, he kissed the void above his right arm, tenderly.

On the third night, I had the malice of placing a chair in the path to the large box. That was an audacious experiment, for if he bumped into the chair and knocked it over, the noise would doubtless wake him up...and then what countenance would he adopt, on finding himself face to face with me, so oddly equipped at such an hour?

Would he confess his terrible secret to me, or would he devise a subterfuge? In any case, I counted on trying hard to put him at his ease and observe him better by simulating a profound sleep: a superb snore, eyelids half-closed. But would he even remember the objective of his expedition? That was not certain. Between the second life and reality the thread of ideas almost always breaks.

The chair did not accomplish much. Although Melanski was walking with his head held high looking directly ahead, he went around it with perfect ease; and, more curiously, when he went back, for fear of bumping it with his pretended burden, he turned sideways.

The fourth night, another stratagem: at quarter past one—Melanski came at half past one precisely—I got up and placed my lighted candle at the exact spot on the mantelpiece where he placed his.

He was no more embarrassed by that than by the chair. He placed his own candle at the other end of the mantelpiece, but when he came back, he took mine by mistake.

As the candles in the study differed considerably from those in the bedroom, and Melanski never alternated their service, he was astonished the following morning to find one of the candles from the study on his nightstand.

That is certainly an astonishment that does not come to the mind of many people, because its object is so insignificant. Only maniacs pick up on such details; so Melanski's mania was fundamental.

He said to Pélagie, in my presence: "How do you explain, Pélagie, that one of the study candles is in my bedroom?"

"Well, Monsieur," Pélagie replied, "it's not always me who carries things upstairs; it must have been you, yesterday evening, when you went to bed."

"I'm sure that it wasn't," he said. "I never make use of a candle like that."

I smiled; he perceived it, and said, gravely: "It's you who played that trick on me eh?"

"How would I do that?" I said.

"By coming into my room and making the swap while I was asleep."

Someone who had loved Melanski less and suffered less from his morbid condition would have been inclined to laugh; I swore to him that I was incapable of mystifying him in a fashion so devoid of ingenuity, and added, not without emotion: "If I were a sleepwalker I'd say to you: 'It's possible that I came into your room while I was asleep,' but I don't believe I am. In fact, you, who are a doctor, examine me a little: have I the appearance of a somnambulist?"

"What an idea!" he cried, excitedly. "Not at all, my friend. Don't go getting that idea into your head. You're no more a somnambulist than I am, thank God!"

"Thank God, you say. Is it a great misfortune, then, to be a somnambulist?"

"A very great misfortune," he told me. I wouldn't want to be one for an empire."

"But I don't see what's so afflicting about sleepwalking."

"Oh, you don't see... First of all, the nervous system is extraordinarily overwrought, just when it ought to be at rest; secondly, somnambulists very often enjoy an incomplete, and hence deceptive, lucidity, which induces them to commit many stupidities; and finally, when they're woken up during their excursion, the abrupt reaction can be fatal to them."

Those final words frightened me by informing me that my experiment with the chair had exposed my friend to the risk of a dangerous awakening.

As for the incomplete lucidity of somnambulists that Melanski mentioned, I admired it in him, in whom I had discerned it clearly, recognized it, and had no doubt that he offered an example of it.

In fact, let us take it from the moment when he got out of bed during the fit.

To light his candle in order to go down to his study was to have the sentiment that he was acting by night; but not to put on his slippers was to be unaware that his feet would be chilled by the steps of the staircase.

To place his candle on the mantelpiece, head for the big box, open it, and, soon believing his arms laden, to use the precaution I described to close it and pick up his candle, etc, etc., was to show an astonishing presence of mind on the part of a man asleep; but not to perceive that he had absolutely nothing in his arms, to imagine the contrary, as revealed by the stressed attitude on which nothing as weighing, was a comical delusion.

And not to remember that I was in his house, that he had put me in his study to sleep, not to see my effects to the right and the left, nor me, whereas he had seen the chair and the lighted candle so promptly, was certainly a vast breach in Melanski's lucidity.

Soon, I had an indication of it even more essential, because it related to the very object of his nocturnal campaigns.

VI

When the initial curiosity was satisfied, I began to weary of being interrupted every night during my first sleep by such a funereally eccentric scene that scarcely changed. On the other hand, although I had nothing to fear, I did not have sufficient placidity to go to sleep as if nothing would happen. Then I almost regretted the discretion that had made me refuse Melanski's offer of his bedroom. I would have liked him to raise the matter again so that I could change my mind, but he did not. The matter was settled. I had questioned his decision several times, but he was no longer thinking about it.

To that concern I added another, less egotistical: that of extracting poor Melanski from his sorry state.

A change of scenery, many fatigues and distractions and the suppression of the damned box seemed to me to be the best specific to employ, and I promised myself ardently to prescribe a departure from Montivilliers.

However, I had not reached the end of the surprises that were in store for me.

One day, when Melanski was traveling the country in his carriage, instead of accompanying him, as I often did, I stayed in the house. I had a headache.

Repose did not soothe it; on the contrary, it aggravated it; I wanted to try a little exercise.

In the garden there was a small patch of land that was absolutely uncultivated and had fallen prey to parasitic plants. It had not occurred to me to ask Melanski why that tiny part of his garden was languishing in that fashion amid well-kept flower-beds and carefully trimmed bushes.

I thought it was because he was planning some important plantation, unless something prevented him from digging it up...and I went to fetch a spade, and started work, taking a childish delight in plunging in my spade with the aid of my foot, lifting the clods of earth and turning them over, disheveled, moist and embalmed.

Suddenly, I felt a rather strong resistance. I parted the earth and I discovered a little box two or three feet square, buried at a mediocre depth.

What could that box contain? Was it money? Who had put it there? Was it Melanski?

Well, yes, it must be him. First of all, the box was too intact to have been there a long time. Secondly, although it was a false calculation, the presence of the box explained why Melanski left fallow the plot in which it lay. But in that case, it wasn't money that it contained, because I knew very well that Melanski did not have the mania of hoarding.

What was it, then?

The lid was only stuck to the box by two pins, and the adherence was imperfect. I was able to slide the blade of the spade into the interstice, and a slight pressure was sufficient to lift out the two pins and raise the lid.

Full of fright, I lowered it again very rapidly. I had just perceived, in a heap, all the bones of a human body; and what had struck me the most in the curse of the rapid glance was the skull, the frontal bone of which no longer presented anything but a void carefully cut out in a rectangle, like the envelope of an ordinary letter, and exactly the same size.

"A crime!" I exclaimed. "And perhaps Melanski's! Oh, great God! No, not him, it's impossible. Anyway, he hasn't been in the house long enough. A cadaver can't be reduced to bones in six months.

The author of the crime, evidently, was the person who had lived in the house before Melanski. But how was it that Melanski had left that precise plot of land uncultivated? It had to be admitted that if it was pure chance, it was a strange coincidence.

I spoke to myself thus while nailing the box shut again, reburying it, and even trying to replant the grass that my spade had uprooted—in sum, trying to efface the marks of my ill-judged labor as much as possible.

When I had accomplished such a reintegration, I walked pensively from path to path, very anxious as to the course of action I should adopt with regard to Melanski. The reader can imagine my embarrassment.

One of two things had to be true: either Melanski was guilty or he was not. I was reasoning, of course, in the natural hypothesis of a crime.

If he was guilty, the best thing was to appear to know nothing about it, for fear of causing him a terrible shame, of compromising my own dignity, and of rendering official, so to speak, the intimate scruple I felt in not denouncing him.

If he was not guilty—and in that case, he must have no suspicion of the already ancient deposit of the box of bones— it was better to inform him, in order that he did not bear any longer the latent responsibility for a crime that someone else had committed.

After much hesitation, I decided to tell Melanski what I had done, because I could not doubt that he was innocent.

Not only did his heart, the noblest that I had ever encountered, seem to me to be impenetrable to the idea of any crime whatsoever, but he had a veritable theory, confirmed many times by my arguments, that a criminal ordinarily harms himself more than his victim, and, in consequence, is acting like a madman.

It is true the Melanski had perhaps gone completely mad...in which case...

Suddenly I saw him come through the door to the garden and advance toward me. I was so absorbed that I had not heard the sound of his carriage when it had arrived.

"Come on," he said to me. "Let's have dinner."

His face was less somber, almost cheerful. He added: "I'm pleased with myself this evening. I've carried out an operation that has succeeded marvelously. I removed a polyp bigger than your thumb from someone's nose; and it's an operation that I was scarcely expecting to perform this morning. Can you imagine that on the road from Montivilliers to Harfleur, I spotted a peasant with an extremely swollen nostril. I made him a sign like this, by touching my noise:

"'That's troubling you, eh?'

"'Yes, Monsieur.'

"'Would you like me to get rid of that swelling for you?'

"'Very well, if it doesn't cost me too dear.'

"'I'll take a nice chicken from you—is that too much?'

"'Will it hurt much?'

"'No.'

"The peasant lived in a farm next to the road; he took me to his house; I took out my instrument-case and extracted his polyp in no time. Oh, I missed you. I would have put it off to the next day so that you could come and watch if I hadn't feared that my man wouldn't want it any longer."

"Me too," I said, trying to maintain my composure. "I've carried out an operation—look."

And I extended my arm toward the patch of ground that I had shifted recently.

He went very pale; his gaze wandered; his lips trembled: so many accusatory symptoms. The amazement into which I was thrown gave me a countenance little better than his.

"Oh, well! You've seen the box?" he murmured, dully.

"Yes."

"You've opened it?"

"Yes."

"So you've discovered a specimen of my madness?"

A specimen of his madness! There was something terrifying in that emphatic phrase.

"You can count on my discretion," I told him, "although I'm exposing myself thus to sharing your remorse; never, I swear to you, will I reveal what hazard has revealed to me. I shall be content silently to curse the unfortunate inspiration that I had to do some gardening. Oh, I wish to Heaven that I was still unaware...if I had only settled on the idea that the box had been put there by you, I would have had the tact to hide my discovery from you, but I thought that it would come as a complete surprise to you."

"Why would I be surprised?" he said, staring at me.

"I assumed," I said, "that you were incapable of committing such an action, and I accused the person who lived here before you of having done it."

"Eh? Who else but me would have been mad enough?"

"Mad!" I cried, withdrawing my arm, on which he had been leaning for a moment. "Mad...you're priceless! Rather say criminal, all that there is of the most criminal!"

"You're harsh," he said to me. "In truth, I've ceded to a culpable impulse."

At the phrase "culpable impulse," I shrugged my shoulders in a gesture of indignation.

He continued: "Look, my friend, the proof that I have seen clearly what might have been odious to my charge in the drama from which I've just emerged is that I would have blushed to tell you about it. But since you've lifted one of the corners of the veil, it's as well that you know everything. I'm much mistaken if, when fully informed, you aren't also more indulgent."

"No, no, Melanski, if you please. I'm only too embarrassed to know the reality of your crime, without also knowing all the details of it."

"What do you mean by my crime? Do you imagine, perchance, that I've killed someone?"

"Or hidden the evidence of a murder committed by someone else, which comes to the same thing. Don't you perceive, then, wretch, that for fear of dooming you, I'm almost becoming your accomplice? You're putting me in a fine situation, you know."

"Shh!" said Melanski, for Pélagie was coming to tell us that the soup was on the table.

"I'll leave this evening," I said, as soon as Pélagie had gone away. "It's impossible for me to stay any longer under the roof of a…friend like you."

"You won't leave," said Melanski, to whom, remarkably, calm had returned as it had abandoned me. "You won't abandon an unfortunate whose only crime is to have a soul in turmoil. What is it you're claiming, then? That I've concealed the evidence of a murder? Either you're crazier than I am, or you haven't examined those bones. If I didn't fear that Pélagie would come and stick her nose in what we're doing. I'd open the box in front of you immediately, in my turn, and I'd show you the ridiculous injustice of your suspicions."

"Monsieur, Monsieur, you're talking too much; the soup will no longer be edible," shouted Pélagie, rendered impatient by her own impatience, or the solicitude of a cook.

VII

While walking toward the house in order to obey Pélagie's injunction, Melanski said to me: "It seems to me, however, that the symmetrical section in the cranium"—and he gestured toward his own forehead—"ought to have leapt to your eyes."

"Indeed," I replied. "I wondered for what reason it had been carried out. One might think that the piece had been removed by a stamp."

We sat down at table. He went on: "And the copper attachments?"

"What?" I said, although I had heard him quite clearly, the last words having taken me by surprise.

"He did not reply because of Pélagie, who planted herself in front of us throughout the dinner, somewhat indiscreetly, the dear woman. Both too preoccupied to say anything outside of our subject, we let Pélagie give tongue as she pleased, and even had the benevolence to pretend to be listening to her.

Immediately after dinner he asked me to accompany him to his room. I followed him there, not interrogating him but impatient to learn something that would permit me to restitute all my esteem to a man whose affinities with me were so great.

He opened his writing-desk, took out a small box from one of the drawers, and took out a miniature from the box, which he handed to me.

"Go over to the window," he said then. "Dusk is falling; you don't have enough light to see clearly."

The miniature represented a woman whose original beauty caused me a kind of interior dazzle: a delightful and gripping beauty, but completely indefinable.

In fact, no sort of beauty related to the physiognomy can ever be defined or explained even by the most skillful writer. In order to comprehend it, it is necessary to see it, and even then, one can see it without comprehending it. Why? Because extralinear beauty is nothing but a relationship, that of the spectacle to the beholder.

So the miniature of the woman that delighted me would, I'm convinced, have left many others cold.: all the more reason for me not to attempt to describe its charms, for that procedure, by its futility, seems to me to be unworthy of both the reader and myself.

I had been holding the miniature for a minute or two when Melanski, who had not taken his eyes off me, said: "Well, what do you observe?"

"What I observe first of all," I said, is that the model for this portrait is one of those women, very rare nowadays, who exercise an absolute fascination upon me."

Melanski shook my hand with a feverish affection. "You feel as I do," he said. "I expected it, moreover. Is it not our habit, many times over? Then again, what do you observe about the painting itself?"

"I observe that it must be the work of an exact and saga-cious portraitist, rather than the work of a man adroit in the manipulation of colors. It seems that the brush-strokes are a trifle gross for a miniature."

"But don't you see that the fault is in the rough substance on which it is painted?"

"In fact, what is it painted on?" I said. "One might think it was wood, but which has the artist chosen a convex sur-face?"

"Look at the back."

I turned the miniature upside-down.

"Is it possible?" I cried. "Yes, God forgive me...that's a terrifying bizarrerie! It's the fragment missing from the skull...yes, yes, of course! I'm not mistaken?" I added, inter-rogating Melanski, although I was certain that I was not wrong.

"You're not mistaken," he replied, phlegmatically. "The portrait you see there has been made on the frontal bone of its model."

"On the frontal bone of its model?" I repeated. "What does that mean?"

"It means that the bone belonged to the skull of the per-son whose portrait it is."

"I'm damned if I understand!"

"You really don't understand?"

"No."

"Well, imagine that you died and your cranium as carefully stripped, and a painter who knew you took it into his head to draw your portrait thereon."

"But that's the most absurd thing in the world. With what objective, pray?"

"It's not a matter of the objective, although I could offer you one that your philosophical humor would easily admit."

"Yes, doubtless, there's a kind of profound facetiousness in our fibers."

"It's a matter of what happened to that miniature of a woman. And pray to Heaven that such an idea didn't occur to the artist, for that's positively what has driven me mad."

"Ah!" I murmured, like a man trying to grasp something. "But how is it that you have this miniature?"

"Because I have the skeleton on the skull of which it was painted."

"Good," I said. "It was painted on the skull, and it's you who have extracted it. But how is it that you have the skeleton of the woman represented here?"

"How? Oh, that's very naïve. After what I've told you, you haven't guessed?"

"No, in truth."

"Well, it's because those bones made up a ready-made skeleton that I had the misfortune to buy from Monsieur Guérin, the skillful naturalist of the Rue Racine."

"Has anyone ever taken it into his head," I asked him, "to hide underground a ready-made skeleton, since there's no risk in exhibiting it and it is even constructed for exhibition? One only has an interest in hiding the skeleton of a former victim."

"In principle, you're right," said Melanski. "When one isn't mad, your argument is incontestable. But when one is mad…! Anyway, I have a good response to make to you. If I show you the little ring fixed to the occiput of the skeleton, designed to suspend it; if I show you the glue that reconnects the ribs, and the copper wires serving as articulations for the limbs, you'd be forced to believe that the skeleton has been prepared, that it cannot be that of a former victim, but simply that of someone who died in hospital.

"The miniature alone," he added "ought to have sufficed, by virtue of its relationship with the skull, to edify you against the idea that there had been a murder. That is why I began by presenting it to you, not yet having the strength to tell you the mystery of my madness in all its details."

It would have been impossible to see a madman endowed with more solid logic. The odious suspicions engendered within me vanished.

"My dear Melanski," I said to him, taking his hand, "I believe you. Forget, I beg you, that on the basis of superficial appearances, I was momentarily able to suppose you the author of an abominable act; but it's necessary to admit that the excessive disturbance that took possession of you when I told you that I had dug up the plot of land where the box was, was furiously accusatory."

"I admit it," replied Melanski, squeezing my hand. "What do you expect? It was the surprise that you were on the trail of my secret, the chagrin of being forced to answer your questions, the shame of showing you the pusillanimous traverses to which I have been subject. Now, I've changed my mind, and I'm not averse to humiliating myself before you; so I shall tell you everything."

VIII

Melanski continued in these terms:

"Two days after I sustained my thesis, less than a week after our departure, I was passing along the Rue Racine and I stopped in front the shop-window of Monsieur Guérin, the naturalist, in which a number of comic scenes were represented by frogs. I noticed two of them that pleased me, and I went in to buy them. In the first there was a female frog with a rose in her paw, posing very modestly, while a painter-frog was sketching her portrait, not forgetting the rose. In the second, there were the same two characters, but the model, no longer posing, was allowing herself to be embraced tenderly by the painter, and the rose had fallen to the floor. Nothing was more droll than that fable in action.

"There was a crowd in Monsieur Guérin's shop. While waiting for my turn to come to ask the employee the price of the two caricatures, I was darting distracted glances to the right and left.

"Against the wall at the back of the shop, partly in shadow, three human skeletons of unequal size were placed. One of them attracted my attention more particularly, because I perceived something on the frontal bone that looked, from a distance, like a stain, but so harmonious in its ensemble, so well-denied in its lines and so odd, that it was worth taking a closer look at it.

"The so-called stain was the admirable portrait of the woman that you're holding. Judge my amazement by yours. It was even more vehement, the object being there before me, gripping me, so to speak, suddenly imposing itself on my divination by virtue of the contrast between a fictitious living being grafted on to the last vestiges of a consummate dead one.

"Imagine the effect of that gaze and that singular smile, which render the portrait so animated. Imagine their effect above the hollow orbits, a nasal cavity, fleshless jaws and the summary scaffolding of the bones.

"At first, I had a sort of vertigo; then, capable of reflection, I admired the fantasy that the author of the portrait had had. Yes, in accordance with the Byronic poetics that are so dear to us, my poor friend, a similar fantasy had to procure me a lugubrious joy, the sole species of joy that you and I experience.

"I recalled that Lord Byron, so Stendhal recounts, was very impressed one day by the sight of a painting by Daniel Crespi representing the following scene: Inside a church, the mass for the dead is being sung around a bier; suddenly, the deceased, who was a canon, raises the mortuary sheet, emerges from his coffin and cries: 'It is by just entitlement that I am damned!'[9]

"Why that memory came back to me while I was face to face with the skeleton bearing the portrait I cannot say, for there was only a very distant analogy between the two—what I call an analogy of tendency.

"I assumed that the skeleton must have come from a sale made after the decease of an artist who, dominated by the maxim 'All is vanity,' had found it both sinister and humorous to paint his mistress.

"I was so absorbed in the contemplation of my skeleton that the shop gradually emptied, without my perceiving it, of all those who had business there.

"Monsieur Guérin's employee, seeing that I had prolonged my wait beyond the necessary time, came toward me and said, with a slightly ironic politeness: 'What does Monsieur desire? Monsieur is a physician, no doubt?'

"'Freshly cast,' I replied, 'for I've only just passed my doctoral thesis.'

"'Well, Monsieur,' the employee said, 'you'll need a skeleton, for when bones are presented that are in need of resetting, it's useful to be able to palpate the skeleton first in the corresponding places. Simple plates in a book cannot enlighten osteological studies like the sight of a skeleton. Is it a skeleton that Monsieur desires?'

"'Yes,' I said, completely forgetting that I had come in for the frogs.. 'This one, for example.'

"'Because of the portrait, Monsieur' said the employee, smiling, "you're not the only one whose caprice has fallen upon that little skeleton. It's already been sold to several times. The portrait aside, though, it's a pretty framework, very well-prepared, as you can see, and furthermore, that of a pretty woman.'

"I had not even noticed that it was the 'framework' of a woman, because my attention had been concentrated more on

---

[9] The painter cited is Daniel Crespi 1598-1630).

the skull than the iliac bones, but how did the employee know that the woman had been pretty? I expressed my surprise to him..

"'Well, Monsieur, you can judge it as well as me from her portrait.'

"'What! That miniature...?'

"Like you, just now, I had not wanted to believe that there was any other relationship between the skeleton and the miniature than that between a canvas and paint. I had not imagined that it might be, in a sense, the fictitious flesh of the deceased individual, covering at a given spot her own bones. The more I thought about that assertion, the more I contested it.

"'There's scarcely any way of admitting,' I told him, 'that such a remarkable painting hasn't been made according to nature; but if it were the portrait of the woman reduced to the state of a skeleton, it would obviously have to have been made from memory.'

"'Oh, permit me: from memory or from a copy,' said the employee, swiftly. 'Nothing prevented, in fact, the artist from having made a portrait of that woman on canvas or enamel while she was still alive, and copying it subsequently on to the very skull of the model, dead and dissected. Now, that's exactly what happened. We obtained it from the author in person, who sold us the skeleton of the unfortunate woman, whom he had cared for and painted while ill, and whom he dissected and painted again when dead. But you must know him; it's Monsieur Onfroy, interned at Lariboisière.'

"I did not know Monsieur Onfroy, whose promotion was doubtless very recent and dated after the moment when my withdrawal from the Internat had been obligatory. Perhaps, however, a month after that, I had encountered the name Onfroy among those of our successors, although it had not made any other impact on me.

"That was what I replied to Monsieur Guérin's employee in expressing to him how astonished I was that Monsieur

Onfroy had not kept such an original work for himself, and in which I, personally, saw even more heart than mind.

"'What do you expect?' said the employee. He needed money. You know…a young man, and an artist more than any other, is argentivorous. In any case, I don't presume that he put into the execution of that portrait the sentiment that you think…he was playing a game, nothing more.'

"'Let's go!' I said to the employee, who had no need of sales talk to convince me. 'I'll buy your skeleton. If you want to send it to me with a settled invoice a few hours from now, I'll receive it myself and pay the commissionaire.'

"Having left my address, I went out. An hour later, I had my skeleton, but the poor two hundred francs that were awaited to settled the bill had bled my writing-desk dry. No matter! I no longer cared about the comical frogs. I had my skeleton. I possessed it. I was free to contemplate, as much as I wished, the strange object that had apprehended my soul, a liberty as deadly as all those one abuses!

"Instead of amusing myself, as I had the right to do, during the few days following the one on which I had sustained my thesis, I remained constantly in the house, not to work, but because—what became frightening subsequently began by being ridiculous—because my skeleton was there beside me, and *we were keeping one another company.* Perhaps you've noticed that large glazed box that is in the room where you're sleeping?"

"Yes, I replied, with an excited curiosity. "Well?"

"Well," he continued, "I opened the curtain and, sometimes walking around the room, sometimes standing still, furtively, in front of it, I gazed incessantly at the skeleton and the portrait."

"Oh my God!" I cried, alarmed. "So your skeleton occupied that glazed box? Oh, my God, what are you telling me?"

The reader, while judging my perspicacity severely lacking for not having already sensed the mysterious relationship between the big glazed box and the skeleton, will nevertheless understand the reason for that maladroit exclamation, which Melanski could not imagine, unconscious as he was of his somnambulistic life.

Thus, he replied to me, slightly astonished: "There's nothing in that to warrant a cry of 'Oh my God," as you've just done, my dear friend. Of course, it's not very easy to see that the glazed box in my study is a skeleton box...but that doesn't enter into consideration. Wait a while and you'll have reason to be seriously astonished."

I bit my lips at having interrupted Melanski. He went on:

"Initially out of simple curiosity, a vague application of our chronic sadness, a pretext for I know not what sentimental irony worthy of Heinrich Heine, that spectacle soon interested my heart. My gaze no longer went alternately from the portrait to the skeleton; it embraced them simultaneously. By virtue of one of the phenomena that the imagination has the gift of producing, the portrait gained ground over the skeleton—which is to say that the tender and incomparable face, on the frontal bone by which it was circumscribed, extended before by charmed eyes, covering the entire death's-head like living flesh, and then the rest of the bony framework was closed as gracefully as any in the world.

"Thanks to the important gift I had of the features of her face, I reconstituted the dead woman around her own remains: an envelope certainly more vaporous, but doubtless also more perfect than her primitive envelope. An alchemist of a superior species, I had made a woman hatch from a few colors and a few bones, under the constant incubation of enthusiasm. And it was precisely the physical woman that I wanted.

"Fundamentally, I did not doubt that that pretended resurrection was vain and deceptive, but I allowed myself to begin to believe it, and abused my senses voluntarily—to such a point, my friend, that I fell in love with my skeleton, translated into a beautiful body by an imagination a hundred times too irritable.

"You remember the passion that Bernardino Luini's Hérodiade inspired in me.[10] I told you that she was one of my feminine types. The ferocious placidity that she expressed attracted me by repelling me. I found her odious but ravishing, that Hérodiade; I languished before her in a culpable admiration. I begged her to condescend to love me, even though she was a truly damnable soul.

"Alas, from the canvas on which Luini represented her, she did not listen to me any more than she would have listed to me in Antipas' court if I had been her contemporary. There was only one advantage in declaring my passion to her at a distance of centuries, which was that in the anticipated case of a rejection, the formidable capricious woman was no longer able to have me beheaded for having wanted to please her, as she had had John the Baptist beheaded for not having feared to displease her. Every day, for a month, I went to contemplate her in the Louvre. Wasted effort!

"She was not occupied with me. Her vague and floating gaze, entirely given over to the interior intoxication of a long-desired possession, did not encounter mine. That was, to tell the truth, Luini's fault. He could have put into Hérodiade's eyes the line of sight that goes directly to the spectator. I became discouraged by loving at a total loss, without the object of my amour even darting a glance of pity at me.

"So, reawakening pride within me, by a supreme effort, I ceased to go and sing my laments beneath Luini's splendid painting. It's the everyday story of unrequited love; it grows weary and turns in another direction.

"Mine turned as soon as it could toward the female skeleton, and with her, it received full satisfaction.

"I dare to assure you, my friend, that she loved me even more than I loved her during the artificial life that she owed to

---

[10] "Hérodiade receiving the head of John the Baptist" (c.1530) by Bernardino Luini (c.1480-1532) is in the Uffizi Gallery, but the Louvre has another study of the same subject, in which the character is given the more usual name of Salome.

me for more than five months, and that her extravagant passion alone forced me to take her out.

"All the phases through which two lovers are accustomed to pass, we passed through.

"To begin with, when I gazed at her fixedly, her countenance seemed to me to be gauche, timid and fearful; but when I peered at her from the corner of my eye in passing, I surprised in her eyes an infinite softness in my regard.

"Then I came to take her poor body hand, which became animated and plump n mine; then I held her from time to time to emerge from her box, sit down on the sofa next to me and chat. She always spoke in a low, very low voice, which did not prevent me from hearing her marvelously, inasmuch as the play of hr physiognomy brightened her slightest speeches. A day came when, very emotionally, I became bold enough to kiss her on the forehead, exactly on top of the portrait. Thus I inaugurated between us and eternal betrothal that marriage did not take long to crown.

"Paris seemed to me to be too noisy an abode for fiancés like us, who liked to meditate on our happiness. In addition, although there was scarcely sagacity in it, I was importuned there more than I counted on being elsewhere by a sort of jealousy against Monsieur Onfroy, who had known while perfectly alive the woman I had come to revivify as best I could.

"It was then that I went to establish myself in Montivilliers. A month had sufficed to reduce me to that insane vision of a skeleton that had become a woman again, and a woman as loving as beloved.

"I have already told you, my friend, that I was to some extent a voluntary insensate, for to anyone who had contested seriously that pretended metamorphosis, I would have replied: 'Are you making fun of me? Is such a miracle possible? You can clearly see that I'm the dupe of an illusion that I'm not stupid enough to want to impose on you. There's nothing there but bones and a few colors on the forehead arranged in a portrait.'

"However, incessantly attracted to my box, I had scarcely opened the door than, instead of the skeleton that I knew it positively to be, I saw with a sensation of indescribable joy the graciously rounded forms of a young fiancée, especially her admirable head.

"Perhaps, if I had commanded my organs, I would have observed through them, as I did through my reason, what there was in the box; but I carefully refrained. I preferred to see what was not there. I found myself as well as could be in those moments of hallucination behind which the empty and vulgar moments of real life faded away. Alas, I did not know what terrible punishment was reserved for me, what a frightful awakening I was to have. It's necessary to believe my friend, that a superior power really is occupied in equilibrating our penalties with our sins.

"The grave sin that I committed was that of giving myself complaisantly to that transmutation of a skeleton into a woman, and attempting a work that God himself would not have been able to accomplish."

"You're forgetting," I said, that the resurrection of the flesh is a Christian dogma."

"In fact, you're right," he said, with a melancholy smile; "well, in what happened to me I see a rude lesson of the Holy Trinity, justly irritated because I anticipated in part the labor of the end of the world...unless it was all simply a magnetic phenomenon...

"But no," he added, as if talking to himself, "if it were a pure magnetic phenomenon, why was the spell that had tenderly protected me until then against the horror of my amour vanish precisely when that horror was to strike me hardest?"

"What happened to you, then, my poor friend? Come on, you're not mad. At the time, I let your illusion regarding Hérodiade pass; I assumed that it wouldn't go any further. As for your story of the skeleton, it's absurd. It's not a case of an insensate dreamer, it's that of a veritable idiot. That the portrait should have impressed you deeply, I can conceive; that it engendered in you an admiration confining I know not what mystical tenderness, all well and good again…but to treat as a living woman the skeleton of a woman is…"

"Yes, yes, you said it, it's a case of veritably idiocy. So that's what I was; and yet, I've pointed out to you that, in that regard, my sensation alone had deviated; my reason remained straight."

"What does it matter? Since in you, reason does not prevail over sensation? That's where your disdain for simple living women led you, and your frantic quest for the ideal…it's lugubrious."

"What! You, my Synnoëte, don't understand," said Melanski, "how seductive and profound an amour like mine might be? Founded on death, it has no fear of it. One the other hand, it cannot provide grounds for treason or even for jealousy, like others. Finally, everything being at the discretion of the sole actor who plays the double role of lover and mistress, it isn't susceptible of engendering lassitude. Thus, it is ineradicable."

"So scantly that it has been vanquished—at least, that's what you gave given me to understand, and for the sake of the amity I have for you, my dear Melanski, I'm very glad that you're liberated from that unhealthy sentiment. Come on, tell me about that. What happened to you, then?"

"Oh, my friend, you'd refuse to believe it; you'd claim that I'd mistaken a dream for a reality. You'd say harsh things to me, as you did a little while ago. Haven't you jeered at me already because, with telling you anything precise, I judged it possible that a certain amorous impulsion could be communicated to inanimate beings that inspires amour, and, contrary to all natural laws, sets them in motion and attracts hem? Now, that's exactly what happened to me, to my great misfortune."

IX

"One day," Melanski continued, "two months after I had settled in Montivilliers, and consequently three months ago—it was the twelfth of May, a Monday morning; I could live a hundred years without ever forgetting that date—I felt something resistant in my bed, alongside my body. I felt it without being able to determined what it was. I opened my eyes. Horrible spectacle! My skeleton had come to lie beside me; our limbs were overlapping, its head was resting on my left shoulder, while my left arm was wrapped round it entirely, folded over its ribs.

"I uttered a cry. I leapt out of bed in order to escape that sinister proximity, for—take note of this bizarrerie—it was at the moment when the *motion* of my skeleton appeared bound to plunge me further into the illusion that it had given me that I reduced those few prepared bones to their veritable significance.

"In addition, even when that illusion was at its height, and had produced scenes of tenderness between my skeleton and me, it had never gone far as to give me the desire for a monstrous possession. I respected her as my fiancée, that ex-woman, but in sum, I loved her ardently...

"On the morning of which I'm speaking, disillusioned as I was, and although I judged the skeleton for what it was—which is to say, absolutely inert and insensible matter—I couldn't suppose that anyone had carried it into my bed in order to play a practical joke, given that no one but me slept in the house. In truth, Pélagie had a key to the door to the street, but that key, which she used during the day, would not have been any use to her at night, because I bolted the door on the inside every evening before going to bed. Then again, Pélagie, whom I had only recently taken into my service, did not even know that I had a skeleton, and even if she had known, would not have been capable of playing a trick on me.

"What, then, ought I to admit? I admit, and will continue to admit until I have found a more satisfactory explanation, that in my intimacy with the skeleton I had, so to speak, electrified it, unknown to myself; that my will had poured its motivating force into it by some means, and that it had come to me drawn by the fraction of my life that it had absorbed and which was returning to me. That is stupid, from the viewpoint of our vulgar axioms, or the official science of locomotion, but perhaps the phenomenon will be verified one day by a new science, still occult today: the science that table-turning implies—which, in parentheses, is a much less rational phenomenon."

The reader would have been able, as I was at the time, to give Melanski the more satisfactory explanation for which he was waiting, of the skeleton's supposed visit. So I was tempted to say to him: *My poor friend, you're a sleepwalker, and it's you who, at half past one in the morning, go in search of your skeleton and have carried it to your bed.*

I feared, however, that the rectification might be worse than the error, all the more so as Melanski had testified to me that he considered it a great misfortune to be a somnambulist. It was better, I thought, to leave him in ignorance of his condition, since, by informing him of it, without taking away the old pretext for his black moods, I would be offering him a new one. To know that every night, he came to exercise in effigy the abduction of his skeleton, and not to have any means of freeing himself from that mania—that might be enough to cause is already-tottering reason to collapse. I loved the unfortunate fellow too much to run such a risk; so I limited myself to replying that in thinking that he had seen the skeleton in his bed he was probably the victim of an illusion analogous to and consequent upon the one that had shown him the skeleton in the form of a beautiful young woman.

Naturally, he did not want to concede the point. He protested his clear-sightedness at the moment of his awakening on that Monday the twelfth of May. He added:

"And the proof that I wasn't hallucinating is that when I took the skeleton out of my bed, I saw very clearly, with an increasing horror, that it had three broken ribs, which you can still verify. Confused by the realization of the enormities to which a reprehensible excitement had taken me, indignant with myself and disgusted with the skeleton, I resolved to finish with those false appetites of the heart, and above all to take precautions against any further whim the skeleton might have to come in search of me. I thought that the best means was to break its harmonic entity, which established attraction between us.

"It was early. I had time in hand before Pélagie arrived. I employed it in committing the crime whose traces you discovered this evening. It was a matter of expelling the spirit that haunted the skeleton and had transported it in such a miraculous fashion to my bed. Now, to achieve that, what could I do? Kill...kill my skeleton! I plunged a scalpel into its forehead and by drawing it along carefully in for straight lines, forming a square, I removed the portrait. I could have left it there, for, in losing the portrait, the skeleton had lost its artificial existence, it really was dead. But, not believing that I was sufficiently secure as yet, I disarticulated the limbs and lodged them in a box, which I nailed shut and buried in the garden, due to an excess of pusillanimity.

"Yes, pusillanimity! That is exactly what determined my confusion when you told me about your discovery. I felt ridiculous for having raised that last unnecessary obstacle to the frightfully tender demonstrations of the skeleton.

"As for the portrait, I did not have the courage to separate myself from it. I kept it in my writing-desk and looked at it frequently. In any case, its isolation rendered it inoffensive. It would not contribute any longer to representing a living woman; it simulated within me the memory of a woman I had known while she was alive.

"However, I was not absolutely rid of my infernal amour. It continued to obsess me during my sleep. I dreamed that the skeleton quit its box and came to me... I dreamed that again last night, alas, and every morning for the last there months, when I've awakened, thinking that I see the skeleton by my side, I've started with the horror that escapes me. Vain fear! The bones are really in the box, and the box is in the garden, and I really am alone in my bed. That persecution is no less ferocious for being a nightmare that vanishes with the coming of day, and, I fear that it is insurmountable. I summoned you here, my friend, in the hope that your company would rid me of the phantom, to which I am prey. It will be necessary for you to stay with me for a long time," he added, smiling, "if you want to break that spell."

"What, my poor friend?" I said to him, a trifle naively, "you can't prevent yourself dreaming about that wretched skeleton?"

"A fine question! If I could, I wouldn't have failed to do so, I assure you."

"You're right, but I don't have the leisure to stay with you forever, and besides which, I'm no great remedy. It's absolutely necessary or you to get away from here, to return to Paris or travel—in sum, to distract yourself."

"How can you expect me, who only have a meager patrimony, to quit a position already very advantageous? The life of pleasure in Paris is costly; nomadic life costs even more. My tiny revenues wouldn't be sufficient. Then again, how do you know that would cure me?"

"In that case, my friend, you only have one recourse. I only indicate it to you tremulously, because I know your opinion in that regard, and that's to marry. When you're in control of a pretty living woman, very much in love with you, as her duty obliges her to be, you'll soon forget your skeleton. Try, damn it, try."

"Never. I know your pretty living women, very much in love, and it's because I've made the experiment that I don't want to do it again, ever."

"But, obstinate as you are, you don't know the woman who will be your wife. She'll be very different from others, believe me."

"Yes, there'll be the difference that, instead of being insupportable to me for a day, a month or a year, it will be for a lifetime, according to the authority of Monsieur le Maire. The prettiest living woman you could find would only give me, on average, five minutes of pleasure a day and twenty-three hours fifty-five minutes of ennui. Thanks. Whatever it costs me, I prefer to do without the five minutes rather than subject myself to the twenty-three hours fifty-five minutes. That's relative wisdom."

"It's a pure joke," I cried, "and if I once laughed on hearing you say things like that, it causes me pain now that a real and serious amour might be the only thing that can extract you from your detestable mental situation."

"A real and serious amour! That, my friend, can be put with living skeletons. Pretty living women, as you call them, are as incapable of feeling it as they are of inspiring it."

I responded nevertheless: "And your skeleton, what does she feel, then, poor dreamer?"

"Nothing any longer," he said, "but once, everything that pleased me and only what pleased me. Do you know anything about homoeopathic medicine and the fashion in which its medicaments are obtained?"

"Very little. Why?"

"One takes, does one not, a grain of the medicinal substance, which one mixes with ninety-nine grains of milk sugar, and then one grain of the mixture, which one mixes again with ninety-nine grains of sugar, and so on. By means of repeating the dilution of the mixtures thirty times over, the dose of the medicinal substance is infinitely small; it does not even equal a quadrillionth or a quintillionth of a grain..."

"What relationship has that with what we're talking about?"

"A very great one. There is in almost every young and beautiful woman one delightful grain. It is exactly that grain that renders the woman so desirable. Now, in living women, by virtue of passing through different mixtures from vices into faults, and from faults into imperfections, the virtue of the grain ends up disappearing, whereas, thanks to my imagination, my skeleton offers me the delightful grain—which is to say, amour pure of any diminishing dilution. Do you understand?"

"I believe so, yes, but what if that diminishing dilution is necessary? What if the delightful grain, to employ your term, is only appropriate to our human temperament when it is reduced by a successive passage from vices into faults, and from faults into imperfections? If God thinks that we ought to follow with regard to our sex, which is no more irreproachable than the other, the methods of homoeopathic physicians with their patients? For example, how do you know that the unattenuated love of a woman would not be too much for you? For, after all, admit that it's a ridiculous pretention to demand of women what we are incapable of rendering to them. We don't contain any more of the ideal than they do, and what we can contain is as extended as theirs in stupid discourse and evil deeds. Beside a moral beauty such as you imagine, your soul would scarcely be beautiful; near to that giant of virtue, you'd be tiny."

"Oh, my God," said Melanski, "I'm not reproaching women for being imperfect. I'm reproaching them for spoiling love for me by mixing so many things with it that they prefer, very inappropriately. The woman would be the true half of my being who, not losing sight of the fleeting nature of life, would take nothing seriously therein but amour—the only thing that is worth the trouble of being born—who would count our minutes by kisses, with whom I could say in all the profundity of our intoxication, but also in all certainty that life passes and that annihilation is at the bottom of the jar: *amor, morituri to salutant.*"

"But you're not worth that!" I exclaimed. "Once again, you're not worth that. For every moment when you have a head elevated to that Byronic lyricism, there are a hundred when you will be flat, and you would be the first to let your absolute amour overflow into a hundred wretched preoccupations."

"Yes, yes, it's true, that if women are sad donzelles, we're sad sires. Ah, look, I've had enough of you, of me, of the skeleton and women. My head's burning; I need air. Would you like to go for a walk?"

"At his hour?" I said.

It was dark, and the moon, frequently veiled by clouds, was giving hardly any light.

"Are you afraid of the calm?"

"Me? Not in the least."

"Well then, get your hat and cane. We'll go all the way to Harfleur."

X

We left the house at the same time as Pélagie, who had just concluded her daily labor.

He set off at a rapid walk, and I matched his stride. We were soon outside the town, beating the road with our soles noisily and cradling our sullen silence to that melancholy rhythm. I looked to the right and left of the road. Here there were fields of wheat with yellowing heads, freshly laid, there, buildings surrounded by apple-trees; further away, a clump of beeches; but I was less concerned with the landscape, graciously enveloped with shadows by the night, than the preoccupation into which Melanski had cast me.

The omnibus service that went back and forth from Le Havre had long ceased. The road was deserted. We only encountered one or two private carriages and four joyful companions, arm in arm, singing at the top of their voices and aiding one another charitably to carry a doubtless exaggerated ration of Calvados with aplomb. Meanwhile, on the right-hand edge of the road we soon reached a long row of linden trees forming, by their junction with the thorny hedge that serve as an enclosure, a few arches of the most charming effect. I had already noticed that row in passing when I had come that way by day with Melanski, and I had been sorry to see the beautiful trees dusted by the rolling of carriages; but by night, the blanching of the dust on the foliage produced a silvery reflection that was one more grace.

I stopped, and then, like a curious child, I tried to look over each of the hedges that opened on to the pathway.

"Come on," Melanski said to me in a low voice. "It's not late yet and there might be someone on the path."

"A woman?" I asked, rejoining him on the causeway.

"Perhaps. Shh!" he added. "Mademoiselle Bénin is, indeed there. Don't look; you'll force me to greet her."

There was something so imperious in the manner in which Melanski said that to me, gripping my arm sharply, that I could not help obeying him.

"Who is this Mademoiselle Bénin, then?" I said to him, when we had passed the pathway.

"That's another one of your naïve questions. She's Mademoiselle Bénin, of course."

"I was trying to ask you whether she's pretty?"

"Very pretty."

"Whether she belongs to a rich family...?"

"Yes. So what?"

"Whether you think she has a few qualities of heart and mind...?"

"Certainly, but why?"

"Finally, you've had occasion to approach her and talk to her?"

"Of course. Her mother has called me a few times to care for one of her domestics, and on those occasions I was able to judge that the young woman has, as they say, everything going for her."

"And her health?"

"Oh, health you'd credit to her. Impossible to be fresher and more appropriately plump: like a freshly-ripened peach."

"So she's a delightful person?"

"As much as a woman can be."

"And you think that she'll render her husband happy?"

"I'm sure of it."

"Then it's necessary to be her husband."

"Who? You? As much as you wish."

"No, you, Melanski."

"My dear friend," exclaimed Melanski, in a voice slightly afflicted by a sudden anger, "leave me alone, I beg of you. In the mental situation that I'm in, it's cruelty on your part to make a happiness gleam before my eyes that I can't realize."

"And why can't you realize it?"

"Why? He asks me why, when he knows everything! Present the finest water to a rabid dog, and you'll see that he won't drink it, that it's impossible for him to drink it."

"That," I said, "is one of those comparisons that has absolutely no justice. Because you've just traversed a period of madness, it doesn't follow that now, reestablished in the integrity of your reason, you can't replace an absurd amour with a reasonable amour for a beautiful young woman. Life, Melanski! Think of it: a blossoming of strength, of beauty, of tenderness in your arms; tangible kisses, no longer imaginary; always a return for a loan, and sometimes a more generous return. You've exhausted your soul in deviating a substantial part of it toward an inanimate object; you have an opportunity to repair it now by means of the superabundantly animated being that you call Mademoiselle Bénin and you're not going to take advantage of it?"

"No."

"But you said just now that she would make the man she marries happy."

"Certainly: you, another—but not me."

"You're imagining that..."

"So be it; but you can't imagine how insupportable you're being; so, once and for all, let's leave it there."

There was no point in persisting further at that moment. Having arrived at the pretty little station in Harfleur, we retraced our steps, almost without unclenching our teeth all the way to Montivilliers. I was heart-broken. My poor friend seemed to me to be incurable, or, at least, I did not know what remedy to attempt.

He completed my discouragement when he said to me, shortly before going up to his bedroom, and point blank: "I loved my skeleton because it loved me as much as I wanted; but it will be the most eccentric, the most satisfying and also the last of my passions. Good night!"

I had hoped that our walk, in fatiguing Melanski and putting back the hour of going to bed might free him for that night of his habitual pilgrimage. Harassed by fatigue and drowsiness myself I went to sleep in that hope. Alas, I was mistaken; my poor friend came back again. I woke up just as he turned round, with a start.

This is the place to add an observation to those I have already made about the non-lucid aspect of his nocturnal actions. How is it explicable that he did not recall that his skeleton was no longer in the box, but persisted in coming to look for it there, and thought that he was carrying it away with him?

The following morning, at about six o'clock, I saw Melanski arrive again, but this time awake, fully dressed and holding the box of bones in his arms.

"I'm sorry to disturb you," he said, "for it's still early, but before Pélagie arrives I desire to repair a pusillanimous action at which I blush." At the same time, he opened the box and took out the various bones one by one.

"What are you going to do, then?" I asked him.

"I'm simply going to rearticulate the limbs of my skeleton and place it in the case from which I should never have removed it."

"Don't do that, I beg you!" I exclaimed. "Don't do that, Melanski! You're right no longer to leave the box buried in the garden, because it might lead to questions that are always annoying, even when they're explained, but for God's sake leave the bones in the box and put it in the attic."

"What inconvenience do you see in my remounting the skeleton here?" asked Melanski, with a sad little smile. "Do you fear, by chance, that a tenderness might develop between the two of you that would supplant me? Well, I'm not jealous; although, to tell you the truth, your proximity to one another authorizes some jealousy on my part. I'm not jealous, because I know full well that my skeleton's life is entirely artificial, and without the portrait it can no longer go to your bed any more than it can return to mine."

I tried to persist, but all my efforts were vain.

"Are you afraid?" he said, finally. "It's not possible! You wouldn't be a man."

"Well, yes, I confess it," I replied, glad to have found that pretext, however humiliating it might be for me; I'm still subject, like children, to vague fear; and now, after the stories you've told me, if it occupies its case two steps from my bed, I wouldn't be capable of closing an eye."

"Really?"

"Truly," I said, with some difficulty, for I don't like to lie, even about the most insignificant things."

"So be it. I'll transport the case and the skeleton to my bedroom—or rather, you can take my room, and I'll come down here, as I should have done long ago."

That was even worse, because that way, I would have no means of preventing the unfortunate Melanski from taking possession not any longer of the skeleton's phantom but of the skeleton itself, and waking up every morning alongside such disagreeable company. It was absolutely necessary to change my mind.

"You understand that I was joking just now," I told him. "Since you don't want to leave the bones in their case, which would be wiser, edify your skeleton here; that's not what will prevent me from sleeping."

He picked up a small pair of pincers with which to twist the metal wires, and he had soon finished reuniting the tarsals, tibias, fibulas, demurs, iliacs, etc, in a harmonious whole. Once the slender human framework was established from head to toe he suspended it from the peg inside the case. Then he stepped back a few paces to observe his skeleton, as he had been accustomed to do before.

"There we go!" he said. "I was right to believe that without the portrait the skeleton would lose its borrowed life. The flesh with which my imagination clothed it, I can no longer perceive today, no matter how hard I look. The mirage has vanished; thank God, I'm free now of an amour my reason condemned, but which, like all the poisons of mysticism, slid into my heart through my false senses in spite of me."

Pointing at the skeleton, he added: "You can see the purpose of what I've just done. As long as it remained underground I would have retained a certain fear of its supposedly marvelous nature, which is no longer possible now." Then he closed the door of the case and said to me; "Let's go! Sleep, idler, while I go into the garden to finish what you started yesterday evening, and when the little patch is dug, I'll place flower-pots there, as it isn't the season for planting or sowing."

But he had no sooner left the study than he came back in. "By the way, the weather's superb. If you wish, we can go have lunch in Le Havre. Is that all right with you?"

"Very good, very good. I don't know Le Havre, since I've only passed through it. I'd planned to go there someday; perhaps I'd even have gone today in your absence. Your proposal to accompany me there is perfect."

"Yes, but you need to get up right away."

"Right away?"

"Yes, certainly, and it won't be too early, because we're go on foot, because we'll be obliged to stop at the home of the man with the polyp, and we'll take the grand tour over the heights of Graville and Ingouville. So, presto! Get dressed."

"Yes, yes—go into the garden and I'll join you there in a minute."

Instead of following that perfidious advice and giving my sloth time to rejoice, Melanski employed violent means and pulled my bedclothes away.

An hour later, we departed, Pélagie knew that she was not to expect us for lunch, or even dinner.

XI

The morning was radiant. We reached the road by the shortest route and were soon going alongside Mademoiselle Bénin's property. I darted a glance over the hedge between the linens and saw something very pretty: two blue tits pursuing one another and hopping—but no young woman, alas. The house was situated at the far end of the driveway; two windows were visible from the road. Now, at one of those very windows, in a pose like Polyhymnia, Mademoiselle Bénin was standing.

In order to feel out Melanski and discover whether he was prepared to talk about her, I said with a feigned negligence: "That house must be very damp,"

He replied with a malicious smile: "Yes, very damp. That's why, among other reasons, you and I would act wisely in not seeking to live in it, even for one day."

"There's no question of it for me," I replied, "but that habitation might be healthier for you than your house in Montivilliers."

"Here we go, you're beginning to catechize me again. I tell you, my friend, that I won't marry at any price, even if you offered me the best, the most beautiful and the richest woman in the world."

When we had passed Harfleur, whose ancient port has fallen into an abandonment so merited and yet so sad, with two or three poor devils of barges, Melanski made me veer to the right and go up to the Abbaye de Graville by a broad winding path bordered with trees, and then by tombs, at the end of which stands the Église Saint-Honorine, flanked by its old abandoned tower, which gives it an entirely romantic aspect. Having arrived in the courtyard of the abbey, with a double row of linden trees behind us, we leaned on the balustrade of the terrace, from which a magnificent view extends. Afterwards we traversed the abbey, between the lodgings of the curé and the girls' school kept by the sisters, and, inclining to the left of a lovely avenue planted with apple trees via a grassy slope accommodated in the rocky hillside, we returned to the cemetery whose first tombs we had seen on arriving.

The accidents of the terrain, the abundance of the grass and an entire vegetation, sometimes cleared and sometimes heaped up at the whim of nature, that infallible artist, formed the most desirable refuge that a dead man could desire.

"Turn round," said Melanski. "You can see over there the panorama that we were enjoying just now from the terrace; and two paces from here is the orchard where the pupils play during their breaks. If the light filtered through the tombs, and if the dead had eyes, what a fine spectacle they'd have, eh? And what satisfaction for the mothers buried here, if exterior noises could reach them, to recognize among others the voice and laughter of their granddaughters."

"I'd like to die in the commune of Graville," I said.

"I've already made the same reflection," said Melanski, "the first time I saw this lovely cemetery. The skeleton of a man and that of a woman would go a long way before encountering a more charming locale to celebrate the honeymoon of their fresh espousal."

Always, as you see, the unfortunate Melanski returned to the object of his lugubrious folly. I made no reply and drew him outside the perimeter of the abbey.

We went through Graville, and then Ingouville, and an hour and a half of walking took us all the way to Le Havre and a comfortable restaurant in the Rue de Paris.

After dinner, he took me to visit the curiosities: the town hall with its beautiful square, the jetty, the citadel, the docks, the dry dock, and finally the various basins filled with ships. In the Eure basin there was a superb American three-master with a fine name that rang tenderly in the ear: the *Love*.

"Would you like to try to visit it?" Melanski asked me.

"I'd like nothing better."

"Well, that stout gentleman smoking his pipe on the deck while overseeing the loading of those barrels of wine must be the captain or the first mate. I'll ask him for permission in English in order to flatter him."

"That's right," I said, "ask..."

Melanski formulated his request with a grace that was familiar to him.

"Captain, will you please allow us to board your ship?"

To which the stout gentleman replied, with an amiable smile: "Z Naywiçksza przyemnoscia."

I have rarely seen a man more bewildered than Melanski was to hear a blunt reply in Polish to a question formed in English—for without being able to speak Polish fluently, he knew enough to discern it from another language, and even to comprehend those few words.

"Thank you very much, Monsieur," said Melanski, in French this time, "for the permission you've been kind enough to grant us."

"And I perceive," said the captain, also in French, "that I've made a error, although not very serious, since you understood my anyway. I replied to you in Polish thinking that was your mother tongue, but you're French, aren't you?"

"Yes, Monsieur," said Melanski, "by birth; but originally, I am indeed Polish. It's necessary to believe that a few of my facial features revealed that to you. Thank you, therefore, for the pleasure you've caused me by reminding me of my poor father's mother tongue."

The voluminous American with the awkward manner awoke three admirations in me. I admired the extraordinary tact that he had shown in discovering at first glance, in Melanski, the Polish type that had never seemed very evident to me. I admired that he had grasped my friend's delicate flattery and responded in kind. And finally, I admired the fact that he knew a single word of Polish, for Polish is not one of those international languages that men in commerce find it advantageous to speak. Melanski did not hold back from expressing that final admiration to him. He replied, simply, that the little Polish he knew he had from his wife, who was Polish. Was it not Byron who remarked that the best grammar from which we men can learn a foreign language is a woman's lips?

The captain wanted to do us the honors of his ship personally, and took us everywhere. We asked him a few questions about the tonnage of the ship, its crew, the merchandise it transported, etc., etc. Finally, Melanski said to him: "I imagine that you have a surgeon attached to your crew, Captain?"

"Unfortunately, no," the captain replied, "but I'm authorized by the company to take one on, and we suffered a too much from not having one during or crossing from America for me to do without one on the return journey. I wrote to

London yesterday asked them to send me one...no matter who...I'm waiting."

"Is it necessary, Captain," I said, "for your surgeon to be English?"

"Not at all, Monsieur, and I'd even prefer that he wasn't," he added, with a smile pierced by the old Yankee rancor against England. "All that I ask is that he knows a little of our language."

"When are you leaving, Captain?" I asked.

"We'll be setting sail in eight or ten days at the latest, if the wind continues to be favorable."

"What conditions would you make for your surgeon?"

"Why are you asking all these questions of the Captain?" Melanski asked me, looking at me with astonishment. "What interest do you have in that? Can you offer him a surgeon?"

"Perhaps."

"What conditions?" repeated the American. "Pardon me, but I don't understand exactly."

"I'm asking you, Captain, what salary you'd give a surgeon who has all his diplomas and proof that he is a doctor in medicine?"

"Oh, right!" exclaimed the Captain. "He'd be engaged for two years to the service of the ship, with the faculty, while the ship is in port, of having an independent clientele, and he'd receive three hundred and fifty dollars a year, plus, of course, nourishment aboard. He'd eat with the first mate and me and have a cabin similar to ours." He added: "If you have someone to propose to me, Monsieur, it'll be necessary to hurry, for an English surgeon might arrive at any moment."

"But he doesn't have anyone," murmured Melanski.

Without replying to my friend, I said to the American: "Tomorrow morning, perhaps I'll have the honor of seeing you again, Captain, and proposing a candidate to you."

"Good," said the Captain. "You can find me until midday at the Hôtel de Normandie. Ask for Mr. Betly."

With that we took our leave of the Captain, who was veritably a very commendable man, and we headed for the Place

Louis XVI, where the omnibus from Le Havre to Montivilliers stopped.

"Who have you in mind, then, to be a surgeon on the *Love*?" asked Melanski.

"You haven't guessed?"

"No."

"Too bad, for it's you, here present, and on whose arm I'm leaning, my old comrade."

"What an idea!"

"I'm only astonished that it didn't occur to you at the same time as it did to me."

"Are you mad?"

"I'm wise, and furthermore, I have an affection for you that you can't doubt, I hope. Well, since you don't want to get married, I believe, as I said to you the other day, that you can only purge your mind of the dangerous chimeras that have been oppressing it for six months by making a long voyage. You've previously objected to me that long voyages cost more than your resources, but here's the prospect of a two year voyage that you can make, all expenses defrayed, and even paid. The opportunity is unique; seized it by the hair."

"But I already have a clientele, which can only increase, that's certain."

"Bah! Your clientele...have you even taken in a thousand francs in your six months of practice? I doubt it—and if you've taken them in, how many have you lost? Instead of which, you'll earn as much in six months of the *Love*, without any possible losses and without any expenses."

"And my house, which I've rented for three years, and my furniture, my horse and my cabriolet?"

"No problem! In a week you can sell your horse and cabriolet. As for your furniture, you leave it in your house, confide the key to the house to Pélagie, who seems to be a very honest woman, and promise her a nice fee is she manages to sublet the house during the three-year period to some temporary employee, such as a collector of indirect taxes, or a commercial agent. She'll find someone, I assure you. In any case, if the house in Montivilliers remains on your hands, you can console yourself by thinking that you're not paying rent on the *Love*. As for your papers and little things you want to keep, you can confide them to me until you return."

"And my skeleton?"

"Oh, that! I'm separating you from that forever."

"And the money that's owed to me? For I'm owed something like a thousand francs, as you said."

"I'll have it collected and invest it for you; or, even better, you can take charge of that yourself in two years."

"And what will people say here, where everyone thinks that I'm definitively installed, about such an abrupt departure, which resembles a flight?"

"Is it really you, Melanski, who's worrying about what people might say? They'll say, of course, that you had a yen to travel, and that you haven't been stupid enough to let the excellent opportunity that was offered to you escape."

"It's certain that a two-year voyage made in that fashion is very tempting."

"And its even greater advantage," I proclaimed, "will be to exercise a fortunate influence on your mind, to give another direction to your ideas."

"Well, I'll think about it. I'm not saying no…I'll think about it tonight, and you'll receive a response tomorrow morning."

We spent the entire evening discussing that new project. Melanski presented me with objections; I replied to them—and I saw with pleasure that he was only asking to be convinced. We separated very late and each retired to our own room.

XII

Very preoccupied with the embarkation I was meditating for Melanski—for it was, after all, a serious matter—half rejoicing and half troubled, balancing the good and bad possibilities that might result from it, I completely forgot that he had rebuilt the skeleton in its case. Under the impression of the conversation with the captain of the *Love* and with the aid of its future consequences, my anxiety of the morning had disappeared. So, I was asleep and dreaming about maritime episodes when poor Melanski arrived at one thirty, as was his habit.

I woke up at the first sound, thank God. He had not taken two steps into the room when, suddenly remembering the re-edification of the skeleton, I thrust my legs out of bed and wanted to run to the case in order to remove the skeleton before he opened it, while he as placing the candle on the mantelpiece—but I judged that I did not have time to prevent him, and that I would also be running a great risk of waking him. I therefore remained there, inert and dejected, murmuring *oh my gods* that could not ward off the misfortune.

He opened the case, really taking out the skeleton this time, and carrying out, in order to take it away, reclose the case and pick up his candle, all the rational movements that I have already described.

What should I do? How could I prevent the accursed skeleton being face to face with Melanski the following morning, and driving him mad completely?

Seized by a blind inspiration, I got up and stealthily, while the poor sleepwalker was picking up his candle, I enlarged the gap in the doorway of the study, slipped out and plastered myself against the wall of the corridor.

Melanski came out slowly, his candle in one hand and his skeleton extended over both arms, taking the greatest precautions not to bump the head of the legs of his precious burden. He placed the candle on the floor, disengaged his left arm, which was supporting the skeleton's legs, replacing that support with his raised left thigh, so that he was only standing on one foot, and closed the study door. Then he bent down, picked up his candle, which he held his right hand, carefully keeping it away from the skeleton, as if he were afraid of burning it. Finally, he went upstairs. I followed, barefoot like him, in a night-shirt, like him, with one hand in front of my mouth to muffle the sound of my breathing, and the other dangling.

He arrived in his bedroom, the door of which he had left wide open...I arrived on his heels. I went to put down his candle; then, by one of those delicate attentions that one has for invalids, he set the feet of the skeleton on the floor beside the bed and put an arm around its waist in order to support it; then he pulled back the bedclothes, took his skeleton over his arm again, laid it down on the far side of the bed and pulled the covers back over it.

I was in the middle of the room and I watched, full of anxiety, not knowing what to expect, hoping that he would soon fall asleep normally beside the skeleton, and that I could then, with the aid of skill, deliver him from his lugubrious companion.

Horror! I see him kiss its forehead, exactly in the hollow formed by the excision of the portrait.

Then he turns round; one might think that he's looking at me. I'm afraid. He comes toward me—directly toward me. I move aside, frightened. He heads for the door. I divine what he wants to do; he wants to close it. With a promptitude equal to his methodical, somnambulistic slowness, I go to the bed, and snatch the skeleton out of it, holding all its limbs against one another in order that they don't rub against one another and make a noise. Melanski returns to his bed in a straight line. I return toward the door, prowling along the wall opposite the bed. I'm at the door. Melanski climbs into his bed, and kisses the bolster at the place where the skeleton's skull was placed a moment before; then he emerges partly from the bed.

It seems to me that he is looking at me and is about to ask what I've done with his skeleton. Not at all—it's to extinguish his candle, which is burning on the night-table.

Now I'm in the dark.

Fortunately, I'm holding the doorknob; I turn it very gently, very gently. The catch yields, and Melanski doesn't wake up. I go out.

Should I close the door again or not?

A grave question. If I don't close it again, tomorrow morning, he might notice that it's open and be astonished. If I close it, the noise might wake him up.

I close it again, awkwardly. The catch grates, and I hear Melanski call: "Who's there?"

I make no reply, as you can imagine. I refrain from moving; but I'm trembling that he might light his candle and come to see.

Nothing.

Groping my way, carrying the skeleton in one arm like a weapon and guiding myself with my right hand I reach the stairway. I go down. I got to the door of the study, I pen it, and I set the skeleton down on the floor. I reach the chair on which my candle and my matches are placed. I light up, and am finally delivered from what is fundamentally one of the most puerile of anguishes, but nevertheless the cruelest that I have ever experienced in my life.

As I had just carried out the counterpart of Melanski's maneuvers, I wondered whether I was really awake or whether I too might be under the influence of a fit of somnambulism. I had some difficult in collecting myself—after which I replaced the skeleton in its case and went to bed.

As for going to sleep, I couldn't. I repeated incessantly that it was imperative that Melanski embarked, and that if perchance he continued to hesitate, it would be necessary to put everything to work to convince him. Then too, the fantastic march that Melanski, the skeleton and I had made from the study to the bedroom, which had been as terrifying as it was ridiculous, occupied my mind strangely.

Perhaps some impatient reader wants to tell me that I had a very simple means of stopping Melanski's nocturnal visits...and what would that have been, reader?

"It would have been, Monsieur, to bolt the study door from the inside—if, that is it had a bolt."

It did, in fact, have one, but I would never have dared to make use of it, for fear that Melanski, exasperated by the resistance of the door, might shake it, wake himself up thanks to his efforts, and discover himself in such a pitiful state.

XIII

At seven o'clock, Melanski came into my room with a smile on his lips, and waking me up, as he had done the day before, he said: "I've decided to embark on the *Love*, all the more so as the Captain is a man with whom I sense that I can sympathize a great deal. I'm going to depart for Le Havre in my cabriolet, which I'll try to sell there, along with the horse, and I'll sign an engagement with Mr. Betly this very morning. Do you want to accompany me?"

There was nothing I would have liked better, and we soon set off, to the great astonishment of Pélagie, who was annoyed, the good woman, by not having to prepare lunch for us for two days running.

Melanski took with him a few documents he had from his father, his birth certificate, his diplomas, certificates from his professors—in sum, everything required to demonstrate that he was an honest and capable man.

With a perfect ease, he negotiated in English his admission to the *Love*. Mr. Betly declared himself more than satisfied. In any case, he was attracted to Melanski, as Melanski was to him, and I had the pleasure of glimpsing that the worthy American, so distinguished and so cordial, would substitute for me with my friend.

"We're almost compatriots...by marriage," he said to Melanski, as he shook his hand, since my wife and you were born of Polish fathers."

As soon as their little treaty was concluded, the captain drafted a telegram to his correspondent in London to countermand the request for a surgeon that he had sent him. I wanted to take the telegram to the office, but Melanski insisted on taking it himself—I have no idea why, but I was glad deep down, for I took advantage of is absence.

"Your new surgeon, Captain," I said to Mr. Betly, "is a fellow full of heart and intelligence. I'll be much mistaken if, when you've known him for a while, you don't accord him your entire affection. As you don't know me, any more than him, it's not for me to offer you a caution in his regard, but you'll verify the justice of my words. You must have noticed that yesterday, when, by virtue of an almost indifferent question from my friend, we learned that you had no surgeon on your crew and that you wanted one, it was me who spoke to you vaguely about being able to provide one, whereas the one that I intended for you was there, and didn't say a word. It was, therefore, me who convinced him to embark. Why?

"Just now, you had the discretion not to ask him what motives he had for quitting a residence where he had begun to practice medicine under the best auspices. He would have replied to you that he likes travel and the adventurous life. But that's not all. It's also a matter, Captain, of effacing the last persistent traces of an eccentric amour that nearly compromised my friend's reason, and which it would take too long to recount to you. Perhaps, in the long hours that you spend on the ship together, he'll take you into his confidence. In any case, I beg you, Captain, in the name of the amity I have for that excellent fellow, to treat him with a very particular care."

"I promise you, Monsieur," Mr. Betly said, "That I'll neglect nothing to make this period of two years agreeable, and perhaps also salutary, for your friend, who will certainly become mine if he doesn't refuse to do so."

With that, Melanski returned. Mr. Betly invited us to lunch. After lunch we occupied ourselves with selling the horse and the cabriolet, which was done more rapidly than we had hoped, because there happened to be a buyer at the Hôtel d'Ingouville, where we had lunch. Melanski got away, I believe, with a loss of two hundred francs on the price he had paid two months earlier.

We returned to Montivilliers by omnibus. How surprised Pélagie was on seeing us return with neither cabriolet nor horse! Everything was explained to her, since, according to my plan, adopted by Melanski, she had to play the important role of letting agent, and her surprise became amazement.

A week passed in packing up everything that Melanski was to take aboard—which is to say, garments, underwear, books, instruments—and everything that I was to put in storage in Paris, including jewelry, private papers, duly tied up and sealed; and in making a list of the objects that were to remain in Pélagie's custody, such as bedding and kitchen equipment.

As for the skeleton and its case, I did not want to pack them until the morning when Melanski was taking to the sea and I was returning to Paris. I was careful, however, every evening before going to bed, to put the skeleton inside the divan that served as my bed. And although Melanski did not fail once to render his customary visit to the case, at least he always went away, thank God, with empty arms.

There were also, during that week, a few adieux to make, notably to his landlord, who, with the calmness of a sage, was careful to have his three years' rent paid in advance, on the pretext that Melanski might not come back, but he authorized the sub-letting as compensation.

My friend's departure excited, I believe, veritable regrets as well as astonishment. He had already put down roots in that pretty region. Pélagie, in taking way the keys of the house, shed large tears. She did not understand why Monsieur was quitting a place where he was living so peacefully, to confront the countless perils of a long-haul voyage. After that, I imagine, her emotion also reflected a few advantages that Melanski gave her, like the gift of a hogshead of wine—a precious thing, especially in Normandy—the faculty of picking the fruits in the garden and a commission of ten per cent if the house was let.

XIV

As you can imagine, our separation did not take place without a great constriction of the heart. Poor friend, the last words he addressed to me were the melancholy lines from Lord Byron: "If I see you again, adieu; if I never see you again, adieu, and adieu again."

I embraced him; then recommending that half of my soul one last time to Mr. Betly, I quit the deck of the *Love*, for they were casting off the moorings. I ran to the jetty, where there were many curious people gathered. I succeeded, not without using my shoulders, in reaching the front rank. The ship, with its sails furled, advanced slowly into the bay, towed by the tug *Alcide*. I waved my handkerchief, and a few other spectators, who apparently had friends aboard, did likewise.

I can still see dear Melanski saluting me tenderly with his head and hand; then, when the ship is already too far from the shore for anyone on board to be recognized, I can at least recognize a handkerchief that I believe is being waved by my poor comrade, to which mine responds until, eventually, having nothing more to do, it wipes a commencement of tears from the edges of my eyelids.

Two hours later I climbed into a railway carriage in order to return to Paris, taking with me a long parcel wrapped in straw, which intrigued the baggage-handlers at the two stations greatly. It was the skeleton case, in which the skeleton, extended as in a coffin, was maintained by wads of paper.

At the Gare Saint-Lazare, two baggage-handlers, as they delivered the said package to me, murmured between themselves as if to interrogate me indirectly: "What's that?"

The customs employee was more explicit, as was his right, and he asked me straight out.

"It's a skeleton," I told him. "Do skeletons play an entry fee, perhaps?"

A policeman who was prowling around whispered in the customs man's ear: "Have him open it."

I showed the messieurs the copper wires, which immediately freed me of the disagreeable suspicion that I had provoked.

That fatal item of furniture, and its even more fatal inhabitant, of which no cab wanted to take charge, and for which

I was obliged to send two commissionaires to the station the following day, are now visible in the museum of osteology at the École de Médecine, to which I made a gift of it on Melanski's behalf. Equally visible in the middle of the frontal bone is the portrait, which I glued back as neatly as possible.

I advise all people to whom things do not appear other than they are, all those who never mistake balloons for lanterns—all the sane, in brief—if they want to jeer at Melanski's inconceivable aberration at close range, to observe how little that portrait combined with a skeleton resembles a woman, and how *stupid* one would have to be to be deceived by it. *Stupid* is the epithet found by Mauplaisant, who is a man of common sense, clear-sighted and antichimerical. Thus the reader, convinced not only by my story but by sight, that Melanski was stupid, will be able to award himself a considerable certificate of superiority over the poor hero of the story.

What more can I tell you? I wanted to talk to Monsieur Onfroy, the dissector of the woman and the painter of her portrait. He does not know very much about the life of the woman, but he gave me a few details about her demise and has put me on the track of learning the rest. Now, as there is no novel, in my opinion, that equals in interest the exact biography of the humblest among us, if that of Armandine Dedeman—as the skeleton was called when it was moving within living flesh—is revealed to me, I shall gladly give it to the public, rather than fatigue my head inventing more or less plausible fiction.

I am waiting for a letter from Melanski, for he promised to write to me from the first port in which the *Love* drops anchor, and another from the Captain, who is supposed to write to me without Melanski's knowledge in order to verify, with regard to our friend's mental health, his personal testimony.

And I shall know, for example, whether, contrary to my conjectures, his fits of somnambulism have continued in an environment completely different from that in which I saw them produced.

The malign reader who interrupted me once before has interrupted me again at the moment when I was about to stop speaking for myself.

"Pardon me," he says, "but there's something you haven't thought of..."

"What's that, Monsieur?"

"You appear to be insisting that your friend Melanski doesn't know that he is a sleepwalker, or at least, that he was, for you feared that he might be affected unduly by learning that he is afflicted by that partial mental alienation, and yet here you are crying out to all and sundry that 'Melanski is a sleepwalker, and he does this and that while asleep,' Do you think that your story will never fall into his hands some day?"

"Yes, Monsieur. It isn't on the Atlantic Ocean, or even in America, I assume, that my story will find him. When, after two years, Melanski returns to France, as I hope, and cured, as I'll wager, if someone is uncharitable enough to reveal to him what it is better that he does not know, he will not be afflicted by it nearly as violently as he would be today. But the best response I can make to you, Monsieur, is that in two years' time, no one, including you, will remember the little story that I have just told."

THE MUTE WOMAN OF THE CHAMPS-ÉLYSÉES

I

I have a very good friend named Alphonse Méril, who has a mania for knotting intrigues in the street—a deplorable and truly reprehensible mania.

It is how he spends his time.

He has nerve to say that he is not wasting it; that he is working in the most intelligent manner; that he is studying, not in the stout books in libraries, from which he does not learn very much, but in the little book with the double lock entitled The Heart of a Woman, from which one can learn everything.

Poor Alphonse! With that paradox, he has never done anything...except stupidities.

For ten years now he has been exercising his art, and in that ultimate art of pleasure he deploys, in truth, a fine talent. Today he is a consummate virtuoso, the Paganini of the genre.

How many times he has quit my arm in order to launch himself in pursuit of a blonde, a brunette, a chestnut or a red-head, or even an African woman! How many times I have been surprised to see that women, apparently very honest, do not disdain to reply to him and sustain his conversation!

He explained that to me himself:

"I conduct myself," he said, "as if in a drawing room. I'm extremely polite, somewhat witty, and thanks to the habitude I have in discerning women, I immediately find the first word that it is necessary to say in order to make them listen to me. When the first word has passed, the others follow. Then I have another first word to find, the word that ought to force them to respond to me; I find it, and the conversation is engaged. It often happens that my adventure is limited to that, but it's still charming—and instructive! Oh, my dear, what a treasure of observations you, who are a man of letters, would amass in my place! What subjects for novels, comedies and dramas would be offered to you! And how you would hold human nature under your hand! It's a pity that such beautiful psychological materials remain unemployed."

"Why don't you employ them?"

"I'm too lazy; and then too, I probably wouldn't have the genius. I can bring the quarry-stone, the wood and the iron, but when it's a matter of building the house, of making use of then, I can't do any more."

"Bah!"

"I'm erudite, but not a historian, you understand."

"You're modest; I know many erudite men who believe themselves to be historians, as if by grace of the estate. In any case, my dear, I deem our kind of erudition a hundred times preferable to that of pedants who have only studied life in archeological tomes—except that you're a frightful libertine and that spoils everything."

II

Now that I've introduced Alphonse Méril to you, reader and you know what kind of man you're dealing with, know that last July, as I was going along the Rue de Richelieu at one o'clock in the morning in a fiacre. I perceived Méril walking alongside the houses in the rain. At the same moment, he called out to my driver:

"Driver, are you free?"

The coachman replied: "No."

In my turn, I shouted: "Stop, driver!"

An agreeable surprise for Méril. When he had climbed in beside me, I said to him: "My dear, you were walking head down just now like a man under the empire of some preoccupation. What's happened to you today?"

"I've had a strange encounter," he replied. "You see me still great troubled by it."

"An encounter with a woman?"

"Of course! And a woman who has turned my mind upside down."

"Get away!"

"I assure you that I haven't got over it."

"You're amusing yourself piquing my curiosity, eh?"

"I'm not amusing myself at all; I don't have the slightest desire to amuse myself. I'm submissive to a very serious and entirely fresh impression, for I was with that woman only a few moments ago."

"Come on, tell me about it."

"Pooh! I fear that it won't have the same effect on you as on me, and that you'll think that the strangest thing about the encounter is that I remain so afflicted by it. You see, my dear, a story, even very skillfully told, can't translate certain vibrations that operate directly on the animal fibers of the spectator. In addition, it's quite possible that I might have been particularly disposed just now to sense it excessively."

"You're wearying me. What happened?"

"Well, at about half past ten I was walking in the Champs-Élysées, on the right hand sight, around the café-concerts. A star was singing at the Alcazar. I stopped for moment with the crowd in order to listen, and then, the last bravos having did away, I started walking again, darting glances his way and that, as always, in quest of adventures. Level with the Café des Ambassadeurs, at the foot of a tree, a woman was sitting, profoundly veiled. Her pose had something very melancholy about it. Her feet on the crossbar of a chair, her elbow on her knees, and her chin in her hand—a marvelous hand, brilliant with gemstones—she was maintaining a complete immobility.

"Her attire was both simple and expensive. I noticed that she did not have the chair next to her that all women seeking fortune reserve. In any case, her attitude was not at all provocative; it was, on the contrary, because of that manner of isolating herself that she was provoking surprised glances from the passers-by.

"A monsieur, seduced liked me by such strangeness, started walking back and forth in front of her with the evident design of attracting her attention and finding a commencement of discourse. I was conducting myself in accordance with the same principles. He must have noticed that, so, each of us was wondering who would take the initiative. It was me. I approached the lady and, in my softest voice, I murmured: 'If one had to make a statue of Discretion, Madame, I believe that you would be a good model!'

"And as she did not reply, I added: 'Undoubtedly, you judge that in speaking to you thus without having the honor of knowing you, I depict well enough the marionette of indiscretion.'

"And as she made no reply again: 'Isn't that true, Madame?'

"She didn't say a word, or move a muscle. I started to walk on, but then I changed my mind. 'You give the impression of being infinitely sad. I assure you that I'm in the same boat. A bad thing, being sad! If you'd like to aid me, we could make single parcel of our respective chagrins and go and throw ourselves in the Seine.'

"Same silence.

"Slightly disconcerted to see sallies that, if not witty, were at least gallant and original, welcomed so coldly, but resolved not to admit myself beaten yet, I continued idling there, while observing her at close range. However, it was eleven o'clock. The café-concerts were closing; the crowds were flowing away. That entire section of the Champs-Élysées was deserted. There was no one left but the veiled lady and me. She did not show any sigh of leaving.

"I went back to her. 'Madame,' I said to her, 'here we are, all alone. A moment ago, if you didn't reply to me, perhaps it's because you feared the curious. Now that peril has disappeared. Tell me squarely to leave you alone, and I'm certainly too polite not to obey you; on the other hand, if it wouldn't displease you to chat with me, say so with the same sincerity.'

"I was standing there in front of her, and I was very fearful that she would send me away. Nothing—except that she extended her lovely hand, as if to discover whether it was raining. 'Yes, Madame,' I told her, 'it's raining, and you can't go home on foot. Would you permit me to hail a cab for you?'

"This time, the veiled woman shook her head, and then got up...and I followed her. We were walking side by side. I said many things that came into my head, all polite, delicate and capable of making the most serious woman smile. She continued to remain silent, but at least she responded by signs of the head that showed me that she was tolerating my presence.

"We took the Rue Rivoli, and then the Rue du Dauphin.

"The veiled woman stopped outside a travelers' hotel, on the threshold of which the proprietress was standing. Was she staying here? I didn't know, but out of discretion, I kept my stance.

"After a couple of minutes, she came back and we continued walking forward. She led me into the garden of the Palais-Royal. She sat down. I sat down next to her. The evening was hot, as you know. In spite of the commencing storm, there was an absolute lack of air. I was stifling; so was the lady. On the far side of me, she moved her veil from time to time in order to wipe her face.

"'Why,' I said to her, 'don't you get some air here? What a passion for incognito! And what is the purpose of all the mystery? Lift your veil, Madame, I beg you, Lift it.'

"She contented herself with a slight shrug of the shoulders. And as, on seeing that movement. I advanced my head mischievously in order to perceive her revealed profile, she let her veil fall and placed her hands over it.

"'Oh.' I exclaimed, 'don't think that I want to see you against your will. But please, speak to me. What's the point of this comedy? You've amused yourself long enough. Come on, burst out laughing, so that I can hear the sound of our voice.'

"Again she shrugged her shoulders slightly. It did not seem to me that those shrugs signified any disdain; they rather seemed to express a mild reproach that she had addressed to me because I was understanding things so poorly.

"I had believed until then that it was only an affectation on her part. I began to suppose that, if she was so profoundly veiled and did not speak, it might perhaps be for very serious reasons.

"About her face I dared not say anything, but on the question of her silence I was less uneasy.

"'Can it be that you're mute, Madame?'

"She nodded affirmatively two or three times.

"'It's because of an accident, then, for you're not deaf?'

"Same sign.

"'But just now, I saw you chatting to a hotel proprietress in the Rue du Dauphin?'

"Energetic sign of negation and a mime of sorts, which signified: *I didn't say anything; it was only the mistress of the hotel who spoke.*

"Still incredulous, I went on: 'Well, since you're mute, talk to me with the aid of the deaf-mute alphabet. I know it and I'll understand you.'

"Immediately, she took the glove of her right hand, and made me the sign that corresponded to the spoken instruction: 'Go away!'

"'You want me to go away,' I said. 'That's harsh of you. You can't imagine how you interest me, not how much joy I experience, being a dreamer, in encountering someone who isn't like everyone else. No, Madame, you can't imagine what magnetism, perhaps fatal, drew me toward you.'

"Third little shrug of the shoulders.

"'Listen to me; they aren't vain words that I'm going to say to you—the words that one says to just any woman. I'm perfectly sincere. So, Madame, without loving you yet, I already experience for you a bizarre sympathy—let's call it romantic, if you like...at any rate, a sympathy such that I can't bear the idea of not seeing you again.'

"Fourth little shrug of the shoulders.

"'I consent to go away, since you order me to do so; but promise me that tomorrow, at eleven o'clock in the evening or any other hour you wish, I'll find you in the Champs-Élysées, near the tree where I saw you think evening. Will you promise me that?'

"Negative sign."

"'Would you care to do it another day?'

"Second negative sign.

"'So I'll never see you again?'

"Third negative sign.

"'Do I displease you? Oh, be frank; it would afflict me, but it wouldn't surprise me.'

"Fourth negative sign, and fifth little shrug of the shoulders.

"It was midnight. By a few rolls, the drum announced the closure of the gardens. She got up. I did likewise. But, extending her arm in the direction of the Rue de Valois, she indicated that direction to me, while she headed for the Rue de Riche-lieu.

"'Yes, yes,' I said, and I continued walking by her side. 'Anything you wish, as long as I see you again. Don't give me to understand that it's impossible. What would render it impossible?'

"She stopped dead in front of me, and, with an abrupt-ness of gesture of which you can have no idea, and abruptness that surprised and alarmed me, she put the tips of her fingers almost level with my eyes.

"I made an involuntary movement of recoil as if before a dagger; then, recovering from my foolish fear, I examined the hand. On one of the fingers, among three or four rings, there was one that had the crown of a marquise attached to it by a little chain. And the veiled lady advanced the crown along her finger with a singular gesture that had something about it like a gesture of attack or malediction.

"'Well,' I said, 'it's the crown of a marquise.'

"Affirmative sign.

"'But I don't see very clearly, Madame, I confess, what that crown has to do with it. What does it matter that you're a marquise? I might not have a title analogous to yours, nor any heraldic title, but I'm quite certain that that doesn't leap to the eyes.'

"I had said those few words in a slightly piqued tone, because I found it strange that her quality as a marquise appeared to her immediately to put a distance between us.

"She hastened to make a very energetic negative sign with both her head and he hand, signifying: You're absolutely mistaken. Nothing is further from my thoughts than such vanity. I willingly consider you as my equal.

"'Perhaps you mean to indicate that you're married?'

"Affirmative sign.

"'That's still not a reason.'

"Little shrug of the shoulders.

"'I'm very unfortunate then, for you have already given birth in me, Madame to a sentiment that merits some reciprocity. You will leave me with a persistent memory. I shall deplore not having known you. I shall not be able to console myself for it.'

"With a charming grace she made her hand rotate in front of her face, which meant: *Get away! Your persistent memory will, go up in smoke.*

'That's a very pretty gesture,' I said to her, 'but you're mistaken if you think that I'll forget you so quickly. How could I, with my turbulent imagination?'

"On that, she resumed walking in an impetuous manner. I observed her gait more closely than I had done previously. There was something jerky, nervous and almost automatic about it, which, combined with her real or simulated mutism, the mystery with which she enveloped her face and the gesture that she had shot at me—that's the right word—to show me the crown, lent her a slightly frightening quality.

"We went out through the wicket-gate of the Théâtre-Français. She took the Rue de Richelieu, went along it as far as the Rue Villedo, and there made me another sign to go away. Enormous drops of rain were beginning to fall, while the black sky was split by immense lightning-flashes. She lifted the hood of her cloak, which was lined with white satin, over her hat. Instead of going away, I helped her with that little operation.

"In the Rue Villedo, as I said to her: 'I don't want to compromise you; I only want to see where you live...,'" she stopped abruptly on the sidewalk, and, backing up against the wall of a house, she lowered her index finger toward the pavement.

"We were absolutely alone. Although it was not yet half past midnight, no one was about; we were alone amid the lightning. At the moment when she made the gesture, a flash of lightning spread over her veil, and I thought that I might glimpse the features of her face in the bright light, but the veil was too thick and I couldn't. I was face to face with her. She could see my marvelously from behind a retrenchment that my gaze couldn't penetrate and which a good education prevented me from breaking through. Ideas came to me that filled me with fear and gave me gooseflesh. At the sight of the obstinate veil I asked myself: *Is the woman a hideous monster?* And at the gesture by which, when I asked her where she lived, she pointed at the ground, I asked myself: *Is the woman mad?*

"However, in the most reassured tone that I could muster, I said: 'Madame, I declare to you, even though you might think I lack propriety, mat it please God, I would like to know where you live, without having the slightest intention of coming to importune you in your home. Believe me, don't wait here, go home. I'm very stubborn and I won't give in.'

"She remained immobile for a few moments, then, making her decision, she went into the Rue Thérèse and rang the bell of a beautiful house.

"While someone came to open it I repeated my plea: 'Give me a sign that we'll see one another again, and tell me when. Tomorrow, perhaps?'

"Negative sign.

"'So you don't want ever to see me again?'

"Same sign.

"The door closed again heavily, and…here I am!"

III

I had listened to Méril's story with a scrupulous attention and an increasing astonishment.

When he had finished...

"What do you think of that woman?" he asked me.

"What do I think of her? I think that I don't know what to think of her."

"Do you believe that she was veritably mute, or that she was pretending to be mute in order to amuse herself at my expense?"

"Well, what if she wasn't really mute and only wanted to make fun of you, it seems to me that as she shut the door of her house in your face she would have burst out laughing and shouted in a mocking voice; 'Bonsoir, Monsieur!' given that when one plays tricks on people one usually likes to make them feel it."

"That's true. And what do you augur from that opaque and permanent veil?"

"Alas, I augur that your lady is at least ugly; for, if a woman is pretty, if it isn't before hiding herself that she wants to be seen, like Galatea, you can be sure that it's after she's hidden. Now, this one kept her veil to the end. A bad sign."

"I fear so. And what do you think of her marquise's crown? Is it authentic? Is it apocryphal?"

"Oh, you're embarrassing me a great deal. However, I wouldn't see anything extraordinary in it being authentic. I know that it's not very frequent to see a marquise, profoundly veiled, going to sit down all alone, by night, in the Champs-Élysées and the garden of the Palais-Royal, but after all, it could happen."

"So, we're admitting that she's a real marquise?"

"Or at least believes herself to be one in good faith."

"What do you mean? You're scaring me. Do you suppose that she's mad?"

"I wouldn't be surprised if she were half way there."

"Her gestures, no? Her gait?"

"Yes, exactly."

"But then it might enter into her madness to veil herself, without her having any reason to hide her features."

"As you'd like her to be pretty, rogue? What does it matter to you, pray, since it's understood that you'll never see her again."

"Of course, of course! Not much."

"Right—and then, a mad woman, that wouldn't be such a treat."

"There are kinds of partial madness that might serve amour rather than posing an obstacle to it."

"I know full well that amour is a kind of madness itself; but not all mad women are fitted for living together. So, in the lunatic asylums they're carefully secluded."

"You're a disenchanter."

"And what if she's an old woman?"

"How can she possibly be an old woman? She was slim; an abundance of blonde hair was over flowing from her round hat, and the skin of her hand was smooth, with the pink whiteness that makes her no more than thirty—I say no more because I believe her to be younger."

"You're completely amorous, my dear Alphonse."

"In truth, no; but I think that supposing the woman to be young, pretty, a marquise and, at the most, eccentric..."

"And mute...."

"Oh, mute! That's almost a quality... Supposing all that, my dear, there would be a great romantic savor for both of us in the prelude to our amour."

"Then you're definitely not intending to leave it there? You intend to see her again, even though she's declared that she doesn't want to?"

"Because of that."

"And how are you going to do that?"

"Ah! That's it! When I was twenty, I would have mounted watch on her door for entire hours every day, in order to take advantage of the moment when she went out. Now that I'm thirty, that would be too much for me. It will be necessary to find another means... What, I don't know."

Méril and I were neighbors. He lived in the Rue d'Assas; I lived in the Rue du Cherche-Midi. Thus, my fiacre took him home along with me. The reader will now understand why Méril got into my cab without any ifs and buts. As he quit me he shook my hand, and promised to inform me of the steps he would take in order to encounter the veiled woman again, and the result of those steps.

IV

A few days passed, during which I heard no mention of him, nor of the veiled lady. I wasn't overly astonished, for I had known for a long time that there's nothing in this miserable life that doesn't end in a fish's tail...*desinit in piscem!*[11] Yes, even the most seductive things. The infinitely great, infinitely just, infinitely good but infinitely ironic Being treats us according to our merits and makes fools of us infinitely. Because we have the misfortune of having a soul and imagination, he tempts us in a thousand ways.

By means of I know not what Robin mirrors,[12] he shows us the specter of objects that appeal to our desire. We stretch out our hand...

Empty! In sum, to employ an energetic expression of Parisian argot, we think we've "got it made," but we never have;

---

[11] The full line from Horace's *Ars Poetica* translates as "The beautiful woman ends in a fish's tail."

[12] An obscure French conjuror by the name of Robin demonstrated the illusion better known as "Pepper's ghost," which employs a mirror, during the 1870s, as reported in *Chambers' Journal*.

we never will in this word, which is all phantoms and simula-cra.

However, Méril, less imbued than me with those discouraging thoughts, had not let go, and was striving to terminate his adventure. Fundamentally, he only wanted to satisfy a curiosity awakened by chance, and, expecting some disappointment, he wanted to know of what it would consist.

The day after the day when he had had his singular encounter, he went past the house inhabited by the mysterious woman repeatedly. He needed a pretext to get in, to talk to the concierge, above all to make him talk. An apartment to let furnished him with it. But I prefer to give him the floor and let him repeat to the reader what he told me.

V

"You have," I said to the concierge, "A large apartment to let?"

"Yes, Monsieur, one the first floor, overlooking the courtyard."

"How much?"

"Two thousand francs."

"Composed of?"

"Six rooms."

"Oh, damn! Six rooms isn't very many. I'd need eight."

"There are two large bright cabinets."

"If there are two large bright cabinets, let's see it anyway."

My aplomb was sublime, given that I can scarcely pay my rent of five hundred francs...

"And who occupies the apartment at present?" I asked, in a distracted manner, as we went upstairs.

"It's a lady; I've given her notice because her manners don't suit me..."

"Aha! Some joker?"

"Monsieur, there are no jokers in my house."

"Pardon me—I thought that's what you meant. Anyway, I'm sure that if one slipped in by accident, you wouldn't tolerate them for long."

"To be sure. As for that one, one can't say that she's guilty of bad conduct, but she's a little…you know."

And he tapped his forehead.

"Oh dear."

"Yes—and I don't like that…no, I don't like that at all."

At the same time, he rang. A little dog stated yapping.

"I don't like animals much either," said the concierge.

You can imagine my difficulty…was the lady in question mine. I thought yes. Would I see her? I wanted that…and I dreaded it. Would she recognize me? Undoubtedly. What would she think of my trickery? It seemed to me that she ought to be flattered, in spite of the prohibition she had mimed against my seeing her again.

An aged domestic came to open the door.

"Monsieur," the concierge said to him, "desires to see the apartment."

Without breathing a word, the old domestic made an affirmative sign and I went in with the concierge.

"Monsieur Baptiste," added the latter, "if you have things to do, don't put yourself out. I'll show Monsieur around."

Thus addressed, Monsieur Baptiste was content to shake his head.

Is he mute too? I wondered.

Without articulating a syllable, he opened the doors one after another, and I traversed several beautiful and richly furnished rooms, where I noticed the particularity that all the corners were hidden by curtains, either of velvet, silk, or woolen damask. Furthermore, there was no one in any of the rooms, except for a black and white cat in one, which was sitting on a side-table, conscientiously licking the fur of its belly. I looked for Monsieur Baptiste. Disappeared.

I went straight to the cat in order to stroke it. A writer celebrated for his wit has made the fine and very just remark:

"A cat does not stroke us; it strokes itself on us." I'm very much afraid that we're becoming similar to that cat—which is to say that in stroking one we're absolutely in quest of an agreeable sensation. And when a tender woman stretches her husband's beard between her delicate fingers; and when a man, with an emotional gaze, smoothes his wife's tresses or plays with the little curl under her chignon... What is the tender woman doing? What is making the man's gaze emotional? She's caressing herself; he's caressing himself. That's amour!

"Isn't that your opinion?" concluded Méril.

"Alas, yes, but what does it matter? Amour judged thus is still a very beautiful thing, a very desirable thing. Suppose that the cat, whose back you've stroked, prefers to stroke itself with you rather than someone else, even suppose that it's preference is exclusive, and that it only wants to stroke itself with you—isn't that already a great success? A complete success? What more do you want? Aren't you enjoying the greatest joy that human nature permits? Be careful. There's less egotism on the part of a person who loves in you the object of her joy than there would be on your part in claiming to be loved, according to other principles."

"Undoubtedly," Méril replied. "You're right. Well, in order to continue my story..."

As the black cat raised its head, and then arched its back under the pressure of my hand, agitating its long silky tail, I perceived next to it on the side-table a partly written page. The temptation was strong; I did not, I confess, have the courage to resist it. I looked at it, while recognizing that it was acting badly, and I read these few lines, the last to be written:

I would be a woman like any other; I would be able to uncover my face; I wouldn't have lost the faculty of saying that I judge it impossible to see him again. An honest and sensate woman would say to herself: What is a liaison commenced in such conditions worth, very probably with a liber-

tine who is not in search of amour but a temporary intrigue, who only came to me because I happened to be in his path and he needs some woman with whom to amuse himself a little? However, when one wants to love, when one has sought in vain in one's entourage for a man one can love, and one encounters one by chance one evening, to banish him once and for all by pronouncing the words "I never want to see you again...," is perhaps stupid. He had such a benevolent gaze, such a frank voice! "I'm perfectly sincere," he said, "without loving you yet, I experience a bizarre sympathy for you..." A bizarre sympathy! That's what I experience too, for him. If I were a woman like any other, if I could uncover my face, if I hadn't lost the faculty of speech, perhaps I wouldn't have judged it impossible to see him again._

There the writing stopped, which I've reported to you the letter, or very nearly. It was neat, and large rather than delicate, with the consequence that I could read it very easily while stroking the cat.

I picked up the pen that was lying near the piece of paper and I wrote thereafter:

See me again anyway. Keep your veil on; don't talk. If you believe that I'm a man of honor you have nothing to fear, have you? I'll know your name in five minutes I already know your address, since I'm in your home. It's therefore just that you also know my name and address, even if you don't do anything. My name is Alphonse Méril and I live at no. 2 Rue d'Assas.

During the brief time that I took to write that, the concierge's attention was distracted by a rather large crack that he had found in the ceiling, the ramifications of which he was following with a certain anxiety. I heard him grumbling loudly about the tenant in the apartment above, and the dancing soirées to which he attributed that damage.

I had finished writing before he had finished grumbling, so that, having not perceived anything, except that I had stroked the cat, he said to me: "Monsieur likes cats; that's like my wife; me, I wouldn't touch the beasts with a barge-pole..."

"What do you expect? Everyone has their own tastes, and it's necessary not o hold it against your wife that she likes cats."

And after having darted a last glance to the right and the left, I headed for the door of the apartment.

As I was crossing the threshold, he said: "Did you notice, Monsieur, the curtains that were in the four corners of every room?"

"Yes," I replied. "So what?"

"Well, it's an invention of that old madwoman..."

At the phrase "old madwoman," I shivered.

"It's an invention of that old madwoman in order to have somewhere to hide right away."

"Oh?"

"Yes. She doesn't show anyone the tip of her nose. As soon as anyone goes into her apartment, it appears that she hides behind one of those curtains, the first that comes to hand. And every time she goes out into the street she wears a veil so thick that I wonder how she can see where she's going."

"It's necessary for you to have seen her, however," I said, with a certain effort, "to know that she's old..."

"Oh, old, I don't know—but I think so. Or if she isn't old, she must be horrible, for it isn't natural that a young and pretty woman would hide like that."

"You're right, it isn't natural..." And in pronouncing those words with the slowness of a disappointed man, I said to myself: *How ridiculous I'm being! Where will my romantic intrigues end? I'm madder than this old madwoman. As long as she doesn't take me at my word! What the devil possessed me to give her my name and address?*

"What is her name?" I asked.

"She calls herself Madame Peyrol."

"De Peyrol!" I exclaimed. "The Marquise de Peyrol."

"Marquise, I never heard any mention of that. On the letters that come for her, which only come rarely, there's just Madame Peyrol."

"Really? And her husband?"

"Her husband? Don't know. Has she ever had a husband?"

"You haven't seen a man with her sometimes?"

"My word, no. Who the devil could want that woman?"

"Indeed," I said, forcing myself to smile.

As we had arrived at the door of the lodge, the concierge asked me whether I found the apartment to my taste.

"Oh, the apartment…," I said. "Yes, undoubtedly, I like it well enough, but I can't settle anything without consulting my wife. As I said, six rooms, even with cabinets, seems to me a little small, for I have a numerous family…"

"Monsieur has young children?"

"I have seven of them," I replied, with aplomb, "and the eldest isn't yet nine…"

"Damn!" murmured the concierge, clicking his tongue in a significant manner. "The proprietor doesn't much like renting to people who have seven young children…"

"That's sufficient, then; let's not talk about it any longer. In any case, I think, in truth, that the apartment wouldn't suit me. Adieu, Monsieur."

VI

After having told me the preceding story, Méril added:

"I nearly came right away to bring you up to date with my intrigue, but I feared your mockery."

"You were wrong. I wouldn't have made fun of you at all. And after all, if I'd have made fun of you then, why wouldn't I do it today?"

"Today, it's not the same. There's something new."

"Ah!"

"Three days later, I received this letter."

I took the letter that Méril was holding out to me, and I read a few lines traced in the neat and rounded script that he had mentioned to me:

If I had not seen you in my home the other days and recognized you as the man of the Champs-Élysées, I would have believed that a practical joker had wanted to trick me by responding to my notes. In fact, perhaps you are that practical joker; I hope so, for your sake. I hope that you don't attach any importance to what you wrote, with a certain conceit and indiscretion, you'll agree. For you would truly lament at having given your affection to a woman who is worse than dead, to a woman who, for two terrible reasons, can no longer be the object of any man's amour. Remember that I do not speak; remember that I do not show my face.

"What do you say to that?" exclaimed Méril.

"I find it very singular.

"But what do you understand by it? What dispositions do you think she has in my regard?

"There aren't two ways of understanding things," I replied. "It's obvious that the woman is in the best dispositions in your regard. You please her. She would be ready to love you, if she doesn't love you already. Her notes told you that; her letter confirms it. Except that, with the common sense that shows that she isn't mad, she makes the observation to you that, being deprived of speech and obliged to wear a veil, she cannot involve herself in amour."

"Why can't she?"

"Oh, my dear friend, you're priceless. Think about it. I suppose that with a woman who can't articulate a single word, but shows you a pretty face, you can spend your time giving her kisses and receiving them from her, and that conversation is as good as any other. I suppose too that if you can't see her face, but she speaks to you and you make charming replies in a sweet voice, that's worth almost as much as kisses. On the contrary, if the face and the voice are both lacking in a woman, what remains for you? Nothing, or almost nothing."

"There's still her hand, which is the most beautiful I've encountered."

"That veil eternally placed over her face and which she doesn't want to lift at any price, doesn't worry you? You're not wondering what it's hiding, and that question doesn't make you shiver?"

"Yes, of course. Shut up—you're frightening me..."

"Admit, however, that curiosity is driving you..."

"I admit it—a ferocious curiosity. There are frightening probabilities, which, by virtue of the mystery that envelops them, attract me toward that woman more that the greatest beauty open to the sky."

"Then you're determined..."

"I'm determined," said Méril, firmly, "to use all means possible to see her again..."

"Seeing her isn't precisely the right word," I said, "since she hasn't uncovered her face before you, and it's understood that she never will uncover it."

"So be it—I mean to find myself facing that living enigma again, in order to be able to penetrate it with a gesture, and not to make it; in order to live in anxiety, in the unknown, in I know not what mortal charm. Oh, you don't understand me. That's not astonishing; I'm rambling."

"I understand you very well—and that's astonishing, because you really are rambling. But what do you expect? I've always understood people who are rambling—it's an idiosyncrasy of mine—rather better than those who claim to be reasoning accurately So all your ramblings don't catch me out, believe me. Would you like proof? To what you've just said, you could easily add this: 'And I'd experience a ferocious pleasure in being loved by this woman who, for two terrible reasons, to use her own expression, cannot be the object of any man's amour.' Isn't that so?"

Méril allowed one of those prolonged cries of "Yes!" to pass between his teeth that are the marks of a keen passion.

"Do you know that it's abominable?" I continued. "You're dreaming about that woman's unhappiness, neither more nor less."

"And mine too; that's my excuse. It's necessary that we both suffer, equally. It's necessary that our meetings be tortures, and yet filled with tenderness—but an infernal tenderness."

"Perfect! When is the first torture? When is the first infernal tenderness?"

"I don't know. She has my note. Will she come, or won't she? Would you like to know what I wrote? Here's a copy of my note."

"Let's see..."

Méril handed me a piece of paper, on which I read:

I am not a practical joker; I am an extremely serious man. Forgive me for the "conceit" and "indiscretion" with which I wrote a few words after your notes. Moreover, I attach a great importance to those few words. You are worse than dead, you say, and for two terrible reasons you can never be the object of any man's amour, because you do not speak and you do not show your face. That is an error. There is one man for who those two reasons are absolutely insignificant, and that man is me. Rue d'Assas, second floor, the door facing the stairway. Every day from two o'clock till six, I'm alone.

"Well?" he asked.

"Well, you expect her to come to you?"

"I expect so."

"The very precise address you give her doesn't signify anything else, that's evident."

"Nothing else, that's evident."

"In spite of the desire she has, she might not dare."

"Bah! A veiled woman—and take note; she arrives at my door, she enters my apartment without asking anything of any intermediary. I'm sparing her the most disagreeable part."

"You're a thoughtful fellow."

"I flatter myself on it. But now I think about it, it's quarter to two; what if she comes while I'm chatting to you? I have to run. Adieu."

VII

I don't believe that there exists in this poor world a role more disagreeable than that of confidant of a fortunate man, especially when one has the same taste as him without the talent to satisfy it. He shows you the way, at a pure loss; he is opening horizons that you cannot attain. He can explain to you how one lays siege to a woman, how she defends herself, how she capitulates, but you, the man with your skylarks ready roasted, nevertheless remain at home, waiting for the woman that will fall amorously into your arms. And you're enraged, waiting in vain, with your legs crossed and your chin in your hand for what he, the fortunate man, has gone to great pains to obtain. And do you complain about being unlucky? Of course you do!

Amour, the most beautiful of careers, if not the most lucrative, resembles others in that one doesn't succeed in it without hard work. To enrich oneself, to acquire a reputation, to have success with women, it's necessary to act, and to do a great deal.

Usually, all kinds of activity go together, like all kinds of idleness, but I believe that in the case of my friend Méril, in the matter of activity, he only has amorous activity. It is, in any case, the sweetest and, all things considered, isn't the least important or the least profitable. People have been seen who, because they had it, could achieve anything. Méril himself, unambitious by nature, doesn't care about achieving anything...but it's rare that he doesn't achieve anything...

Anyway, more than a week after the day when he was hoping to receive a visit from the mute woman, having not received any news from him, I went to see him one morning.

"Oh, it's you," he said, as soon as he saw me.

That locution I have often experienced; Méril greets me with it regularly every time he is in a bad mood; no matter how courteous his tone might be, I'm never deceived by it. If, on the contrary, he says: "Ah, there you are!" it's because everything is going as he wishes, that he is well, joyful and content with life. I believe that in both cases he experiences pleasure in seeing me, so I can't be any more annoyed by his "Oh it's you," than by his "Ah, there you are!" but in the former case I know that he will have nothing to relate to me butt disappointments, while in the latter, he will have the satisfaction of telling me some story in which he played an agreeable role.

"Well, how goes it?" I asked him.

"It's going badly."

"I suspected as much."

"Life is decidedly stupid," he said, after a momentary pause.

"Why is that?"

"Pooh!"

"Your mute has been deaf, eh?"

"I'm not in a mood to hear witticisms, you know."

"And yet you can't help laughing, grump. She hasn't come, then?"

"No."

"Well, my dear, one might be mute and obliged to wear a veil on one's face, but running to a young man's home at the first invitation is a bit strong. It's necessary to arrange a rendezvous on neutral ground to begin with."

"It's a fine time to tell me that. You always give me advice after the fact. It seemed to me that, after her letter, I didn't have to hesitate—but women are such strange creatures!"

I went into Méril's small drawing room, while chatting. On the small table in the middle of the room, a large bouquet of roses was lying in a melancholy fashion, already half-faded, and beside it a blank piece of paper with a pencil on top.

"Méril?"

"What?"

"I'll wager that you had prepared the language of flowers next to the language of handwriting."

"You're right, my poor friend, and the paper has remained free of writing, and the flowers are dead."

He had uttered those words with a certain sadness—but as if he had suddenly been pricked by a needle, he added in a very animated and slightly angry tone: "For a week I've been *posing*; for a week I've been staying in my room regularly, like a studious youth. Oh, I've had enough; it's too much. Today, I'm taking back my liberty, I'll run around the four quarters of Paris..."

"And today is perhaps exactly when she'll come!"

"Too bad."

"Believe me, stay at home and renew your bouquet."

If Lucretius, the great Lucretius, has to conclude this chapter—may his gigantic memory forgive me—he would willingly conclude it, I think, as I began it, but with this variation:

I don't believe that there exists in this poor world a role more agreeable than that of confidant of a fortunate man whose good fortune turns bad...

Suave mari magno...[13]

VIII

Well, Lucretius would have been punished for that ungenerous sentiment, on receiving the following day the visit of his friend Méril, triumphant.

"Finally!" he cried. "I did what you said. I waited for her yesterday. It was the good day, apparently."

---

[13] The quote is from Lucretius' *De Rerum Natura*. The line translates as "It is pleasant [to watch from the shore] in a great sea [stirred by the wind]...."

At about three o'clock, a brief ring at the door made me shiver. I opened it. She was in front of me.

"How I've been longing to see you!" I cried, taking her hand.

She withdrew it, and went straight into my drawing room as if she already knew the way. I followed her there. She stopped in front of each of the objects that furnish or ornament it; she looked at everything through her veil; she leaned over the faded bouquet, which she respired at length. Then she made me a sign that she wanted to write. I showed her the paper and pencil, and this is what she wrote:

I hesitated for a long time before coming to see you; I only decided to do it because of the good opinion I have of you, the confidence that you inspire in me. To lift my veil would be to deliver me a mortal insult; it would be to commit a cowardly act. You have no reason to deliver me a mortal insult; you are incapable, I believe, of committing a cowardly act. Thus, I'm tranquil. But tell me, how is it possible that you could derive pleasure in receiving in your home a woman as disgraced as I am? My first visit might pique your curiosity; so be it. The second would exasperate you. For me, it is different. During the few minutes in which I would sense you near me, it seems to me that the species of tomb in which I am imprisoned would open slightly. Let the dead seek out the living; that is their affair—but the living have reason to avoid the dead.

"I'm a living man of another sort," I replied to her, "A living man who has always had a weakness for the dead. You will be welcome every time you come, and I will love you as you would like me to love you."

I sat down at the table, next to her; I squeezed her little hand, which responded to my grip, and I started to take off her glove. She let me do it complaisantly. It's decidedly one of the prettiest hands there is, of a fleshiness so firm and so bursting with freshness that one cannot suppose it to be more than thirty years old. I saw once again all the rings of the other evening, with the crown of the marquise that she had aimed at my eyes so well in the garden of the Palais-Royal. I looked at that crown for a long time, smiling in spite of myself; the Mute perceived that and she wrote:

Why are you smiling? It seems to me that there is malice in your smile. The concierge will have told you that my name is Madame Peyrol, and you see no relationship, do you, between a Madame Peyrol and a marquise? I am both, however. I chose the name Peyrol in order to hide in its shadow. As for the title, it has been too fatal for me to keep it, and I would much prefer not to have it—but in sum, I have it.

"You're misinterpreting my smile," I replied to her. "I was smiling at your hand, as I'm still smiling at it, as one smiles at a child, in order that it might be favorable to me and allow me to give it a few kisses."

And, indeed, I began to kiss that hand, and I didn't stop. I don't stop, personally, when I'm kissing a beautiful hand. From time to time, that one had a few slight movements of recoil, but I kept hold of it and I treated it in the manner in which one treats a runaway prisoner, and inflicted a double punishment…or pleasure.

Then the marquise wrote something very pretty:

You're kissing me too much. Remember that I have nothing else to offer you, and when you weary of that, nothing more will remain, for you or for me.

"But I'm not a man to weary thus—no, Madame."

She stayed in my drawing room for an hour. Certainly, there isn't anyone who wouldn't judge as painful such a long tête-à-tête with a woman of whom you can only see the hand and who never says a word; nevertheless, I found the hour short. The marquise wrote such fine and profound things, and her hand was so expressive—I say expressive because I saw clearly reflected their confidence, dread, joy and sadness; in sum, all the play appropriate to human physiognomy. It's a truly curious thing for whoever observes it, and few people have observed it: temporary lineaments, mysterious characters in the language of the soul, tracing themselves in the noblest parts of the body!

*

"Do you want to see," Méril added, "some of the fine and profound things that she wrote and, I think, improvised, in my home? I reread them so frequently after her departure, and again this morning, that I can flatter myself in knowing them by heart. But I prefer to show them to you, and for you to read them for yourself."

And Méril took from his pocket a large sheet of paper, folded in four, on which were written in sequence all the questions and all the responses of the marquise—in sum, her part of the dialogue. He showed me with his fingertip the passages on which to concentrate my attention.

*

You're about thirty years old, aren't you? You're beginning to know life. I'm twenty-two myself; that's still very young, but certain events have aged my prematurely. Would you like us to talk in all sincerity?

When one has some experience of things, particularly matters of amour, it's impossible not to mistrust the man or the woman with whom one has made a liaison. You mistrust me.

Oh, there's no need to try to avoid the issue. You mistrust me. And you're right, doubly right. First of all, I'm a woman. Secondly, I'm veiled. What is my heart worth? What does my face represent? You're wondering: Is she a schemer? Is she a monster? At the very moment that you're taking me by the hand and covering me with tender kisses, those ideas are going through your mind, aren't they?

Another evasion! I proposed that we speak frankly about life. You've said that you wanted that. And already you're lying. Accuse women of being insincere, then! See that I'm more sincere, myself. I confess that I mistrust you, and greatly.

Because nothing proves to me that you're good, seriously good; because you might be frivolous, and even because I'm running the risk of loving in you a man who will wash his hands of me as soon as his curiosity is satisfied. That's why.

Terrible, but sage.

No. When one knows that happiness is precarious, one savors it far more. One doesn't let anything escape. One is knowingly happy. Dos it not seem to you, as it does to me, that that condition of the soul, anxious as it is, perhaps because of its anxiety, offers the greats compensations in amour?

It is thus that the traveler passing through a beautiful country finds impressions a hundred times more vivid there than the inhabitant of that country. The former feels that what he sees today he will doubtless never see again, and he embraces everything with a passionate gaze. The latter has seen yesterday what he is seeing today, and expects to see it again tomorrow; so the most sublime spectacle produces hardly any effect on him. He enjoys it without enjoying it. He is astonished that the other, the traveler, is uttering cries of astonishment. He wonders what is the matter with him.

You and I are that traveler. When younger, very young, we believed that we would able to live peacefully in certain splendid regions of amour. The eternal master pushed us forward, crying to us: "March! March!" With sadness—perhaps with despair, who knows?—we have turned our heads in order to contemplate one last time that fugitive horizon, which, for us, has circumscribed pure joy. It is necessary to renounce it henceforth.

"We have begun to march through arid plains where nothing grows but disappointment; except that if, at rare in-

tervals, we happen to encounter a flower that still has some mysterious relationship with those of pure joy, we lean over it, we drink its rich colors with our eyes, we breathe in its perfume; we lend it ten times more tender attention than to all those that once surrounded us. We're not unaware that it will wither before us, and that, in continuing on our way, we shall no longer have anything to the right and the left but disappointments, and more disappointments.

Get away! Entirely natural ideas—at least, I think so. But are they not yours?

Indeed! So, to get back to my subject, I desire to rise with you far above the affectations and hypocrisies that are usually exchanged between a man and a woman. I desire that we know exactly who we are and on what you can count in attaching ourselves to one another. I desire, in sum, that we play with love—play with love is a vile expression—other than with beguiling words and actions. And to begin with, I will tell you my life story scrupulously. I will tell you everything.

Yes, even why I remain veiled and why I am mute.

[...]

It is by virtue of a scruple that the reader will not, I hope, hold against me that I am leaving blank what Méril replied, all that being spoken and, I consequence, not contained on the paper. I know that I would have been able to reestablish it under his dictation, but as his role in the dialogue was only secondary, I prefer to leave it to the sagacity of the reader to substitute for it.

I was reading the conversation of the marquise aloud in front of Méril. When I arrived at that: "Yes, even why I remain veiled and why I am mute." Méril took the sheet of paper from my hands and said:

"At that point she got up. She took a rose from the bouquet and slid it into her corsage. She went around the room again, as she had done when she arrived, she put her hand on my shoulder and she headed for the door.

"I ran after her. 'When shall I see you again Madame?'

"With her pretty fingers, she made me a sign: *In four days*.

"Then she took me by the arm, led me to my piano, opened it, extended on the lectern a melody by Schubert, and made me a sign to sit down and play.

"I wasn't half way through the piece when I turned around instinctively. She was no longer there!"

"That's not very nice," I said, laughing. "To make you play a piece by Schubert and go away in the middle—that's at least disrespectful to poor Schubert and to you."

"It's you who aren't being very nice," said Méril, a trifle piqued. "I am, on the contrary, infinitely grateful to her for that mysterious exit. She disappeared like a dream; it was perfectly in keeping with the situation. The veil and the mutism demanded that it should be thus. A singular woman! Well, her singularity is exactly why I shall love her. My mind is already full of her, as you can imagine."

"You're not coming with me to Trouville, then?"

"When are you leaving?"

"Tomorrow."

"No, my dear friend, the beautiful ladies of the beach have tongues that wag too much and faces too uncovered.

J'aime mieux mon Isis.
O gué!
J'aime mieux mon Isis.[14]

---

[14] The repeated line is improvised, but the "O gué" would have indicated to a contemporary reader that they were being sung to the rhythm of the chorus of a popular children's song "Si le roi m'avait donné Paris."

And Méril shook my hand and wished me bon voyage.

IX

I had made him promise to write to me. He kept his word, all the more willingly because it is a need for a man to talk about his little affairs. In truth, a man isn't sorry, either, to know about the little affairs of others. In that regard, everything is arranged for the best.

I think that the reader, if this story interests him a little, will read over my shoulder the three letters that Méril sent me during the month I spent by the sea. Here they are, in chronological order.

8 August.

She came back yesterday, my dear friend, on the very day that she had indicated to me. I have put my arm round her waist. I have held her against my breast, and my lips have brushed her veil; but I confess, that kiss gave me a chill. To what face was it addressed? I don't know. By virtue of a kind of boasting to myself, I wanted to redouble it, but, having perceived the attractive repugnance that she inspired in me, she interposed her beautiful hand.

Then, pulling away, she went to the piano and played the melody by Schubert, with a rare sentiment, taking it up precisely at the note that I had reached when she left the other day. That is a trivial detail, but which shows an infinite delicacy. It is one of the thousand nonsensicalities that amour produces.

I am reputed, as you know, to be quite a good musician in the group of our acquaintances. Well, frankly, I believe her to be far superior to me. She astonished me. How precious that musical language, the purest and most beautiful of all, will be between us. Everything that she wanted to say to me, I understood. And note how well the mysterious idiom fits in with the other mysteries. We shall veritably have an exceptional life, an exceptional amour. An apparition within reality!

The hardest part for me will be getting used to the eternal veil that makes the unhappy creature a woman without a face. It's better, I know, that she has no face than if she showed one that was distant. In spite of probabilities, I have to suppose her beautiful beneath the veil; more beautiful than anyone is. The entire field of my imagination is free. I can compose for her the type that pleases me most: a broad but not very elevated brow, connecting eyebrows, large dark, almost rectangular eyes; a small nose with quivering nostrils; prominent lips, a chin fading away into the softness of the neck. That's how I want her to be.

And who will belie me? No one—not even me, since I'm condemned never to know her features.

But will I be strong enough and poetic enough to accept that situation, so frightful and so tender?

I fear that I might not. I sense my impatiences, the rages that are familiar to you, the hand that itches to tear away her veil. What I perceive of her, the firm and gracious whiteness of her nape, the elegant slope of her shoulders, the rich slimness of her waist, all cries out to me: how can she not be beautiful? And if she's beautiful, that veil is odious. No more veil!

At one moment, she stopped playing—it was the waltz from Faust—and turned toward me; in order to look at me, I think. I held out my hands to her. She placed hers in them, which I bore to my lips. Then, as if to render me that caress in some way, she ran her fingers over my beard.

"Since you don't want me to see you," I said, "blindfold my eyes, take off your veil, and let me kiss you."

I can here you laughing from here, my dear friend—you find the idea droll; that's a game of blind man's bluff that surpasses your expectation. She laughed at it: a muffled and inarticulate laugh that gave me gooseflesh.

Then she got up from the piano, went to the table and wrote:

If you don't want to be reasonable, I'll go this instant, and you'll never see me again.

"What do you call being reasonable?" I asked.

I call being reasonable never making any attempt on my face.

I felt quite content that she refused the proposal made in jest that made you laugh just now, for I would have had a great anxiety as to what my mouth might encounter.

"You've offered," I said, "to tell me your life story, to tell me why you wear a veil; I'm still waiting."

It's necessary to wait a while. I'm writing for you, at the moment, but you have no need to write what you want to say; let's see first what kind of man you are and what you think of yourself. I'm listening.

It was necessary for me to do it, and this is how I did it. You, who know me well, my dear friend, will be my witness that I judged myself impartially.

"What kind of man am I, Madame? A very complex individual, and, in consequence, not easy to disentangle. What do I think of myself? I don't really know exactly what to think. Sometimes good and sometimes bad, depending on which side of the coin appears.

"There are times when I declare myself to be egotistical, skeptical, proud, cowardly, ignorant and stupid. There are others when I would swear that I'm devoted, naïve, modest, courageous, learned and clever.

Fundamentally, the mixture or alternation of those qualities or defects must make me a weak character, a banal nature, whatever my desire might be to distinguish myself."

A weak character, that's possible, she replied on the paper, a banal nature, no. Banal natures don't look themselves up and down like that.

And I confess to you, dear friend, that I was very flat-tered that she made that difference, legitimate after all.

She added: But you're not telling me what you're worth in amour.

"What am I worth in amour, Madame? A great deal, I believe, if it's a matter of loving. Not much, if it's a matter of being loved."

That's a remark that might be pretty, *she wrote,* but that's not what I want. You're falling into drawing-room preciosity. Frankness, if you please.

"I have more frankness than you think. The great ten-derness of which I'm capable is wearisome for women, and they don't take long to become blasé on my account, whereas I never become blasé for the same reason."

We'll see about that, fine talker; go to your piano and play me a song of farewell.

"Already?"

Yes, it's necessary.

I obeyed her, very sad. But while my fingers were run-ning over the keys I looked behind me. She opened the door, put her hand to her veil as if to blow me a kiss, and disap-peared.
That's where we are, my dear friend.

17 August.
Yesterday evening, when I got home, the concierge handed me a rather voluminous letter, closed by two red seals. I recognized the handwriting of the address immediately.
"Who brought this?"

"A man."

"He didn't say anything?"

"No, Monsieur."

Scarcely was I in my apartment than I broke the seals. It was, as I suspected, the abridged history of her life that the Marquise was sending me. But why hadn't she brought it herself? I'll transcribe a few pages for you, in the certainty that they'll interest you...

X. The Brief Memoirs of the Marquise

I was born in 1864. I am, in consequence, twenty-two years old at present. The first years of my life were spent in the part of Auxerrois known as La Puisaye, where my father possessed a magnificent estate.

My father, a man of great sense, simple heart and mild mores, much preferred the country to the city. He had, moreover, a pronounced fondness for hunting, which was to be fatal to him, since he perished miserably during a hunting party, killed by one of his maladroit companions.

My mother's character was very different. Superficial, loving intrigue and a riotous existence, she had always dreamed of living in Paris. I cannot remember ever having seen her and my father in accord for five minutes on any subject whatsoever. I lived between them, more saddened than one can suppose in a child by that perpetual discord.

All my instincts drew me toward my father, and naturally I inclined in his direction. His unexpected death, although I was only twelve years old at that time, caused me a pain of which I was only relieved by other chagrins a long time after. Why, I said to myself, did death not fall upon my mother instead?

In truth, that regret was impious, and I accuse myself of it as an evil sentiment, but I believe that in my place, few children would have been virtuous enough not to feel it. The detached fashion in which my mother welcomed her widowhood contributed, in any case, to giving me that sentiment, and, it appears to me, to excusing it.

The first act of authority accomplished by my mother was to prompt the sale of the land that was as odious to her as it was dear to me. A thousand memories attached me to it, especially the saddest: the violent death of my father. I addressed the most touching supplications to my mother in vain; she took no account of them. She had her idea, an obsession, which was to double her income by capitalizing a property that did not have a high yield by comparison with industrial shares, and to go and live in Paris. The sale was held by auction and in total.[15]

My mother claimed that it was a great advantage for us, but that consideration, which has scant effect on me now, had none then. What moved me to tears was leaving, once and for all, the meadows in which I had often played during the haymaking with Bog Tom, my father' favorite dog; the woods where I had so often, for pleasure, aided the poor to collect firewood, especially old Catuche, saying to her: Don't worry, Catuche, about breaking dry branches that are still on the tree. If I were tall enough...;" and the river on the bank of which I sat so often to make crowns of myosotis; and our good farmers, who found that I wasn't proud with them and had such a mild and affectionate way of calling my Mam'zelle Julie.

Oh, when I think about all that, I still weep.

It was also necessary to say adieu to my friend Tom, and that wasn't the least cruel adieu. Poor dog! I pleaded his cause with all possible fire and emotion, in vain. My mother wouldn't consent to taking him with us. He was given, at my request, to a neighboring small landowner, half-monsieur and

---

[15] Author's note: "Although the marquise does not say so, it is evident that the property in La Puisaye cannot have belonged entirely to her father but must have been owned jointly with her mother, who, in order to avoid dividing it between herself and her ward, must have obtained a judgment of sale from the tribunal."

half-peasant, who had known my father well and liked him a great deal.

My mother only took her trunks.

Having arrived in Paris we did not live together for long. My mother had nothing more urgent than to get rid of me by putting me in a boarding school.

If my father had been alive, the idea of boarding school would have horrified me; with him dead, I almost rejoiced in going there.

Thanks to the notions that good an enlightened man had give me, since the first glimmer of reason had appeared within me, I immediately found myself on a level with the other pupils of my age, and superior to them in some respects. The method of education employed by my father produced that superiority. He had not limited himself, as is almost always done, to instructing me in the rules of grammar, the elements of arithmetic and a few details of history, geography and literature. He reasoned everything before me, forcing me to do likewise. The slightest thing that we encountered in our studies, the simplest spectacle offered to us, was for him a subject of reflections so clear and precise that a child's mind could only profit therefrom. He formed my mind and my conscience in the image of his own mind and conscience.

My mother, who never forgave him for his qualities, could not bear to see them reflected in me, and drew away further from me as I drew closer to him.

Bizarrely enough, I had exactly the same features as my mother, but the soul of my father, and, in consequence, his physiognomy, had passed into me. When she began to look at me, my mother, at the sight of the features that I had in common with her, seemed glad of that resemblance, but she did not take long to discover in the midst of those features an expression that was foreign to her, and that chilled her tenderness. I believe now that she was jealous of the fact that I did not have her character, as I had her face.

For my father it was the complete opposite. He had been very much in love with my mother. She still inspired a sort of passion in him, mingled with bitterness. In seeing represented in me what she had of beauty and what he had of goodness, he had everything he could wish. I was what he had dreamed of my mother becoming.

Sometimes, at the same moment, if I happened to express one of the petty current ideas obtained from my father, he caressed me with a sad gaze and my mother shot me a hostile glance. It was easier to sense than to explain my mother's discontentment.

Although her attitudes generally displeased my father, he treated her with a rare mildness and indulgence. She could not hate him, therefore, or hate me for marching with him. I imagine, however, that she had the chagrin typical of people who are in the wrong, who sense that they are in the wrong, but who do not want to conform.

My father had not only taken care of my moral education but also my physical education. He played with me as young comrade would have done. We ran, we jumped, and we devoted ourselves to gymnastic exercises. I was with him more frequently than with my mother.

In the boarding-school, it was necessary for me to live an enclosed life, entirely new to me. I had some difficulty accustoming myself to it. Music, which I began to learn at that time with all my heart, was perhaps the good fairy that aided me. Music operated another miracle; it filled to some extent the void that my father, in dying, had left within me. In addition, my mistresses and my companions did not take long to show me a keen sympathy—one of those sympathies that can be embarrassing, in that they set you apart. I was very pretty and very benevolent. That is the whole secret. In good faith, I would have liked to be a little less pretty, in order no longer to have been the cynosure of all eyes. People sensed that— without my saying anything, naturally—and loved me more because of it.

My mother sometimes came to visit me. I say "visit" because that is the right word. It was, unfortunately only too evident to me that she was not yielding to the impulsion of her maternal heart, but acquitting an obligation to society. And I was not alone in perceiving that. People talked about it at the school; they felt sorry for me.

In the reception room, if I darted a glance at the other groups, I saw all gazes turned in my mother's direction, and I blushed crimson.

Since we had been in Paris she had released the bridle on her worldly and vainglorious instincts; in the beginning, whenever she came to see me, I observed that her attire was enriched by a more pronounce charter of coquetry. She did not stop until she was on a level with the flashiest elegant ladies. Her language, even the timbre of her voice, also changed gradually. I had never really recognized a mother in her; I ended up fining her a stranger who deigned to honor me with her protection.

The worst thing was that she sought to inspire me with her taste for frivolous luxury. She never talked to me about anything but fashion; she wanted me to arrange my hair in a certain pretentious fashion, and that I wear make-up. I listened to her without making much response. Irritated, angered, perhaps mortified, she claimed that I would never be anything but a simpleton. That was the clearest of our conversations.

After my mother's visits it often happened that I thought about my poor father and mourned him again. Life with her seemed to me, in any case, to be scarcely enviable, since, from my first year at school, I manifested the desire not to take vacations. She was I think, piqued that the idea came to me, but delighted not to have me on her back for a month and a half. What would she have done with a little girl already growing up in Monaco or Luchon? Or how could she have consented not to travel?

In the following years it went without saying that I would remain at the school. One year, however, when I was sixteen, my mother, having decided to spend the summer in the vicinity of Paris, insisted that I accompany her. It was in a little cottage at Chalou. We lived there, quite secluded, not receiving anyone, but my mother went to Paris twice a week where she spent the day. The other days she employed either lying asleep on a sofa or getting dressed in from of her mirror.

As for me, I occupied myself with the housework, reading and going for walks; most of all I walked, as I had once done in La Puisaye, not with poor Tom any longer, my first canine amour, but with a pretty little white griffon belonging to my mother, who testified to it all the affection of which she was capable, of a certain cold and disdainful variety.

One afternoon, my mother was in Paris, the chambermaid was tidying the drawing room and I was strolling in the garden in front of the house. I was stripping the rose-bushes of their dead flowers, and in order to tease Bibi, my mother's dog, who was lying on the sand of the pathway, I threw them at him as I went along.

Suddenly, Bibi got up, bounding with an incredible joy, and at the same time an elegantly clad young man cried: "Bonjour, Bibi, bonjour, bonjour! Oh my God, what caresses! You'll devour my legs."

During the brief times that I had spent with my mother, either in Paris or in the country, I had never seen that visitor. However, the manner in which he spoke to the dog, and in which he had been welcomed by him, immediately designated him to me as an habitué of the household.

He came toward me, bowed to me gracefully, was momentarily nonplussed—I was exceedingly nonplussed myself—and then, having stammered a few words about what I was doing, he said: "In Madame de Framée here, Mademoiselle?"

"No, Monsieur, my mother is in Paris."

"You mother?"

"Of course, my mother," I relied, blushing. "You didn't guess on seeing me that Madame de Framée is my mother? People say, however, that I resemble her."

"Certainly, Mademoiselle, certainly—but I thought..." He added, rather awkwardly: "I'm the son of one of Madame's friends, the Marquise d'Ingrande."

I bowed. *How is it*, I said to myself, *that this young man is the son of one of my mother's friends, but has never heard mention of me?* And I was very confused to discover that my mother surrounded my existence with such mystery, without my being able to penetrate her reasons.

In any case, I knew no more about my mother's friends than they knew about me. The name of the Marquise d'Ingrande awakened no memory in me."

Monsieur d'Ingrande was looking at me with astonished eyes, as if I were the eighth wonder of the world.

I knew nothing about the usages of society. I did not know how to receive a young man, and he was, so to speak, the first one to whom I had ever talked. He addressed the compliments to me that one addresses habitually...

He told me, I believe, that my mother must be happy to see a young person as gracious and as amiable as I was...

And that, although I had not said or done anything gracious, and had not been amiable at all.

"Mademoiselle has left boarding-school?"

"No, I'm still there. I'm only taking a short vacation.

"Still at school!"

"Yes, Monsieur," I said, blushing. "I'm only sixteen."

"At the Oiseaux, perhaps?"

"No, in a smaller school, with Mademoiselle Berthelot."

"Oh, I know it...Rue Blanche."

"No, Monsieur, Rue de Vaugirard."

All those questions, I discovered later why he was asking them. At the time, I didn't suspect any motive, and I imagined that he was only making conversation. Soon, he asked me whether Joséphine, my mother's chambermaid, had accompanied her mistress to Paris. I said no, that she was tidying the drawing room. He saluted me and, to my great astonishment, went to find Mademoiselle Joséphine. I went up to my room in order not to be in his passage when he went, but to be able to see him go nevertheless.

Alone in my room, I became bolder, and I examined Monsieur d'Ingrande mentally, as I would never have dared to do with my own eyes. His face, his attire and is manners appeared to be those of a very respectable young man.

Young women have a prompt glance, and their little mind is an objective lens in which the image of a handsome young man has the custom of being fixed instantaneously. Without that marvelous photographic procedure their situation would be truly too cruel; thanks to it, they have a compensation. It is forbidden for them to look a man in the face, especially and above all one that is dear to them, so be it! They will gaze at him internally, and he will still be there, perhaps flattered, for they operate marvelously, and with a brand new apparatus.

When Monsieur d'Ingrande passed through the garden again—and that did not take long—surprised not to see me, he looked for me everywhere with an anxious gaze; I watched him through my Venetian blinds and laughed. Finally, he bent down, picked up a couple of the dead roses I had thrown from the ground, and slipped them into his wallet.

Immediately, I was no longer laughing, and without knowing why. I felt my cheeks turning crimson and my brow darkening.

Scarcely had Monsieur d'Ingrande gone that Mademoiselle Joséphine ran into my room.

"Well, Mademoiselle?" she said to me, with a smile that appeared to me to be quite new on her rather pinched lips, a trifle dry and inexpressive.

"Well, Joséphine?" I said, a trifle embarrassed.

"You weren't expecting, were you, to see a handsome young Monsieur today?"

"That's true. He knows Maman, then, that Monsieur?"

"Yes, yes…and how do you find him?"

"Pleasant."

"He finds you charming…"

"Oh."

"He'd like to be able to come back here.

"What's preventing him, since he knows Maman?"

"In fact, Madame doesn't want him to come."

"Why not?"

"Because of you."

"Because of me?"

"Because of you."

"That's singular..."

"And in fact, it would be a good idea not to tell Madame that he came today."

"What an idea! Didn't he come to see her?"

"Of course, but she'll be annoyed that he encountered you alone."

"Joséphine, I don't like hiding things, and besides, I have no reason to do so in that matter. I'll tell my mother what happened."

"You're making a mistake. Madame will be very discontented."

Mademoiselle Joséphine's prediction was accurate. My mother listened to me with an affected indifference, beneath which I read the greatest annoyance. She usually went to Paris twice a week, on Monday and Thursday. Unusually, she returned the day after Monsieur d'Ingrande's visit. And from that moment on she treated me even more coldly than before.

As for me, I did not see Monsieur d'Ingrande at Chatou again...but I thought a great deal more about him...far too much.

Eventually, my vacation finished, and I went back to the Berthelot school. I had been there for about a week when I was told that a lady was asking to see me in the reception room. It was a woman of about fifty, although she looked scarcely forty, tall and robust, with an aristocratic manner.

"I recognized you immediately as Madame de Framée's daughter," she said coming toward me and embracing me in the most affable manner. "Léon was right; you're the living portrait of your mother...dear child! And even prettier. Do you know what my name is? I'm the Marquise d'Ingrande. But you saw my son at Chatou, didn't you?"

"Yes, Madame," I said, blushing to my ears.

"Oh, you've bewitched him! He thinks of nothing but you; he talks about nothing but you. Can you imagine that he keeps dead roses clipped by your scissors? One can't be any crazier, or any more amorous."

She continued to talk to me like that about her son, which was very embarrassing for me, and made me feel awkward as a young woman can. Then, judging that the conversation was putting me to the torture, she said: "Oh, the dear little angel, now she's all troubled! Let's not talk any more about that nasty boy who frightens young women. Let's talk about your mother. It's necessary to admit that it's strange of your mother not to introduce to her acquaintances a child who does her so much honor. But I said to myself: *I'll go to the school. I'll see her anyway, and her mother won't know anything about it—or if she does, too bad.*"

Madame d'Ingrande pleased me a great deal, by virtue of her sympathetic appearance, the gracious things she said to me, by the interest she seemed to be taking in me, and most of all, I think, because she was Monsieur d'Ingrande's mother. I will add that when she left, she gave me a little box full on excellent bonbons.

When my mother came to see me, I did not say anything about the visit I had had, for fear that she would be unjustly irritated. In any case, if Madame d'Ingrande, with whom she must be in continual communication, had kept silent with regard to it, it was because she must have her reasons and, sadly, she inspired more confidence in me than my mother.

Meanwhile, her son was never out of my mind. I had scolded myself for that in vain; there was no means of correcting myself. The less I wanted to think about him, the more I thought about him. Unless one has been a young woman oneself, one cannot suspect the naïve and foolish dreams that constitute amour in a young woman.

The name of Léon seemed incomparable to me, and I practiced pronouncing it in twenty different ways mentally, and sometimes aloud, if there was no one within earshot. I looked at it in the calendar beside the date of 10 April, or I wrote it spontaneously, without noticing, in the margin of my notebooks when I was roughing out my impositions—but I erased it immediately in order not to betray my secret to the junior mistress, who might perhaps have scolded me roundly for mingling my work with entirely heterogeneous matters.

For Madame Berthelot's birthday we put on a play in the school. One of my companions, a tall brunette named Clémence, whom I contemplated, to put it precisely, because she resembled *him* slightly, had the role of a young man, not at all amorous—Madame Berthelot did not permit amorousness even on stage—but a brother who protected his orphan sister in a touching manner. I was that orphan sister. A masculine costume had been found for Clémence, which only lacked a small beard. She wanted a simple moustache. I insisted that she that she take the entire beard. Why? Because Monsieur d'Ingrande wore his like that. She gave in, and I filled my role of younger sister with a verve and brio that earned me a great deal of applause.

One day, Madame d'Ingrande came and took a few treats for me out of a handbag that I had not seen before.

"Oh, what a pretty bag!" I exclaimed.

"It's a gift that my son gave me yesterday," she said. "It's Russian leather and has a very nice odor—smell it."

I didn't have to be asked twice. I took it in my hands; I put my nose over it and found an odor there ten times better than it had.

Those are examples of the anxious and novel tenderness that attaches itself like a down to everything it encounters.

I had, of course, only seen Monsieur d'Ingrande once—but at sixteen, it is amply sufficient to render you amorous to have seen a young man once, as long as he is genteel. And that amour is more solid than one might think. It can last a long time; it can last forever if the man who inspires it is worthy of it, and if he takes care to cultivate it.

Toward the end of the school year my mother gave me a great surprise. She brought to the reception room...who? Monsieur d'Ingrande. When I went in and found him with her,

I almost fainted; it was impossible for me to dissimulate my emotion.

Him, smiling in the most detached manner. Oh, men! I wanted to turn around in order to compose a new face, but my mother, who had seen me, called: "Well, Julie?" It was necessary to present myself as I was. I stammered that I had forgotten my handkerchief, which determined between my mother and Monsieur d'Ingrande a knowing smile, and rendered me crimson.

My mother told me that I would be spending the next vacation with her, and that I would, in consequence, have every opportunity to see Madame d'Ingrande, that I would see her much more comfortably than in the school.

"How do you know, Maman?"

"Ah, little mystery-maker! Madame d'Ingrande has confessed everything to me...not long ago, only yesterday."

"My mother has a very great affection for you," said Monsieur d'Ingrande.

"She knows too, I think, how much I like her," I replied, with sufficient aplomb. For aplomb had returned to me on seeing that unexpected understanding between Madame d'Ingrande, Monsieur d'Ingrande, my mother and myself.

My mother was no longer recognizable. Only a week ago, she had still been stiff and cold in my regard. Now she was almost affectionate, and almost tender.

Foolish hopes of happiness immediately traversed my mind. I sensed that I was about to commence a new life, and I was delighted by it. One of my companions, however, to whom I had the habit of making confidences, threw disturbance into my soul and awakened a horrible doubt there.

"You mother is still young," she said to me, "And above all, she appears so. It wouldn't be impossible for it to be her that marries Monsieur d'Ingrande. And if she came here today with him, perhaps it's to prepare you for that eventuality; and if she was so amiable, it must be because she feels the need to have herself forgiven."

"You're right!" I exclaimed, right away. "That must be it. I'm nothing but a fool."

And tears escaped me, and then more tears. Afterwards, by dint of reflection, I ended up in despair. My mother, who was scarcely thirty-seven, only looked thirty. She was very pretty, assuredly more seductive than me, a little schoolgirl, and more capable of pleasing Monsieur d'Ingrande.

Vacation time arrived without any explanation being given to me. I would gladly have gone back to school rather than witness a marriage that would break my heart, but when I said that I did not want to take the vacation and my mother and Madame d'Ingrande asked me why I was very embarrassed.

It was necessary to yield, and it did not take me long to see that my fears were chimerical. Three days after my arrival in Chatou, in the vicinity of the same cottage to which he had come the previous year, a charming scene took place between him and me, which all the subsequent disappointments have not been able to efface from my memory.

He and his mother had had lunch with us. After lunch, at which Madame d'Ingrande had been the life and soul of the party, my mother proposed a walk. We left the house. I was taking a position alongside Madame d'Ingrande when my mother said to Monsieur d'Ingrande: "My dear friend, offer your arm to my daughter; Madame d'Ingrande and I have to talk."

His arm to me—what a joy! Too much joy; I was trembling like a leaf as I rested my arm on his.

At first the conversation was banal, but so banal that it promised a more serious explanation, which was not long delayed.

"Mademoiselle," he said to me, "Madame de Framée has authorized me to talk to you in all frankness, and it is pleasant for me finally to reveal to you the secret that I have kept locked in my heart for an entire year. I love you and I have no desire greater than to marry you. Your mother consents to our

143

marriage, but only if you consent yourself, and I would be the first to make the same condition. Would you like to be my wife?"

Would I like to? Each of his words sang in my ears the sweetest melody I had ever heard. However, I did not know how to respond, so overcome was I by emotion. That emotion must have been evident, and Monsieur d'Ingrande could not have been mistaken in that regard. But men are singular beings; they push conceit to the ultimate limits. They delight in forcing a young woman to say what she would prefer them to divine.

Monsieur d'Ingrande said: "You aren't responding..."

"What do you want me to say, Monsieur?" I said very emotional.

"That you would like to."

"Isn't it obvious?"

"What?"

"Well, yes, yes, yes," I said, smiling.

"Yes what?"

"Oh, that's too much! Will you understand if I go and kiss your mother?"

"You're an angel," he said.

Madame de Framée and Madame d'Ingrande were walking a few paces ahead of us. I made Madame d'Ingrande turn round by tugging lightly on her arm. Then, when we were next to the ladies, I threw my arms around Madame d'Ingrande's neck, saying to Monsieur d'Ingrande: "Do likewise to my mother."

How naïve and confident I was then!

Throughout the time of our engagement—which lasted four or five months—Monsieur d'Ingrande's character always remained the same: noble, good and generous. At least, he appeared so to me. I was proud to love him. I did not believe that it was possible to encounter a man more worthy of love.

My mother had gained all my affection, not only because she lent her hand to a marriage of which I had dreamed, but also because she began to show affection toward me, and God knows that she had not spoiled me with affection.

Less than eighteen years old when I married, my heart was too honest and pure to suspect anything in the three individuals surrounding me—my mother, Madame d'Ingrande and her son—except that they desired my happiness. My extreme youth maintained me in that illusion marvelously. To suppose evil, especially certain complicated infamies, it is necessary already to have observed and seen a great deal.

My mother and my husband treated me a little like a child, and I had felt several times that the household was governed almost entirely in accordance with my mother's will, even though she did not live with us, rarely in accordance with my husband's and never in accordance with mine—which, to tell the truth, was not very definite.

Naturally mild and submissive, I adapted well enough to the humble situation that was made for me, and I was so far from seeing it as a real humiliation that I joked about it with my husband

"A sort of military hierarchy rules here," I said to him. "My mother is the captain; you, Léon, are her lieutenant, and your mother and I are simple soldiers."

"Madame de Framée is an intelligent woman," he replied, "and we don't do badly in listening to her."

Sometimes they teased one another in a fashion that denoted a perfect understanding and the greatest familiarity. Between my husband and me that would have appeared charming; between my mother and him it irritated me a little, but without my seeing anything absolutely reprehensible about it. They seemed to be taking me as a referee. That was the role that my mother ought to have played.

I strove to laugh when they laughed; I certainly did not do so wholeheartedly. Those scenes not only happened before me but also before strangers. A lady who had witnessed some said to me one day, with a malicious smile that chilled me:

"How lucky you are, dear child. Your pretty maman and your husband offer a very touching spectacle. I've never seen a son-in-law and mother-in-law get on so well. One would think that they were made for one another. How rare that is! In that fashion you can't fear that your household will be troubled. Oh, you ought to be very happy!"

I was so happy that when that accursed woman had gone, I began to weep, to weep all the tears I had. Léon incessantly had my mother's name on his lips, Madame de Framée this and Madame de Framée that. One day, there was even her forename, which was even stranger, and when talking to me, instead of calling me Julie he sometimes called me Hortense. I had understood perfectly, but I made a semblance of not understanding, or at least not attaching any importance to the lapse.

A horrible doubt came to my soul, however. My love for Léon received a cruel blow, and I was jealous of my mother. Every time my husband went out I was no longer alive. Where is he? What is he doing?

The state of pregnancy in which I then found myself must certainly have contributed to aggravating my nerves. That state served as an ostensible motive for all my ill humor and sadness.

It was in vain that I did not allow the anxiety and jealousy that obsessed me to show; I did not succeed any better in keeping my husband beside me than if I had revealed them. He neglected me a great deal and I no longer recognized in him the man of the first months of our marriage.

My mother-in-law lived with us. By contrast with what happens more frequently, there was a perfect harmony between her and me, and I can say that her amiable society was my consolation on many occasions.

Fundamentally, I am sure that she had for me all the sympathy that she showed and that it was painful for her to see her son so different from what I would have wished. I even believe that she often made him observations and remonstrations. But with regard to me, although I carefully refrained from accusing him, she had the art of making him appear as white as snow, and it was all the easier to convince me because I desired to be convinced.

My mother talked about going to Vichy for her health. Léon, who sometimes complained of gastralgia, wanted to go with her. I was in my seventh month; all travel was forbidden to me. I wanted to accompany him anyway. He opposed it. I hoped then that he would stay. He did not. His mother intervened in vain.

As for my mother, she said "that she would not get involved in our affairs."

The combined departure of my mother and my husband threw me into a profound affliction. In addition, it was to bring us misfortune. Twenty days later, one afternoon, my mother-in-law was brought home dead. She had collapsed in the street under the influence of a cerebral congestion. The abruptness of that event, for which nothing had prepared me, and the idea that I had to face it alone, caused me a crisis from which I nearly died.

When my husband and my mother arrived, summoned by telegram, they found two cadavers, that on Madame d'Ingrande and that of a poor little creature that had been killed in my womb.

For myself, I was not entirely dead, but it would not have taken much. I was delirious, I did not recognize them.

As soon as I recovered my senses, I represented to myself the sad road that I had followed since my marriage. As if the latest ordeals had suddenly matured me, as if they had shown me things in a clearer light, I judged with horror, thanks to certain memories that became precise in my mind for the first time, that my husband had been my mother's lover before my marriage and had remained so afterwards.

But why, then, had Monsieur d'Ingrande married me? I did not understand it then; later, I did. First of all, I was rich, and if, on the one hand, my fortune had tempted Monsieur d'Ingrande, on the other, my mother must have found it more convenient to render the accounts of her guardianship to her

147

lover than to a stranger. Secondly, I was pretty enough for him to desire me without loving me. Finally, for a wretchedly libertine nature, there could have been I know not what crapulous satisfaction in deceiving a daughter with her mother.

To see those two individuals at my beside, to be cared for by them, what a torture! At every instant my heart urged me to sit up in my bed of suffering and cry to them: "But it's infamous! But I'm the stake in an execrable game! But you're committing a permanent crime!"

I would have liked to succumb to my malady, and I don't know why I got better. It was by a miracle, so many thoughts assailed me, adding to the illness, should have rendered to incurable.

The illness disappeared, however; the thoughts remained. My husband and my mother became odious to me. I required a proof to crush them under the shame of their relationship. I waited for it; I sought it.

An anonymous letter that revealed everything to me arrived conveniently—not that I was able to consider it as proof, but it was because of it that I obtained the most conclusive of all, a confession.

My first impulse was to confront my husband and interrogate him proudly, that letter in hand. My second was less noble, I confess, but at least it was more ingenious. I set my face straight; I hid my emotion with extreme care, and, to put it simply, with the skill appropriate to a woman.

"My dear friend," I said to my husband, handing him the letter, "someone who thinks that they are giving me great pain tells me that you have been and still are my mother's lover. They don't suspect that I've known it for a long time."

Those last words, spoken with a slight smile, did not astonish my husband; they stupefied him. He stood before me, his gaze fixed and bewildered, without saying anything.

I went on: "Between ourselves, I'm not annoyed by that letter, because it serves as a pretext for me to talk to you about something of which you were wrong to make a mystery."

"Julie," he murmured, "What is this comedy? I don't understand."

"Get away!" I said, laughing, and gently taking him by the beard in order to kiss him. "Big baby! You understand marvelously. I can see what's stopping you. You're afraid that I'll hold it against you. I'm not a woman as vulgar as that, thank God."

"Julie, are you mad?"

"Truly, no, I'm not mad; but on the other hand, admit it, you're quite disconcerted. You'd have liked it if, like a petty bourgeois wife, I was red with anger. Why get annoyed? Any other mistress than my mother, I wouldn't have forgiven you, but my mother...!"

"It's not possible, you're making fun of me," he said—and then, squeezing my wrist convulsively, he added: "Or you have infamies to be forgiven yourself."

"Let's be reasonable," I said, with a sang-froid of which I truly did not think myself capable. "You knew my mother before knowing me. She was and still is a very seductive, very coquettish woman. There's nothing strange in your becoming amorous; nothing strange in her yielding to you. Then, as you wanted to marry, you found what you needed in me; nothing strange, either, in that you married me, that you and my mother made your arrangements to render me happy without harming your own happiness. As for me, I repeat, that appears quite natural."

"Well, since you take that tone, you don't merit being spared. Yes, I was your mother's lover before our marriage, and I still am. I had a few scruples about that; you've removed them; thank you. There's more indignity on your part in not suffering from the fact that your mother and I entertain such relations than ours in entertaining them. You're judged by that: you're worth less than others."

"It's you who are judged!" I cried, becoming truly myself again. "You're nothing but a wretch. Not content with committing one of the most ignoble acts that a man can commit, you've dreamed of making it a torture for me, and when I retain my cries of agony, when I stifle them under a feigned indifference, you don't like it any longer, you lack something. Don't worry, it's there. Your ferocity has nothing to regret. For as long as I live, there'll be a bloody wound in my heart."

With that, my emotion burst forth, all the more forcefully for having been held back. I fell into an armchair and dissolved in tears.

He threw himself at my knees.

"Julie, Julie, forgive me," he said. "I'm greatly culpable, I know, but I love you, I assure you that I love you..."

"I don't believe any of it," I replied. "Absolutely none. But if you love me, so much the worse for you—you'll be unhappy."

"Why did you set a trap for me?" he murmured. "Why did you set a trap? If I hadn't confessed...for, after all, you didn't know for sure. There would still have been good days for us. I've said to your mother: 'Julie is an angel, I want to be entirely hers...'"

As he said that he tried to take my hands and kiss them.

"Leave me alone," I cried, sharply. "Don't add the insult of your caresses to your other insults. Henceforth we'll live as if we were strangers to one another, and don't imagine that I'm speaking under the empire of an anger that will pass. I'm full of sang-froid; I'm very resolute. It's no longer a child that you're dealing with, it's a woman. And you know that when a woman sets out to resist something, her resistance is insurmountable.

In fact, from that day on, whatever means my husband tried to get back into my good graces, he could not do it. Tenderness, please, even tears—for he wept—were all futile.

He had begun to love me when I had made him sense that his sins would not be forgiven; and the rigor with which I kept my promise was to exasperate his amour fatally and render it malevolent. So that man, although well brought up, was brought by rage to treat me in the harshest and most brutal manner. That was what I wanted. Several times I attempted to separate myself from him amicably. He used his authority to prevent me from doing so. Finally, the separation was imposed on him by our judge. I thought myself liberated from him. I was mistaken. He did not cease to pursue me, for two years, with his letters and his person.

*

In vain I had searched for a residence in a quarter very different from his; in vain a summoned from La Puisaye an old friend of my father's, an honorable artisan, Baptiste, in order for him to serve as my protector. In vain I took the greatest care to vary the times when I went out. Either Monsieur d'Ingrande came to my home—without Baptiste letting him in—or he followed me

I learned that he had broken with my mother, as I had myself, and in his letters, and in the few words he succeeded in saying to me in person, he tried to weigh upon her all the responsibility for what he called "our misfortune."

One day he said to me: "To be as insensible as you are to my repentance and the memory of your former love for me, you must have a lover. If I knew him, I would kill him. As I don't know him, I'll take it out on you."

"I have nothing for which to reproach myself," I told him, "and I'm not afraid of you."

"I hope you have nothing for which to reproach yourself, as you say," he went on, "for the separation has not taken my name away from you and I don't intend that it should be compromised by you."

"It has already been compromised sufficiently by you," I replied, coldly, "and I wish to heaven that I no longer bore it."

"Do you wish my death, by chance?"

"No, Monsieur, I will not do you that honor; I only want one thing, and that is no longer to encounter you incessantly every time I step out into the street."

"Adieu, Madame," he said. "You will only encounter me once more."

The dry and incisive tone with which he accompanied those words, the emphasis that he gave them, and something precipitate about his retreat, caused me a spontaneous fear,

And when I tried to analyze the words themselves: "You will only encounter me once more," it did not seem to me that the song was any more reassuring than the tune.

What would that final encounter produce? Since he announced it to me so solemnly, was it not because it would have, according to him, a very particular decisive character? But what? I lost myself I conjectures, and as usual, not one of those I formed was verified. Convinced, however, that I could expect nothing good, I no longer went out.

I had been living as a recluse for three weeks when I received the following letter from my husband:

Madame,

I am leaving this evening on a voyage whose duration I cannot foresee. I would have liked to see you beforehand and to attempt once again to reconcile myself with you, but I see that any further step would be futile. You have determination, Madame, and you have my compliments for that. Personally, I am weak. The idea that I shall never see you again has entered into my mind and caused me an extreme disturbance. That I should disappear from your horizon once and for all is, on the contrary, of a nature to fill your mind with delight. That is exactly why I am in haste to communicate it to you. Will you say thereafter that I am wicked?

Marquis d'Ingrande.

Nothing tests human weakness like uncertainty and the contradiction of our sentiments. We do not know, three-quarters of the time, where our heart will take us. Will our justice prevail or our pity? Will we have implacability or indulgence? Such is the embarrassment. There is only one thing that is certain, and that is that whatever we do, we will be unhappy.

Every time I encountered my husband it was a torture for me. It seems, therefore, that I ought to have applauded his going away. Not at all. I wept. And yet I did not feel drawn to reunite with him, and intimacy was impossible henceforth.

Why was I weeping, then? Because there were still secret attachments between us; because beneath my present rancor there as my love of old.

Alas, I did not take long to discover, and in the most horrible manner, the true sentiments that Monsieur d'Ingrande ought to have inspired in me.

His letter was a trap, an ambush.

A week later, at dusk. I was going out in order to go and dine in town. I had not taken ten steps along the sidewalk when someone touched me on the shoulder. I turned round.

To recognize my husband, to feel a frightful pain in the face, to want to cry out but not to be able to do so, was the work of an instant. It was blinding.

I rushed back inside. At the sight of my fear, and doubtless also of the state of my face, Baptiste uttered loud cries. I tried to tell him what had happened to me; it was impossible to articulate a word. I looked at myself in a mirror, and was horrorstruck.

Disfigured and mute! Oh, great God!

Although that first impression of my distress is already a year old, I cannot talk about it without my heart failing. I seem to experience again.

Why did the wretch not kill me? I thought. *It is infamous to let me live in these conditions.* He had wanted to render me hideous by throwing his burning liquid in my face, at the same time he had taken away from me the use of speech, and I did not even have the consolation of lamenting.

Baptiste had gone to find a physician, Dr.***, who found me in bed with an intense fever. I wrote down for him what had happened. He did not think that I had become mute by the effect of the seizure alone; he told me that it was a case of new mutism, that I would doubtless recover the power of speech in a short while, when the crisis was over, that I did not have to worry about that. As for the wounds on my face, he added that they were much slighter than I thought, that they would disappear entirely or only lave an insignificant trace. In sum, he did his best to restore my morale. I was not duped by those obliging—or, to put it better, skillful—procedures. I was very well aware that my beauty was lost forever, and if I hoped for anything, it was only not to remain mute forever.

My adventure had caused some talk in Parisian society, and I refrained in vain from lodging a complaint against my husband. I learned from the doctor that the police were searching for him but could not lay their hands on him. I found out later that he was in England, and I was relieved by that, for it would have been painful for me, whatever harm that man had done to me, to see him dragged before a court and condemned to forced labor.

During the malign fever that followed that terrible encounter with Monsieur d'Ingrande, I did not want to have anyone else with me but the excellent Baptiste. It often happened that I demanded the mirror from him, only to throw it away as soon as I had seen myself. He, the good soul, was astonished then by the movement of repulsion for my image, and he declared that I hadn't changed, not in the least.

I could see, myself, that it was entirely the contrary; I no longer recognized myself. So, as soon as my wounds had scarred over and I began to get up, I resolved no longer to show myself in person without a veil or a velvet mask, and for a year, in spite of Baptiste's urgings, I do not remember having failed once in the promise I had made myself. I only made an exception for him, for it is impossible always to hide my face from him.

In what fashion has that year passed? In the greatest distress, alas, between Batiste, my dog and my cat.

By virtue of an eccentricity of character from which I take no honor, but which I can explain marvelously, I have thus far kept at a distance all the people that I knew before. They believe that I am far from Paris. I am sparing them pity for my condition, and sparing myself the shame of their pity. If I have changed my name, it is to put them off the track.

The double misfortune that has struck me renders me unsociable, so to speak; I am something between a woman and a statue, a hybrid being.

I have encountered a man in the Champs-Élysées, Monsieur Alphonse Méril, who has claimed that I pleased him veiled and mute. If that is not vain gallantry, he must be very eccentric. In fact, I am not astonished that one man had that strange state of mind—only one, for one would not be able to find two.

XI

Here ends, my dear friend, the story of the marquise. Has it interested you? It seems to me that, for being so short, it is very vivid. That is, I think, because the essential things are detailed there, and nothing but the essential things.

As for me, it did more than interest me; it completed rendering me amorous. The honest heart of that poor woman, the disgust in which the marriage was steeped, the frightful disgrace that her pride earned her and her great sentiment of virtue, together with the confidence I seemed to inspire in her, all concurred to make me desire more and more to know her. Yes, certainly, I would have liked her to be my mistress.

Exiled from frivolous society by her mutism and her veil, she would only me more completely mine. Finally, I would realize the dream I had always had and that has given me the false air, the utterly false air, of a Don Juan: that of encountering, not the ideal woman but an ordinary woman for whom I would be the only possible man.

I know now that, far from being a monster, she is pretty; that at twenty-two, her present age, the essential beauty remains to her, the beauty that comes from the purity of the blood and the harmony of the figure.

The stains that the vitriol has hollowed out in her privileged face and mar it, I ought not to see, but were I to see them a hundred times they would appear to me as one more reason for attaching myself to her.

I shall bring her to forsake her veil, first by begging her to substitute for it a mask uncovering the mouth and the eyes, the two principal agents of amour. I have just written to her and I have emphasized everything that I have said to you here. I add that she is making me die of impatience by not coming.

28 August

Finally, she has come. Scarcely had she come in than she whipped my nose with a bouquet of Chinese asters that she had in her hand; then she threw the bouquet on to the table, and, to my great surprise, undid the strings of her hat, which went precipitately to join the bouquet, along with the veil.

I had had a moment of mad hope; I had thought that the vitriol was a fable invented by her to render her beauty more gripping. Alas, I had reckoned without the velvet mask. It was there, the rascally mask, and it hid everything from me with the exception of the gaze, the hips and the ears.

She had also taken off a black silk bodice decorated with jet trimmings. Underneath it there was a corsage as white as snow, which contrasted in the most gallant fashion with the black velvet mask: a divine corsage which served to highlight her pink shoulders, impregnated with a light perfume, and divine by virtue of its curvature full of promise.

The black velvet mask was not simply tied on. It enclosed the face hermetically and a part of the neck, one section of it attached beneath the chignon and the other where little wisps of hair have the habit of straying. It was more like a second face molded on to the face than a true mask. The nose, the forehead, the chin and the cheeks must have been copied exactly. The hair over the forehead and the temples hid the edge of the mask, from which stood out, like jewels in a casket, eyes of sapphire, lips of coral and two dainty ears reminiscent in their form and their color of the rarest sea-shells.

What I could not see was so well modeled by the velvet, and what I could see was so evocative, that I could flatter myself with grasping the physiognomy of the charming woman.

I experience a certain embarrassment in telling you how we spent that day. We had an entire explanation without words; we both sang the most beautiful ballad without music.

So why did she have a muslin corsage and no longer a hat on her head? Whatever her reasons were, I understood them and I showed that I understood them...

Delightful creature!

I did not know yet, before having held her, all the intelligence and heart that a woman can put into certain details of amour, even without speaking.

Sometimes her lips, forcing the door of their narrow prison, dilated in order to smile; sometimes her beautiful eyes allowed great silent tears to fall, like large, warm, perfumed drops of summer rain.

It was thus that she responded to the things I said, and sometimes, if a precise word as necessary, as paper and pencil were out of season, she employed the language of the Abbé de l'Épée,[16] or, more capriciously, she traced the word in the palm of my hand with her fingernail. I felt what she wrote, for want of being able to read it, and I almost always felt it at the first stroke.

Our embraces concluded, before leaving, she sat down at my table and left me by way of adieu, these singular phrases:

If your soul is capable of a veritable amour, you will love me as you have never loved, and that amour, which no disillusionment can ruin, will be a great joy for you. If your soul is incapable of a veritable amour, you will be able to substitute for it, as so many people do a pretty little artificial amour, which will still satisfy me a great deal, for it is necessary not to be too demanding in this world. As for me, I certainly count on giving you one or the other. See what an admirable day we have spent today! And that thanks to a few sentimental grimaces. Would you like to be my little Alphonse for good? But I'm asking you there something that you don't know yourself.

---

[16] Charles-Michel de l'Épée (1712-1789) developed the first sign language for the use of the deaf, which he taught in the Institution Nationale des Sourd-Muets À Paris, which he founded and continued after his death.

We have only to let our two hearts go their own way and see where they lead us. Those sorts of stupidities are not susceptible of direction; and when one spurs them, one renders them surly and restive.

What do you think, my dear friend, of her horoscope? "If your soul is capable of a veritable amour, you will love me as you have never loved." It's necessary, then, that she feels very strong, or that she has already judged me very weak. That naïve excess gives me a frisson. In truth, I reassure myself by taking what my tender sorceress adds thereafter in her letter, to wit, that the veritable amour with which I gratify her will not perish under the influence of any disillusionment.

I wager that you, a man of little faith, are convinced that a veritable amour and I are not made to lodge under the same sign. My vagabond humor is crossing your mind, and you can see filing past all the women to whom I've paid court in the last ten years.

Reason no more, my friend, because today I am attached to one, and I love her as you have never loved.

What do you think of the "pretty artificial amour" and that confession worth its weight in gold that "I certainly count on giving you one or the other"? It seems to me that there is a very piquant frankness in that on the part of a woman, and that it will draw me with regard to Julie to become, as she puts it, "her little Alphonse for good."

If she is only offering me in return a pretty artificial amour, I share her opinion; it will still satisfy me a great deal, for it's necessary not to be too demanding in this world. And a few "sentimental grimaces," grimaces though they are, will defray my days better than many other unsentimental grimaces appropriate to civilized humanity.

At the moment of separation, while I still had her hand on my lips, she suddenly drew it away; then, repeating a gesture already familiar, she thrust her ringed finger before my eyes. I looked at it. The marquise's crown was no longer hanging from the end of the little chain. It had been replaced by two letters, delicately engraved: A.M.

"A.M.!" I exclaimed. "Why those two letters in the place of your crown? A.M.," I added, laughing, that can only signify Assurance Mutuelle. *That's your plaque. You're paying a premium to an insurance company against the disappointments of amour. What is that premium?"*

She lifted her veil and her laughter was audible, like a flutter of wings; and again I saw my beautiful pink lips and my beautiful blue eyes; and I was unable to see them without giving them evidence of all my esteem.

She returned to the table and wrote:

You're a conceited man playing the part of a modest one. You know perfectly well that A.M. means Alphonse Méril. But your idea of the Assurance Mutuelle is amusing, and I thank you for having had it. What premium am I paying? Perpetual suspicion—and it is a heavy premium. Don't take out insurance yourself, I beg you; be confident. I am an exceptional woman, as you will see.

I read that over her head. When she got up from the table, I said to her, opening my arms to her for the first time: "Julie, do you love me?"

She shrugged her shoulders slightly, and headed for the door.

"Julie, tell me that you love me," I repeated, as she disengaged herself from my hands in order to leave.

While blowing me a long kiss she shook her head, but although it has never been the rule, there was reason to think that, this time, her negation was worth two affirmations.

XII

That letter was the last I received from Méril. Three days later I quit the sea and I returned to Paris. There I found Méril very absorbed by his recent passion, and I had been able to imagine.

Having become perfectly happy, he had nothing else to tell me, Entire happiness does not support narration. That is a cliché.

We saw one another at rare intervals. If I mentioned Her to him, if I asked him about his amours, he replied, with a melancholy smile: "She's charming, charming, my black cat; she only lacks speech."

He called her "his black cat" because of the velvet mask. She only came to his home three times a week, in order, he said, to leave him time to desire her. But he was enraged that there was incessantly a day in between, not to mention the nights.

When she was here, they made music with four hands, or made love with four arms.

Six months passed in that fashion: six full months.

It seemed that their happiness was at its peak, and that it could only decline. However, something absolutely unexpected, and quasi-miraculous, opened up a new phase to it.

This is how Méril recounted the event to me himself:

Yesterday, she fainted, as sometimes happens to her during our best moments. Those faints, to which I'm accustomed, no longer frighten me. I know that they only last for five minutes or so. Until then, I had not thought of taking advantage of them to penetrate the secret of that visage, or if I had thought of it, it was a fleeting desire immediately dominated by the idea that I would be committing an abuse of rust, a veritable infamy.

Suddenly, I was seized by a vertigo. Like a criminal gripped by the demon of crime, I felt myself go pale and tremble throughout my being. And in spite of myself, so to speak, attracted by a blind force, taking no account whatsoever of the enormity of the act, I cut the cords of the mask with a penknife.

It was necessary that I see her; I had a ferocious need to sew her. With infinite tremulousness, I gradually lifted the mask. Finally, it was removed. I looked. I cried: "But you're beautiful! You're still beautiful! You've always been beautiful!"

And at the same time, I covered with burning kisses all the parts of her face that were revealed to me, even those that had been spoiled—especially those—at the bottom of the left cheek and the neck, over the breadth of four fingers.

She came round; she looked at me anxiously and, by virtue of I know not what presentiment, sought to put her hands to her mask. I held them back. I wanted her to learn from the contact of my lips on her cheek that she no longer had the mask, since it was also to show her that I loved her no less after having seen her. A futile precaution! She dissolved in tears, pulled her hands way from mine energetically, and plastered them over her face.

In vain I repeated, in every tone:

"My dear angel, forgive me. I confess that I've broken my word; I confess that it's an indignity; but I wouldn't have wanted not to have committed it, since I'm liberating you once and for all from that mask. I don't want you to wear it any longer, you hear? You're crazy to think that you're disfigured. Get up, come with me to the mirror, look at yourself without prejudice. The physician, you remember, the physician...he was telling you the truth, the exact truth, I assure you, my Julie, my beautiful Julie, my adorable Julie...!"

She shook her head and her tears flowed more abundantly.

I got up, I went to fetch a small, mirror, and then. tearing her hands away from her face, I said to her: "Look at yourself. In the name of our amour, look at yourself!"

She darted a fearful glance at the mirror, and then shoved it away with one hand, while touching with the other the few scars that the vitriol had left on her face, murmuring in a voice that seemed to come from the antipodes: "There! There!" And she enveloped me with a gaze of indescribable sadness.

"Julie, you're crazy. Don't look at yourself in the mirror any more, look into my eyes."

They were very moist, and they ought to have rendered three things very eloquently: an extreme amour, a sincere admiration and a flight of my entire being toward her.

"Look into my eyes, I beg you, and enjoy the impression you make on me."

Her gaze plunged profoundly into mine, obedient to a sort of magnetism stronger than her, and stronger than me. Coloring by degrees, it finally took on an excessive, almost supernatural glare, a glare that I had never seen through the mask, and she cried—yes, my friend, she cried:

"Alphonse, I believe you, for I love you. But I'm speaking! That's certain—I'm speaking! Oh, my God, I'm speaking."

The commotion that those words caused me, the first that she had pronounced in my presence, was incomparable, I assure you, to any that I had ever felt before.

When Méril reached that point in his story, I could not help allowing a slight smile to appear on my lips.

"What does that smile signify?" Méril demanded.

"Nothing."

"Be frank."

"What's the point? Nothing, I tell you."

"I'll wager that you find all that strange, don't you?"

"Well, yes, if you need a confession, a little strange. That a woman should think herself completely disfigured by vitriol when her beauty is only trivially afflicted is already bizarre and somewhat contrary to our nature, which leads us to overestimate ourselves rather than depreciate ourselves. But I find the mutism gripping and then leaving the marquise devoid of the slightest scientific reason, for she would have become mute by virtue of terror and would have ceased to be by virtue of joy, would she not?"

"Yes, exactly."

"Is that possible?"

162

"It's a fact."

"Still, it's necessary to suppose that it's true."

"On what do you base your doubt on that matter?"

"On its implausibility."

"Or on your ignorance of the laws on Nature. Oh, my dear friend, how little we know!" Méril added, philosophically.

"Then, she can speak now?"

"Like you and me, and I'm the happiest of men. By the way, I haven't told you what Madame d'Ingrande had to sort out with the hotelier in the Rue du Dauphin on the evening when I encountered her in the Champs-Élysées, if you remember. I asked her today and she replied:

"'I had read in a newspaper an announcement that an English physician, a specialist in maladies of the voice, was in Paris staying at The Hôtel du Dauphin. I had already gone to the hotel once to see whether he had arrived. I went back a second time without suspecting that my real physician was walking alongside me in the Rue de Rivoli.'

"'Are you quite certain of that?' I asked, clicking my tongue in a slightly jealous fashion.

"She didn't make any reply, but she shrugged her shoulders slightly.

"'You're frightening me,' I said, gaily, 'If you don't reply to me immediately. I'll believe that you've become mute again…'

"She threw her arms around my neck and uttered a prolonged burst of laughter, which proved to me well enough that her voice had returned."

XIII

When Méril left me, I immediately went to one of my friends, a physician, and submitted the case of mutism to him, for the tranquility of my conscience.

"It doesn't astonish me at all," he said, to my great astonishment.

And in order to convince me, he opened a medical dictionary, where no less singular cases of mutism and the cure of mutism were cited, on the authority of Stoll, Scheid, Haller, Gaubius and Schencklus.[17]

"Read those authors," he added, seriously.

"Really! You're advising me, dear friend, to...you're very kind, but I'd rather believe you twenty times over than read even one of them."

---

[17] Albert von Haller and Jerome Gaubius were both renowned eighteenth-century physicians ad a physician named Stoll was one of the popularizers of homeopathy in the same period; the other names are elusive.

MRS. LITTLE

Prologue

There are people (I am a sorry example) who generally obtain more ennui than pleasure from social relationships. There are some whose idleness is disturbed thereby, because one has to get dressed at fixed hours; there are others whose vanity is compromised, because one cannot always flatter oneself with presenting the image for which one is ambitious; some suffer from their frankness, because one is exposed to saying, or at least hearing said, many white lies; others, finally, without being retained at home by idleness, vanity, or even a grim integrity, renounce society after a few attempts, for want of ever finding their intellectual and moral milieu there.

When I say "their milieu," I do not suppose in the slightest that no sort of divergence of opinion is produced between the habitués of the same society, which would be monotonous and, moreover, impossible, but I am supposing that there is no magnetic antipathy between them.

And that is quite rare.

For myself, I only know of one salon where I have found my milieu, and which I continue to frequent, and that is Madame ***'s. A little more and I would have named that sovereignly amiable woman, whom one of the most fortunate hazards of my life enabled me to encounter in Rome, in May 18**, and who was kind enough, on my return to Paris, to admit me into the restricted number of her familiars.

We meet in her drawing room every Wednesday, ten persons at the most, among whom are four wives with their husbands, women who are neither prudes nor coquettes, but simple and good, like the mistress of the house.

People chat there at their ease, and if there are sometimes differences of opinion, there is always the same humor. Everyone enjoys themselves there effortlessly, because honesty, benevolence and a certain jovial philosophy are equally shared by everyone.

I doubt that another salon like it exists in Paris. One of us, with good reason, has called it "the worldly paradise." And it is a paradise that we shall not lose, for if we form multiples of Adam and Eve there, at least no one can say that there is a serpent among us, nor any apples, except for the golden serpent with emerald eyes worn on the finger of the mistress of the house, and the pommel of the cane on which the metaphysician Morini has the custom of supporting his chin while he divides the spidery thread of our transcendent conceptions.

One evening we had a full complement. The conversation revolved around the force of habit in amour. The beautiful and virtuous Mina—I believe that I can give the true forename of our hostess—talked to us in an emotional voice about the husband she had lost many years before, and the portrait of the latter, so lifelike was it, seemed to detach itself from the wall and discuss fidelity with us.

In thinking about the great misfortune that had overtaken their friend and which might overtake them in their turn from one day to the next, the women were almost weeping, and not one of the men, I am convinced—even the bachelors—felt born within him the foul and vile desire, so frequent in banal natures, to soil with their caprice or passion a sentiment as sacred as that of a widow's mourning.

Suddenly, the door of the drawing room opened and Mina's chambermaid, the worthy old Gervaise, whom we called between ourselves "the chamberlain," announced Monsieur Le Bref.

The name was unknown to all of us, except Mina. So, in the moment when she got up to go and greet Monsieur Le Bref, with her familiar grace, we looked at one another, and it was easy for me to see, painted on all the faces, the same apprehension regarding the newcomer.

Was he not destined to trouble in some manner the precious harmony that reigned among us? Such is the question that we were asking one another with our eyes.

In order to resolve the prevision as much as it was possible for me, I examined Monsieur Le Bref very attentively

He was a tall and handsome fellow, about thirty-five years old, elegantly dressed, with a simple and grave deportment, of a rare distinction, extremely sympathetic from the outset. The first words he pronounced revealed to me, in addition, the timbre of a charming voice and a good deal of intelligence.

There is a locution that is generally applied to people much less well endowed than Monsieur Le Bref appeared to be: it is said that they have "everything going for them."

He gave the impression of being such an accomplished fellow that I thought, privately: *There's a man who has everything going for him, and quite a lot more!*

A perfection so overwhelming could not help but make me anxious, because of the women. And I feared immediately that it might be an element of dissolution for the circle, if only by giving umbrage to the men, were Monsieur Le Bref to become one of us.

"My dear friends," exclaimed Mina, "I introduce to you Monsieur Le Bref, a nomad who is incorrigible to the point that, in coming to see me this evening in Paris, where he only arrived yesterday from Rome, he tells me that he is departing tomorrow for England. I regret his precipitate departure all the more because, belonging to our school, he would become one of the pillars of the Academy of Joyful Melancholics."

"If you would care to admit me as a corresponding member," said Monsieur Le Bref, I will formulate the wish that everyone resume the conversation that was in progress before my arrival."

"The question that is the order of the day, or rather, of the evening," replied Mina, "cannot interest you."

"Am I not a joyful melancholic?"

"Yes, but…"

"But what, Madame?"

"Would you like to know?"

"Certainly."

"Well, we were talking about the force of habit in amour...now, you travel far too much to have ideas on that subject."

"I have them, however, and the best."

"Oh!! The best?"

"And the freshest," he said.

She started to laugh and said: "I'm sure that you're of the opinion that habit is the greatest scourge of amour."

"Entirely the contrary, Madame, I am of the opinion that the only true amour is born of habitude."

"For a nomad, you astonish me."

"Alas, you know full well," replied Monsieur Le Bref, "that the ideas that are dearest to us are precisely those that we have not been able to attempt in practice—but I have encountered in my travels an English eccentric who has taken the practice of the idea of force of habit in amour as far as, and even further than, it can reasonably be taken."

"Come on, tell us about that," cried Mina. "It will be your speech, or rather your narration, of reception into the Academy of Joyful Melancholics."

"I must warn you, though, that the story is a trifle long," Monsieur Le Bref replied.

"So much the better for us," replied another lady.

Monsieur Le Bref yielded to that graciousness, and, as we all demanded the story of the Englishman, he began to tell it.

PART ONE: IN SPAIN

I

In August 18**, following a cruel family misfortune that had caused me sufficient chagrin to affect my health profoundly, my physician, thinking that I had need of both a tonic and distraction, prescribed the sea-baths at Biarritz for me.

In truth, the listlessness in which I found myself then was so great, and I was so isolated by my sadness from the ordinary course of human things, that I was reluctant to displace myself. My physician insisted. I tried at least to obtain from him that I might simply go to Luc, in Normandy, where I had my habits so to speak, for I had spent several summer seasons there, but he closed my mouth, saying to me that I would derive all the more benefit from my voyage if my destination was more distant and quite new to me.

I therefore decided in favor of Biarritz.

As I had a friend to see in Bordeaux I stopped there for a full day, which also permitted me to rest, for the journey from Paris to Bordeaux cannot help but be somewhat fatiguing.

When I arrived, two days later, on the platform of the Gare Saint-Jean, the train for Bayonne was already full. After having searched from carriage to carriage for an empty seat, I spotted a compartment in which, apart from two good English figures—a man and a women—who were blocking the door, there seemed to be places free.

I approached in order to climb in, but the man exclaimed: "No, you can't!"

I attempted to infringe that order, whose legitimacy seemed all the less explicable to me because there were, in fact, six vacant seats in the compartment.

Immediately in the same way that a guard dog launches itself out of its niche to bark loudly at any individual bold enough to approach, the lady irrupted out of carriage window and an ill-defined screech emerged from between her elongated teeth. I heard something like: "Loa! Loa!"

In my stupefaction, I stood there at first with my hand on the door handle.

What the devil did that Englishwoman mean with her *Loa, loa*?

I thought of Alfred de Vigny's *Éloa*,[18] but without settling on the idea that the Englishwoman might want to compare to that celestial creature a monsieur who persisted in trying to climb into railway carriage.

Then I reflected that she might be insulting me and shouting: "L'oie, l'oie!"—which is to say; "You're a goose!" although I found such an insult excessive.

Finally, I was extracted from my perplexity by the conductor of the train, who, having heard the Englishwoman's peacock screech, approached me and said, politely raising his cap in one hand while he used the other to show me an indicative placard: "You see, Monsieur, this compartment is reserved until Bayonne.

"*Loué*!" I exclaimed. "Ah—I understand."

So, the Englishman, in saying to me "No, you can't" and his worthy companion, in crying "Loa! Loa!" or "L'oie, l'oie!" had simply wanted to signify to me that they had an exclusive right to the compartment.

In fact, did they really? I don't know. Perhaps they had simply brought, in return for a good tip, the complicity of the train conductor—which can be done, so it's said.

---

[18] In Alfred de Vigny's poem, a classic of French Romanticism, Éloa is a female angel who falls in love with handsome male angel, not realizing that he is about to start a war in heaven and be damned, drawing her to damnation with him in spite of her innocence.

At any rate, I did not persist, and I allowed myself to be led meekly by the conductor, guilty or not of private enterprise, to another compartment, where, by some miracle, one seat remained unoccupied, and for his trouble I even slipped a fifty-centime piece into his hand.

In those days the railway did not go as far as Biarritz, but there was a very rapid diligence service from Bayonne station to Biarritz. When, having arrived at Bayonne station, I had reclaimed my baggage, I raced to the diligence and installed myself in a corner of the coupé.

I thought that the coupé was for first comers, but to tell the truth, I was not certain of that, only knowing one thing, which was that I had bought a first class ticket in Bordeaux, diligence included, to Biarritz.

I was therefore, stuck in my corner of the coupé, at hazard, watching the passengers arrive, and sometimes shuddering when the factors threw their heavy luggage up on to the impartial.

Suddenly, here come my English couple again, heading straight for the coupé, and the husband says: "You can't stay," and the wife adds "Loa, loa," or, again, "L'oie, l'oie."

"Good, good," I said, laughing, I should have expected that."

And I got down through the other door and climbed philosophically into the interior.

The Hôtel des Ambassadeurs had been recommended to me as one of the best in Biarritz.

On arriving in Biarritz at the diligence office, I spotted a commissionaire attached to that hotel, the name of which he wore inscribed on his cap.

"Under the tarpaulin of the diligence," I said to him, "there's a trunk and a hat-box with the name of Monsieur Le Bref, will you take them?"

Before he had time to reply, the Englishman, having approached us, asked him: "Boy, you were the boy of the Hôtel des Ambassadeurs?"

"Yes, Monsieur," said the commissionaire, without paying the slightest attention to me.

"Oh, I thought so. Since you were the boy of the Hôtel des Ambassadeurs, come a little, take the trunks of me. to carry them to the Hôtel des Ambassadeurs."

"Yes, Monsieur…I have others to take as well"

"You take those of me first."

On hearing that injunction, I felt a surge of impatience that I could not master. In sum, it was becoming a challenge. That beastly islander, then, had sworn to cut the grass from my feet in every circumstance. Not content with nearly making me miss the train in Bordeaux by forbidding me to climb into his compartment, under the pretext that he had reserved it, and having thrown me out of the coupé in Bayonne under the same pretext, now he was demanding that the commissionaire of the Hôtel des Ambassadeurs serve him before me, although I had commandeered him first.

"In truth Monsieur, in truth," I said to the Englishman, in a very acerbic tone, "you don't inconvenience yourself as much as politeness requires in our land of France. I commandeered this man before you and he has no reason to serve you before me."

"It was you who lack politeness and me I won't suffer it," replied the Englishman. "I had a sufficient motive for demanding the work of this porter. Me I have retained the place of me and my wife for more than a fortnight at the Hôtel des Ambassadeurs."

"L'oie," I said, ironically.

"Oh yes, said the Englishwoman. "This porter is loa."

I had a desire to reply: "L'oie is your husband! L'oie is you!" But I contented myself with saying, with an ironic smile, of which they certainly did not comprehend the full range: "May the god Lord bless both of you!"

And after having given my instructions to the commissionaire I went to the Hôtel des Ambassadeurs in order to book a room, in the event that—which I did not know—the English couple had left any available.

I asked when I arrived whether it was possible to give me a room with a view over the sea, to which the reply was negative, because there was only one vacant with that situation, which had been promised to an English couple who were expected at any moment.

I ought to have expected that. It was added that there was another next door to that one, which did not have a sea view but which was no less comfortable.

"Next door to the English couple!" I exclaimed. "Oh, no, not next door to them, I beg you, I implore you."

It was to the landlady of the hotel that I replied in those terms. She could not help laughing.

"Monsieur doesn't much like the English, I see."

"On their island, yes indeed, on their island. Oh, my God, you're not of my opinion, Madame and you prefer them in your hotel—that's understandable."

"The ones who are going to occupy that room," she said, gaily, pointing at the door, "a lady and gentleman, reserved it a fortnight ago."

"Yes, yes, I know."

"Monsieur knows them?"

"Far too well. And I announce to you that they'll be here momentarily. Try, then, to find me a room a hundred leagues from theirs...a hundred leagues is very little...a thousand leagues."

She evidently found the animadversion that I professed for the subjects of Queen Victoria very amusing.

"In that case," she said, "it would be better to give Monsieur a room in the other wing of the house."

"Yes, Madame," I cried, "that's right... the other wing, if you please."

II

The room that I had been given simply had a view over a small courtyard where there was a small basin in which a few ducks were paddling. It was not the sea, but nor was it the

English couple, and yet the ducks reminded me of the Anglo-French exclamation that had aggravated my nerves so much: "L'oie, l'oie!"

After having taken a few turns around the beach, I came back for dinner. I arrived slightly late; everyone was at table.

There were only two places free, and by virtue of a slightly grotesque fatality, one of those places was next to the English couple and the other facing them.

Between two evils, it is said, it is necessary to choose the lesser. But there was still the question of knowing which was the lesser. That was what I asked myself as I hung my hat on one of the pegs in the dining room.

If I sat facing them the viewpoint would not only be not amusing for me, but exasperating. If, on the contrary, I sat alongside, might I not pick a quarrel?

I made a reflection that cut short my uncertainty.

They're capable, I thought, of having reserved the place next to them, and if I go sit down there, the Englishwoman will doubtless screech once again: "L'oie! L'oie!"

That idea amused me so much that my rancor against the English couple was disarmed and, having arrived at the place that was opposite them, I began contemplating them one after another with a very equable and even cheerful, humor.

The Englishman might have been thirty-five or forty years old, and the Englishwoman not much younger. For faces, they possessed two marvelously matched ruddy balls, which did not lack analogy with a Dutch cheese in their integrity. There existed between them a family resemblance such that one would more readily have taken them for brother and sister than husband and wife. And yet, they were definitely spouses, for the Englishman, in speaking of the Englishwoman during our little altercation in front of the diligence, had said: "my wife."

It is necessary to admit that nothing about them suggested that they were nasty people. On the contrary, their placid gaze was imprinted with bonhomie.

As true English people, of course, they did not have any expansion, although they seemed happy to be beside one another.

At intervals, the husband said a few words to his wife, to which she replied with a single word: "Yes," or "No," depending upon the circumstance—nothing more.

The following morning, as I was looking at the names of the bathers staying at the hotel, I noticed, not far from mine, those of Mr. and Mrs. Little of Chester, with the indication that they had arrived the day before. It was of no importance to me to know what the name of admirably matched couple was, but, in any case, I knew.

From that day on, and for twenty more, I stayed in Biarritz. My life was spent, naturally, on the edge of the sea—all the time that was not spent indoors, that is, for I took the plunge every morning and evening.

And as the life of the other bathers was identical to mine I could not help encountering Mr. and Mrs. Little quite frequently

One morning, when I was walking, after my bath, along the "Côte des Fous," I passed so close to the couple that, in spite of the scant sympathy they inspired in me because of my ancient grievances against them, I judged it appropriate to salute them.

Although his gaze met mine—at least, such was my conviction—Mr. Little did not raise his hat. Nor did Mrs. Little incline her head, as convention would have required, but remained perfectly straight and stiff.

I was choked by that. It remained to be determined where it was intentional rudeness on the party of the English couple, or simple inadvertence. I thought at first of intentional rudeness, and I called both of them bumpkins mentally. Then I reflected that, after all, they had no reason to be impolite in my regard, and I almost arrived at excusing them, on thinking that Mr. Little was too occupied with conversing with Mrs. Little, and Mrs. Little too occupied with listening to Mr. Little, to take the trouble to salute me.

Furthermore, I have noticed that the English, probably because they are islanders, have the very particular gift of isolating themselves in a crowd. It seems that they always have a little sea around them.

That consideration dispelled the slight rancor that I still had against Mr. and Mrs. Little. Nevertheless, I promise myself to isolate myself as well henceforth when I passed within range of them—which is to say, not to salute them again. And I kept my word.

It was perhaps ten days that the English couple and I had been in Biarritz, and we had encountered one another every day, either at table at the Hôtel des Ambassadeurs, or on the beach—or even, as people used to say, in the bosom of Amphitrite—without even looking at one another. One morning, as I was taking my bath at Port-Vieux, and while swimming, I had drawn somewhat apart, I heard cries of distress. As I was on my back at that moment and could only see the sky, I turned over precipitately, and gave the water a good kick in order to rise above the waves, in order to see where the cries were coming from.

I then perceived a crowd of people on the beach who were making signals to me, and a short distance away from me, a small indistinct mass that was struggling against the waves.

In a few strokes, I had reached the object in question, which it was impossible for me to define, while the observation boat arrived from the other direction, impelled by its oars.

I seized the object, which was a body wrapped in black woolen fabric, which the boatman and I hoisted into the boat, to the applause of the spectators.

I climbed into the boat myself, and as the boatman rowed toward the shore, which was not very far away. I gazed with a very sympathetic curiosity at the kind of human package that we had pulled out of the water.

It was a man, and a man whose face was not unknown to me, it seemed, without my being able to put a name to it. But I had something more urgent to do than rack my brains trying to find it. Was the man, whoever he was, alive or dead? It did not take me long to establish that he was alive, for as I bent over him, he opened his eyes to look at me, and his mouth to say to me: "I thank you."

Oh, of course, I should have suspected it. It was the Englishman from the Hôtel des Ambassadeurs, Mr. Little—except that his ruddy face had gone very pale.

Meanwhile, the boat touched the shore, the sailor threw the anchor, and then we both picked Mr. Little up, him by the feet and me by the shoulders, and we carried him on to the beach, where a curious crowd had gathered.

Mrs. Little was there, in tears, with a woolen peignoir in her hands, with which she enveloped her husband, while she enveloped me, I have to admit, with a gaze moist with gratitude. And as if that gaze were insufficient to translate her thought, she said to me, amid sobs that truly went to my heart: "Monsur, you have saved the life of the husband of me. You are courageous gentleman." And she added: "*I bless you.*"[19]

"Not at all, Madame," your words are not made to wound me."

And I slipped away as quickly as possible, for, apart from the fact that my attire was not very appropriate and was even little shocking for the ultra-prudish gaze of a lady, I was beginning to feel cold and was in haste to dry myself.

While running toward my cabin, however, I wondered why the devil Mrs. Little imagined that she might be wounding me by declaring that I was a courageous gentleman.

By dint of reflection I remembered that the English verb "to bless" refers to benediction, and that consequently, Mr. Little had simply wanted to wish me well.

When I was dressed, my first concern was to enquire about Mr. Little, and I learned with pleasure that he was as well as could be. I was told that after he had drunk a glass of

---

[19] Mrs. Little says the italicized phrase in English, which leads the narrator to misunderstand, the French verb *blesser* meaning to wound.

port, he had had himself wrapped in a warm blanket, and that two strong fellows were presently occupied in massaging him.

He has no further need of me, I thought, and I headed for the hotel with all the more haste because I was late for lunch and I had a great appetite.

My arrival at table, where everyone was gathered, was greeted by a sympathetic murmur. Doubtless everyone already knew that I had assisted in the Englishman's rescue, and it even seemed to me that they had been talking about it when I came in. At any rate, in addition to compliments that I could have done without—for, in sum, there was absolutely nothing heroic in my perfectly natural action—questions were addressed to me, to which I could not reply, regarding the cause that had nearly cost the life of Mr. Little, an excellent swimmer.

I left the table before he arrived there, but I met him at the door of the hotel as he was coming back from the beach, accompanied by his wife.

On perceiving me he quit the latter's arm and, extending both his hands to me, he said effusively: "I want to know the name of you, Monsur."

"The name of me," I said, laughing, "is Le Bref."

"Ho ho! That was very good, but can you give to me the little card of you?"

"Gladly." And, taking one of my cards out of my wallet, I handed it to him.

"Perfectly," he said, looking at the card. "Le Bref is the name of you. That name, it was forever written on the breast of me, Tommy Little, cheese-maker of Chester."

"Much obliged," I said to him. And I thought: It's lucky that he didn't tell me that my name is inscribed in his bowels.

"This is the little card of me," he said, handing me his card, "and know, Monsur, that I was at your disposal in my fortune and my life."

"Oh, Monsieur," I exclaimed, "you're too good, a thousand times too good."

"No," said Mrs. Little.

"Go and have lunch," I said, "for you must be hungry."

"I have already had port with little biscuits," replied the cheese manufacturer, "but Mrs. Little, no..."

"Then Mrs. Little must be very hungry," I said to the husband. "It is, in fact, improbable that your port and little biscuits have sustained her."

"No," replied Mrs. Little, seriously, while Mr. Little laughed at my joke.

"But tell me, Monsieur," I said, "did you have a fainting-fit in the water, for you're a swimmer of the first order?"

"Ho, yes, in the water...how do you say it...a fainting-fit?"

"Yes, a fainting-fit...you suddenly felt lost consciousness?"

"Ho, yes, lost..."

"It gripped you in the head?"

"No, no, it gripped me in the belly by a sudden natural need."

"Ah!" I said, stiffening my lips in order not to burst out laughing. "That's truly peculiar. In any case, we won't talk about it anymore. Believe me, go and have lunch."

It was thus that our first conversation concluded; it was to be followed by many others, a perfect intimacy having been established between us thereafter.

III

That intimacy became so warm and so cordial on either part that we decided to undertake a trip to Spain together.

The proposal was made to me by Mr. Little and I must say that I was very hesitant to accept it, for fear of having to suffer more than once in that little plan the British egotism that had to be—at least, I believed so then—stronger than friendship.

However, Mr. and Mrs. Little had become so pleasant, and even obliging, toward me since the rescue that I thought I might risk the trip.

It was therefore agreed that when our season ended, we would take the steamboat at Bayonne for San Sebastian, and from there we would go in stages all the way to Andalusia.

An unexpected event prevented up from completing our journey, but at least we tried and went quite a long way.

You know the Gulf of Gascony, and you know that it isn't always in a good mood. Our crossing from Bayonne to San Sebastian was completed without too much inconvenience, but when we arrived in port, at the very moment when the passengers were disembarking by means of small launches, the waves became very angry.

The launch into which I had already descended was agitated terribly. Our two oarsmen were unable to maintain the boat at the side of the steamer. I extended my hand to Mrs. Little to help her get down, while her husband, who was still on the deck of the steamer, supported her by the waist, and that worked quite well.

When Mr. Little wanted to get down in his turn, however, he recklessly refused the hand I held out to him and, the launch having suddenly sifted, our worthy islander would surely hand fallen into the water if I had not grabbed him just in time by the strap of his marine binoculars.

"Ho, yes," he said, with great phlegm, when he had sat down. "You will still be saving the life of me, then."

"One good turn deserves another," I replied.

"Ho, yes, I liked nothing so much as to see in frightful danger, to show you my gratitude.

"Ho, yes," confirmed Mrs. Little, with the most amusing gravity.

"I'd prefer it, my dear Monsieur Little, and very much so, if you didn't have the opportunity."

"No, no, I wanted absolutely to have it, me, that opportunity, and you disoblige me in refusing it to me."

"In truth, you're very good."

The few people who were about to disembark from the launch with us were laughing to the point of tears at the slightly excessive zeal deployed toward me by the worthy Mr. Little, who, in order to have the satisfaction of saving me in his turn, would have liked me to be on the brink of doom.

Having spent two successive years in England, one of them at the University of Oxford, I certainly knew English far better that Mr. and Mrs. Little knew French, and they recognized fully my superiority in that regard, having judged it for themselves in Biarritz, on one occasion when I had tried to converse with them in English. But, Mr. Little having adjured me only to employ the French language in my conversation with his wife and himself in order to constrain them to learn it, whether they like it or not, I had naturally deferred to his desire.

Scarcely had we reached Spanish soil than Mr. Little, addressing me for the first time in English, said to me: "If I were capable of speaking Spanish, I would say to you: 'Let's speak Spanish, since we're in the homeland of Cervantes,' but I have to admit that I'm incapable of speaking Spanish, at least until further notice. We can now, therefore, if you please, speak English between us."

I was so content with that resolution that I showed Mr. Little how much I approved by an exceedingly prolix response in the language of Walter Scott. Instead of quite simply saying "Gladly, Mr. Little," I made a veritable speech on two points: firstly, the pleasure that he caused me thereby, and then on the merits of his idiom.

Since I had had the honor of knowing Mrs. Little, I had been struck by her scant expansion toward a husband who had the greatest attention for her. It was not that she was insensible to his attentions, for it was not rare when she was the object of them for her to squeeze Mr. Little's hand with a marked tenderness, but she scarcely said two or three words to him at intervals. More often than not she only replied with a monosyllabic "Yes" or "No" to questions, reflections or explanations emanating from her husband.

British coldness being insufficient to explain that constant mutism, I had thought that it might be attributable to the singular obligation imposed on Mrs. Little by her husband only to speak French, which was far from being familiar to her. I was mistaken. When it was permissible for her to express herself in the mother tongue, she scarcely said any more. It was, therefore, a matter of personal temperament. She was what is known in the French Midi—and also in Spain, I believe—as a *sang-mort*.[20]

She was positively not astonished by anything, applying too literally Horace's precept *Nul mirari*.

Mr. Little, doubtless long habituated too that superlative nonchalance, did not seem to be affected by it in the slightest. It was sufficient for him that she listen to him complaisantly, which she did not fail to do.

As for me, on seeing the woman limit herself to being the recipient of her husband's thoughts—and mine, for I had no more success than Mr. Little in getting four words out of her—I sometimes had a muted irritation. *She's not a wife*, I said to myself, *she's an automaton*; and I could not understand why Mr. Little had brought such an insignificant person with him across Europe instead of confining her to his cheese-factory in Chester. I was judging things from my own point of view, without reflecting that Mr. Little's might by quite different—as I learned subsequently, since his wife's principal charm in his eyes was her very passivity.

It is certain, considering things carefully, that such a woman, if not precisely agreeable, is at least very inoffensive. She did, said and thought almost exactly what her husband wanted, while others agitate thoughts of rebellion incessantly against theirs, quarrel with them and behave in such a fashion as to make them discontent.

In the entire course of our voyage in Spain, I never saw Mrs. Little emit a determination, or even a simple desire, but, on the other hand, I always saw her approve of her husband's

---

[20] This dialect term, with translates literally as "blood-dead," has no exact English translation, although the phrase "cold-blooded" is a near equivalent, when used to refers to a person unusually devoid of emotion.

resolutions—which, I ought to say, were perfectly in accord with mine.

San Sebastian is, as you know, one of the most picturesquely situated towns in all of Spain, on the slope of Mount Orgulio, the summit of which, crowned by the citadel, is no less than a hundred sixteen meters above sea level. The little port wedged between the mountain and the island of Santa Clara is a charming sight. Thus we could not help admiring it as we climbed up toward the town, although it had nearly been inhospitable to us.

When we were half way up Mount Orgulio, alongside steep rocks, Mrs. Little, to whom I had offered my arm in order to lend her a little support in her ascendant march, broke her habitual silence.

"It's very singular," she said, in English, "to represent the virgin with a mantilla on her head and a fan in her hand."

The wife of the Chester cheese-maker was thinking aloud in that fashion about a Madonna that we had just seen while passing the Church of Santa Clara, where she was in great honor.

"Do you think so, Madame?" I said. "It is, on the contrary, quite natural, and for myself, I'm only astonished that the Christ on the cross facing the pulpit isn't costumed as a torero."

Meanwhile, we arrived at the tombs of the English officers killed in 1836 during the defense of San Sebastian against Carlist troops.[21] Mr. Little took off his hat, and I did the same.

---

[21] A British volunteer force known as the Auxiliary Legion came to San Sebastian to support a contingent of the French Foreign Legion during the First Carlist War of 1833-37, in which France and England were both lending rather half-hearted support to Queen Isabella; about a quarter of their number were killed in the course of a long and bitter struggle to prevent the Carlists taking the city

"Thank you, my dear Monsieur Le Bref," he said, shaking my hand effusively, "for that mark of respect for the memory of my unfortunate compatriots."

"My dear Monsieur Little," I replied, emotionally, "any Frenchman, believe me, would have the same respect in this circumstance, and if, by chance, there are any who would not, I would hold it against them. I will add that, in saluting those heroes, I intend expressly to salute their fatherland and yours, Monsieur Little."

"Thank you, thank you, my dear sir," he said, wiping his cheeks, which were bathed in tears.

The patriotic commotion that he had just experienced, I experienced in my turn when we reached the citadel so heroically defended in 1813 by the French against the English and the Portuguese.

"Monsieur Little," I exclaimed, "about sixty years ago, a French general, General Rey, after having defended this citadel heroically against your compatriots, was obliged to capitulate, the city being destroyed, but he emerged from here with a carbine on his shoulder.[22] You will permit me, will you not, to evoke his noble memory?"

"And I join with you in honoring him," replied Mr. Little.

"Ho, yes," added Mrs. Little, addressing a small confirmatory nod of the head to me.

There is no doubt that the amity that was beginning to unite me with Mr. and Mrs. Little was strongly cemented by that double homage, rendered with the same sincere emotion, by me to England and him to France.

---

[22] Louis-Emmanuel Rey's defense of San Sebastian during the Napoleonic Wars was ultimately defeated, but became legendary for its tenacity and ingenuity.

IV

At Burgos, the city made up like a café-concert singer, I had a specimen of the truly touching tenderness that Mr. and Mrs. Little experienced for one another.

It was at the Municipal Palace, where we had gone to see the remains of El Cid and Chimène,[23] preciously conserved in a chest, and which consisted, as one might imagine, of wretched dusty bones.

A middle-aged woman, whom I assumed to be the door-keeper of the place, was charged with showing them to us. When she had opened the chest, divided into two compartments, she indicated that pitiful debris to us with a proud gesture.

Immediately, however, Mr. Little, carried away by I know not what interior demon, plunged a hand recklessly into the chest and brought out of one of the compartments a tibia belonging to the Cid, and from the other, a humerus belong to Chimène; then, having knocked them together before Mrs. Little's eyes, he aid to her in English, with a deep sigh:

"Alas, my dear Betty, behold what will one day remain of you and me. Far worse, no one will seek to see our remains, much less will a worthy Spaniard come to Chester to take them out of their box momentarily and permit them to give one another a posthumous kiss."

Like her husband, Mrs. Little uttered a deep sigh, and was content to reply, "Ho yes, Tom."

Mr. Little went on: "It's only as yet a demi-disaster when the bones of those who have loved one another are united, but

---

[23] The Spanish warrior called "El Cid" by the Moors (Rodrigo Diaz, 1040-1099) and his wife Jimena (Chimène in French) obtained a particular significance in France because to Pierre Corneille's play *Le Cid* (1636), which was advertized, accurately as a "tragicomedy," and thus started and argument about generic propriety that raged for decades.

when they're separated, even by the partition in a chest, it's very sad, Betty. We ought, if you want my opinion, to express in our respective testaments the desire that, once deprived of their flesh, ours should be mingled."

"Ho yes, Tom," replied Mrs. Little. "Ho yes."

"That," I said to Mr. Little, "is a rather lugubrious precaution."

"But as well to take, certainly, replacing the bones of the two legendary lovers in their box, "for it's necessary not to expect our heirs, especially when they are not our own children, to care about our bones. Will they even care about our memory?"

"A good precaution to take, you say but that depends on the manner of one's understanding," I objected. "If it is true that there is an immaterial principle within us, it is the souls of faithful spouses that have an interest in drawing together, and not their bones, and if that principle does not exist, what does it matter whether or not the bones are brought together by the hand of a heir?

"Do you believe, in good faith, that the remains of Rodrigo and Chimène feel a very vivid joy in being side by side? Their separation would not be cruel. What is cruel, and truly cruel, is for Rodrigo to survive or Chimène to survive Rodrigo."

"Very cruel, indeed, Monsieur Le Bref. Thus, my wife and I have tried for two or three years now to shield ourselves as much as humanly possible from that eventuality. Isn't that true Betty?"

"Ho yes, Tom."

"But how can you shield yourselves against that?" I exclaimed, astonished.

Our conversation in English was evidently not to the doorkeeper's liking, either because, not understanding it, she saw it as intolerable gibberish, or because she was in haste to get rid of us. Before Mr. Little had time to respond to my question, therefore, she intervened.

"Caballeros and Señora," she said, "here is now the stool on which the first judges of Castile sat, from whom the Cid was descended. For nine hundred years that stool has been here, in that very place."

"What is she saying?" Mr. Little asked me, who scarcely understood any more Spanish than he could speak

I repeated the doorkeeper's explanation in English.

"Nine hundred years!" exclaimed Mr. Little. "Do you hear, Betty? For nine hundred years that stool has been in the place that it occupies today. Isn't it worth the trouble of our sitting on it?"

"Ho yes," said Mrs. Little.

And she made a movement to sit down on it, but before she could put the said stool in contact with her majestic behind, the doorkeeper, who was alert, took her by the arm abruptly, in order to prevent her from doing so.

At the same time, the doorkeeper uttered a flood of words, the sense of which was that it was absolutely forbidden for visitors to pose their humble posterior on a stool that the judges of Castile had honored with their august derrière. And I translated the prohibition for Mr. Little—but instead of resigning himself placidly, as common sense appeared to command, he jibbed.

"It's impossible, Monsieur Le Bref," he said to me, "that we leave here without all three of us having sat in turn on that stool. Isn't it, Betty?"

"Ho yes, Tom."

"But what's the point, Monsieur Little?" I observed. "What can result from it for you? And besides, you've been told that it's not permitted."

Without making any reply, Mr. Little took a duro and two pesetas from his pocket and, holding the duro in one hand and the two pesetas n the other, he made the doorkeeper understand by means of an expressive mime accompanied by a few words in bad Spanish, that he would give her the duro if she would let us sit down, and only the two pesetas if she refused.

It goes without saying that that very British argument caused the doorkeeper to reflect. Her reflection was so prompt, in fact, that it did not last twenty seconds.

"Well, so be it," she said. "Sit down, but don't tell anyone, for you'd lose me my job, for sure."

Mrs. Little and her husband immediately satisfied their desire. As for me, mine was so feeble, that in sitting down, it was not so much the desire in question that I was satisfying as that of Mr. Little.

Afterwards, we went to the cathedral, which is one of the most grandiose and splendid monuments in the entire world. There is such a profusion of riches there that the eye is dazzled by them, and so many things to see that the eyes eventually weary of gazing.

Mrs. Little was particularly impressed by the famous crucified Christ who bleeds every Friday. It is, in fact, difficult to imagine anything more troubling, for that Christ, an admirable mannequin, has nothing of the statue but everything of the man in his gaze, his convulsed features, his lips, which seem to move, his hair, beard, eyebrows and eyelashes, and even his skin, which one could believe to be human, which is even said to be, and which appears to cover, instead of stuffing, true flesh, so much elasticity does it offer to the eye.

When, by the light of two candles, the sacristan suddenly lifted the curtain to show us that horrible spectacle, Mrs. Little let herself fall to her knees and almost lost consciousness.

Without sharing her religious ecstasy, Mr. Little and I were deeply moved.

On seeing her faint, like a true Magdalen at the foot of the cross, we hastened to support her.

"Betty, Betty," said Mr. Little, tenderly, "collect yourself, my dear Betty...it's only a simulation."

But even though he lavished concern and delicate tenderness on his wife, she still did not come round. In order to bring her to her senses the sacristan had to go in search of incense; he burned it under her nose, and she did not take long to speak.

"Alas, my dear Tom," she exclaimed, "I thought I was transported to Golgotha during Our Lord's passion!"

Meanwhile, we drew her out of the chapel.

The sacristan told us then that it was necessary to see Papa Moscas before leaving the cathedral.

What is Papa Moscas?

Quite simply an automaton lodged inside the case of the clock above the principal door, created by a Moorish artist, commissioned by Enrique III, King of Castile,[24] in memory of one of the most romantic episodes of his adventurous life.

Once, a long time ago, that automaton must have been very curious, for at the first stroke of the hour, it emerged from its hiding-place and, at every other stroke, it uttered a scream and made a bizarre gesture. That scream and gesture, provoking laughter from children, and even adults, caused a certain disturbance during religious ceremonies. One bishop, whose humor was austere rather than jovial, considered it as an occasion of scandal and ordered that the secret mechanism that enabled Papa Moscas to cry out and gesticulate should be broken. That is why, since then, Papa Moscas remains silent and motionless.

In response to Mr. Little's request, I asked the sacristan whether, to his knowledge, before having his springs broken, Papa Moscas had done anything else other than cry out, and if, for instance, he had spoken a few words.

"Don Enrique," the sacristan replied, "would certainly have liked Papa Moscas to have been able to repeat the tender words uttered to him by a young woman who loved him in secret, and who expired in confessing that chaste love to him, but the constructor of the automaton was not able to succeed, in spite of his efforts. As for the scream it reproduced, it was

---

[24] Enrique II reigned in Castile from 1390-1406. The famous automaton of Burgos cathedral known as Papamoscas is featured in numerous literary works, including one by Victor Hugo. It can easily be viewed nowadays on YouTube.

the one uttered by the young woman when she saw Don Enrique menaced by three wolves in the middle of a forest."

"In England," Mr. Little said to me, with a visible smile of satisfaction, "I know two automata much more curious than that one, for, in addition to the particularity they offer in appearing to be flesh and bone, like the Christ we saw just now, they resemble feature or feature persons presently alive, a few of whose familiar words they pronounce with the same intonation as their models, not to mention that once their mechanism is primed, they can walk almost as well as them. Isn't that so, Betty?"

"Ho yes, Tom," said Mrs. Little.

"In truth," I exclaimed, "I'd like to see such automata."

"If you come to our country, my dear Monsieur Le Bref," Mr. Little replied, "We'll show them to you. There's nothing more curious in the entire world."

"They're doubtless exhibited by some Barnum?"

"No."

"They're found in some museum?"

"No. They belong to an individual, and cost him very dearly, I can't deny. That's not astonishing, though; a master sculptor and a mechanician each worked on them for four years without respite. The individual had to shell out no less than twenty thousand pounds sterling—isn't that so, Betty?"

"Ho yes, Tom."

"But in sum, what does that individual do with his automata?"

"Nothing, for the moment, thank God, but a time will come, unfortunately, when one or other of them will have its utility."

"One of them?" I said, astonished

"Yes," said Mr. Little.

"But in the meantime he shows them to the curious?"

"No, no," Mrs. Little put in, with an animation that was not habitual to her. "On the contrary, he hides them, and they both repose in the coffins that he has had fabricated in their size."

"What a singular idea," I said.

There is a proverb which says that if one mentions the wolf one sees his tail. Scarcely had Mrs. Little mentioned coffins to me than we turned a street corner and were confronted by a shop devoted exclusively to the sale of coffins.

There were coffins of every size and genre—painted, gilded, sculpted, covered in lace, in two beautiful window displays to either side of the open door, where a young and pretty Castilian woman was framed, plying a needle and singing wholeheartedly.

Inside the shop there were more ordinary ones piled up on top of one another, all the way to the ceiling, as well as little ones designed for children.

We stopped, astonished by that exhibition of coffins, which is no more customary in England than in France.

Although there was nothing amusing about it, Mr. and Mrs. Little were very interested in it, and I even thought I observed them looking one another up and down from the corner of the eyes, as if each of them were measuring up the other for a coffin. But I dare not affirm that.

V

In almost all the hotels in the two Castiles, especially in the one in which we were staying in Burgos, the service is carried out by young women rather than men, and quite lovely young women, believe me. Sturdy, lively and cheerful, it gladdens the heart just to look at them.

If I mention that detail, it is because it was the pretext for a violent scene between Mrs. Little and her husband, which permitted me to appreciate in a new light the true character of the lady in question, which had previously appeared to me to be excessively meek.

The day after our arrival in Burgos, as Mr. Little, who had come to collect me from my room at eight o'clock in the morning, was going down the hotel staircase with me, one of the maidservants named Amparo—Protection—who was just in front of us, wanting to hasten her pace, made a false step and fell backwards, laden with sheets and napkins.

Mr. Little only just had time to catch her in his arms. She was a very cheerful young woman. Although she must have had a moment of fright on suddenly finding herself in the Englishman's arms, she uttered a burst of laughter that resounded all the way to the room where Mrs. Little was putting the last touches to her attire before joining us.

If it had only been Amparo's laughter that had reached Mrs. Little's ears, there would certainly not have been much harm done, and it would not have disturbed the taciturn Englishwoman unduly, but what completed the disaster, what troubled her beyond all expression, was that the loud voice of her husband mingled with that burst of feminine Spanish laughter.

Mrs. Little bounded out of her room, her hat in one hand and her cape in the other, just in time to see this stimulating spectacle: Amparo guffawing with laughter in the arms of Mr. Little, who, I admit, was not in any particular hurry to stand her up again, although I would swear that there was not the slightest frolicsome intention on his part.

As soon as he heard his wife coming, however, he hastened to return Amparo to her feet—too late, alas!"

Mrs. Little had seen everything, and misinterpreted it completely.

As I turned round I was amazed by her expression, which, ordinarily so placid, had become more trenchant than a sharp steel blade. Mr. Little could not see that guillotine gaze weighing upon the back of his neck, because he was turned around, but he must have sensed it, for he shuddered in every limb.

Divining the situation marvelously, I thought that it was up to me to save him.

"Madame," I said, affecting a detached tone, "but for your husband that poor girl might have broken her hip."

"Truly," said Mrs. Little, "the pretext is good."

At that point Mr. Little thought he ought to turn round and defend himself.

"I swear to you, my dear Betty, that it's not a pretext but the pure truth."

"Good, good, one knows your habits."

"My habits!" cried Mr. Little, clapping his hands together.

"Indeed," said Mrs. Little, whose gaze was animated by a singular fire. "You're the vilest of men and I don't know what's stopping me from throwing you down the stairs."

"Calm down, Betty, for God's sake, came down. Don't make a scandal here for no reason."

"For no reason?"

"Yes, yes, for no reason."

As he said that, Mr. Little darted a pleading glance at me, as if to appeal for my aid. I was fearful of his life, but I felt even more pity for him.

"It's certain Madame," I said, "that there is nothing in this to excite your anger in the slightest."

"I'm not angry, merely indignant."

"Yes, yes, I meant your indignation, since you prefer that. Note that what happened to your husband might equally well have happened to me."

"It would have been much better, Monsieur, if it had happened to you."

"I don't disagree, Madame."

"And why, in fact, was it not into your arms, but precisely into Mr. Little's, that this young lady allowed herself to fall, laughing?"

"For the very simple reason, Madame that Mr. Little was behind her, and not me."

"Mr. Little always arranges himself in such a manner as to find himself behind maids!" exclaimed Mrs. Little.

"Oh!" interjected Mr. Little.

Amparo, the maidservant who had caused all that emotion, quite innocently, had not failed to perceive that she was the object of it. She had turned back at the moment of Mrs.

Little's sharpest—or, at last, most ironic—remarks, and, without comprehending a word of the English exchanged between the husband, the wife and me, she had divined everything.

I judged that by a smile, which was immediately followed by a slight artificial coughing fit, but which Mrs. Little, unfortunately, mistook for a burst of laughter.

Thinking that she was being mocked, the latter lavished imprecations upon her husband almost as tragic as those of the famous Camille of the Horatii.[25]

"Man devoid of morality, devoid of decency, vulgar debauchee, knowing your depraved tastes as I do, I ought to have refused to undertake a voyage to the continent in your company. It's not enough to play the rake with my maidservants, now you have to address yourself to hotel maids! And in front of Monsieur Le Bref! Well, you ought to be dying of shame. As for me, I no longer want to look at you."

Mrs. Little had delivered that philippic in a strident voice, save for the final words—As for me, I no longer want to look at you"—which had dissolved in a flood of tears. As she pronounced them she ran to her room, and went into it precipitately, locking the door behind her, with a double click.

"It's a tantrum," said Mr. Little. "It will pass, like the others..."

Meanwhile, he went tranquilly downstairs.

I hesitated to follow him. He noticed that.

"Come on, then," he said. "You know very well that we still have to see the Cid's monument."

"But it's scarcely possible for us to go without Mrs. Little," I objected.

"Why not?"

"In order not to give her a further motive for irritation."

---

[25] Pierre Corneille also wrote *Horace* (1640), based on Livy's account of the conflict between the Horatii and the Curiati, in which Camille [Camilla], the sister of Horace [Horatius] and the fiancée of Curiace [Curiatus], gets caught in the middle

"Come on, then—at least she'll be irritated for something, whereas just now she was irritated for nothing. And then, I know her; after a few minutes, we'll see her fall back into her flat calm."

As we were leaving the hotel, me apparently more worried than him, for the unexpected domestic quarrel preoccupied me greatly, he added: "Poor Monsieur Le Bref, you look utterly upset. You would never have believed in her capable of such an outburst, would you?"

"No, I confess. In my presence at least, Mrs. Little has always been so tender in your regard, so passive, even, that I thought her incapable of being carried away like that."

"Well, yes, she deceives everyone. Oh, my dear friend"—it was the first time that Mr. Little had conferred the title of friend upon me—"you can't imagine how my poor wife's mania has made me suffer in the past."

"Is it habitual to her?" I asked.

"Alas," sighed Mr. Little.

"Perhaps," I observed, "you have given purchase to it in the beginning by exciting Mrs. Little's jealousy. I observed just now that your attitude with regard to Amparo was only incorrect in appearance, but I noticed that Mrs. Little also reproached you with the one you ordinarily have to your maidservants in Chester."

"That's exactly in what her folly consists, my de Monsieur Le Bref. She imagines that I'm amorous of all my maidservants, so she won't keep one of them."

"And you've done nothing to give her reason to believe it?"

"Absolutely nothing, I assure you."

"You haven't had any compromising familiarities with the young women in question?"

"Not at all! Except that being, by God's grace, a good man, I give them evidence of solicitude, as to all my entourage, and it's that solicitude, which is nothing but humanity, that Mrs. Little mistakes for flirtation."

"But she can't to fly off the handle frequently, as she's just done," I said, lightly, for, after all, I suppose she doesn't see you very day with a maidservant, especially a Spanish maidservant, in your arms!"

"She sees worse than that, not in reality but in imagination...so scarcely a day goes past in Chester when she doesn't make little scenes, if not big ones."

"That must make you very unhappy, Mr. Little."

"Very unhappy, as you say, Monsieur Le Bref, very unhappy, and it's in great part to change my wife's unhealthy condition, even more dolorous for me than for her, that I bought her to the continent. I thought I had succeeded, but now, today, her mania has got hold of her again."

"Damn! Today there was a mitigating circumstance...Amparo was in your arms...well and truly in your arms. And I understand why, at that sight, all Mrs. Little's supposed grievances against you were reawakened. Do you know what I'd do in your place? On returning to Chester I'd replace, once and for all, all my wife's young maids with old negroes, since, as well as your not obtaining the pleasure from those young women that Mrs. Little supposes, they are, on the contrary, the source all kinds of trouble for you."

"I've already thought of that," Mr. Little replied, phlegmatically, "and have even threatened my wife with it, but, apart from the fact that she doesn't much care to have a negro as a chambermaid, I confess that the constant sight of a face of that color would darken my ides, which are already too black."

While chatting in that manner, Mr. Little and I, in the company of one of those benevolent but not disinterested guides, who always put themselves at the disposal of strangers, had climbed a hill overlooking the town of Burgos, crowned by the ruins of a castle in which the ancient kings of Castile resided.

When we were in sight of those ruins, to which we were unable to get any closer, Mr. Little had a philosophico-lyrical—or lyrico-philosophical, if you prefer—effusion.

"How I would like my wife to be here with us!" he exclaimed. "I would say to hr: 'Betty, my dear Betty, you see what remains of that royal castle where powerful princes and beautiful princesses once lived, and of those princes and princesses even less remains, nothing any longer remains but a vague memory. Does that not give you pause for reflection? Does that not put a finger on the nullity of human things? And given that, do you not understand that you have been doubly mistaken to quarrel for no reason with a worthy husband like me, who ought to inspire every confidence in you?'"

Without perceiving very clearly the correlation there was between the ruins of the castle of the kings of Castile and the jealous scene that Mr. Little had made a short while before, I was almost moved to tears by the truly pathetic tone in which the worthy Mr. Little had pronounced his little speech. I understood once again that he was an excellent man and I thought that his wife was veritably very ill-advised to torment him.

VI

After having seen, successively, the triumphal arch in the Doric style erected by Felipe II to Ferdinand Gonzales and the stone column erected to Rodrigo Diaz de Vivar—which is to say the Cid Campeador—in 1784, I believe, neither of which are very curious, we returned to our hotel.

The first person who struck our eyes on arrival was Mrs. Little.

She was sitting in the shade outside the door in a veritably very placid attitude. On seeing her, even at a distance, it was obvious that her jealous irritation had completely disappeared.

I said to her, still in English, with a bright smile, which was reflected on her lips: "In truth, Madame, you were truly inspired not to go to see the monument to the Cid. It's not worth the trouble of being seen."

At the same moment Amparo emerged from the hotel in order to run few local errands and she had an absurd expression of slight embarrassment as she went past us, while Mr. Little, troubled by the fear that his wife's mania might take hold of her again, at the sight of the maidservant, affected to be looking in the other direction.

"Would you like us to depart for Valladolid this afternoon, my dear Betty?" asked Mr. Little. "I've mentioned it to Monsieur Le Bref, who is of that opinion."

"Indeed," I said. "I believe we have nothing further to do in Burgos."

"I think so to, Tom," said Mrs. Little, daring a glance at her husband that was, in truth, very mild.

After lunch we packed our trunks and left.

Why the devil did we go to Valladolid?

It is one of the Spanish towns that contains the fewest curiosities, but it is also one of the richest in historic memories.

I wanted to see in it the old city in which Felipe III held his court, where Gongora, Argensola and the great Cervantes lived, where Christopher Columbus died, and which gave birth one of the most brilliant Spanish poets of our era, Don José Zorrilla, the author of the *Cantos del Trovador* and the truly admirable *Don Juan Tenorio*.[26]

As for Mr. and Mrs. Little, one of their compatriots having praised certain colossal statues of painted wood representing the actors and the onlookers of the drama of the Passion, notably a kneeling virgin very lifelike in her dolor, thy had scarcely other objective in coming to Valladolid than seeing them.

---

[26] José Zorrilla (1817-1893) was a leading figure in the Spanish Romantic Movement. Cantos de Irovador was pushing in 1841 and the "religioso-fantastico drama" *Don Juan Tenorio* in 1844. The later became the longest-running drama in Spain, but he had sold the rights outright and he began published scathing criticisms of the play in the hope of killing it off so that he could write a new version, but in vain.

When we arrived there, as we were surrounded at the railway station by hoteliers who were trying to capture us, Mr. Little said to me: "Above all, let's not go to a hotel where the service is carried out by women, as in Burgos. You speak Spanish better than me; have the goodness to ask these fellows before anything else whether the service in their establishment is by men or women."

Several of those to whom I posed that question, in replying to me that their service was carried out by women, had a expression both mocking and engaging, which showed me the extent to which they misinterpreted my motive in asking, and which was succeeded by a keen disappointment when they saw me turn away.

One of them changed his mind then, and said: "Caballero, there are undoubtedly women who contribute to the service in my hotel, but it is primarily carried out by men, as in Paris."

That was the Hotel of the Redemption. We booked rooms there, and for the day and a half that we stayed there, there was, fortunately, not the slightest scene remotely similar to the one in Burgos.

On the other hand, in Madrid, to which we went thereafter, I saw Mrs. Little in a much graver state of effervescence. It is true that her Tom had nothing to do with it this time, and little maids even less, given that it was difficult to glimpse the skirt of one in the hotel where we were staying.

It was during a bullfight, the first and last that Mrs. Little witnessed.

Although I had warned her about the horror of the spectacle, with which I was already familiar, she had wanted to confront it, not supposing it to be as horrible as it really is. As for her husband, he was no more eager than I was to watch the contest, for he had taken me at my word, but he yielded in order to company his wife, and I went with them.

At first, Mrs. Little, without enthusiasm taking hold of her, seemed keenly interested. The sight of ten thousand spectators heaped on the steps of an immense circus, the rutilant costumes of the women, and even the men, the noise of joyful conversation and he arrival, to the sound of the music of cuadrilla, of the ceremoniously-clad toreros, the parade of the three espadas dressed in the splendid costume of Figaro in The Barber of Seville, the banderillos and capeadores covered in silver and gold, picadors in horseback proceeding in pairs holding long lances, with broad-brimmed gray hats and yellow buffalo-hide trousers, and, finally, the chulos, or servants, and even the entry of the bull, all appeared to strike her imagination vividly and capture it.

But as soon as she had seen a horse, its belly punctured by the bull's horn, buckle and collapse in the arena and then, lifted up by the picador's spur, try to walk, impeding its feet with its dangling entrails, she stood up, gripped by a nervous tremor and started abusing the alcalde who was guilty, in her eyes, of permitting such atrocities in the most virulent manner, in English.

It often happens in arenas that the Spaniards abuse the alcalde, and very violently, but it is to reproach him for tolerating the slightest remission in the massacre.

Have you ever heard of *banderillas de fuego*? They are arrows of a sort furnished with a rocket, which ignites just at the moment when the point penetrates the flesh of the bull, and burns the wound, causing the poor animal atrocious pain.

Now, when a bull, certainly having more courage and common sense than that inept and ferocious multitude of men and women, disdains to respond to the bloody provocations of the picadors and banderilleros, who initially sink their lances into it, and then shoot their arrows into is neck, when it only seems to be demanding one thing, which is for the door to be opened so that it can return to the pen, cries ring out from all directions: "Banderillas de fuego!"

And if the alcalde, who is the only one who can authorize the employment of those banderillas, is still reluctant to do it because of a residuum of humanity, and if, in spite of the furious cries of "Fuego! Fuego!" the alcalde is obstinate in his refusal, popular rage turns against him and one can then hear cries of *"Las banderillas al alcalde! Fuego al alcalde!"*

Let us return to Mrs. Little. At first her indignant voice did not penetrate, so loud was the hubbub, any further than the nearest steps, but as it was still increasing in volume, in spite of the efforts that Mr. Little and I were making to stifle it, general attention did not take long to awaken, and all gazes quit the bull momentarily in order to fix upon the foreigner from whom an avalanche of words and gestures was flowing.

What the devil was wrong with her? It was even possible to believe, at first, that she was exhaling her wrath at the picadors, who might have seemed to the public a little slack and maladroit when they struck the bull with their lances. But her neighbors, particular fanatics of tauromachy, eventually understood by the virulent manner in which she was shouting at them that she was condemning tauromachy itself.

From then on, Mr. Little and I, like Mrs. Little, were the object of a disorderly protestation on their part. I wondered whether those fanatics were not about to throw all three of us into the arena, and all was all the more authorized in the suspicion because a few cries could be heard threatening us with exactly that, when an incident came to our aid.

Fortunately, Mrs. Little, vanquished by emotion, lost consciousness.

Her faint was very opportune, since it extracted Mr. Little and me from a great embarrassment

But what we needed most of all was to be able to get her out of that furious crowd, and us with her. Alas, we absolutely could not do that, so compact was it, even flooding the corridors.

For want of anything better, the prolongation of her unconsciousness, if it would not have disturbed Mr. Little, would have appeared to me to be entirely desirable. Yes, I would have been delighted if the worthy woman had not come round before the end of the contest.

However, she came round after a few minutes and manifested the unrealizable desire to get out.

We made her understand the impossibility of succeeding in that. Then she started to weep.

"Nothing forces you to watch," I told her. "Put your fan in front of your eyes."

Vain advice...she could not help looking, from time to time, as if fascinated by some invincible charm; she looked, and she glimpsed all the horrors.

As for Mr. Little and myself, possessed of greater will-power than her, we had imposed on ourselves spontaneously, without the slightest preliminary agreement, the obligation to watch the spectators rather than the actors of the scene of carnage.

Although the general attention was entirely devoted to the scene, our excessively unenthusiastic attitude provided our nearest neighbors, of both sexes, with a distraction that they held against us. I heard some suggesting worse things than hanging us. In order not to find the slightest attraction in those bloody games, to dare to allow the repulsion they inspired in us to show, we were wretches, we were going so far as to insult the proud Spanish nation.

Finally, our torture ended, along with that of twenty horses and five bulls, victims of inept and disgusting human ferocity, and we were able to quit the circus, not without being jeered somewhat.

Fortunately, there are other things to see in Madrid than the Corrida. One is far from having said everything when one has cited the admirable Plaza de la Puerta del Sol, where the movement of the capital is concentrated, where the noisy genius of the Madrilene people is summarized, the Prado and the Buen Retiro, which are magnificent promenades, the museum of painting and the naval museum, each the most beautiful of its genre in Europe, the convent of the Escurial, a unique ensemble emerged from the grandiose and funereal petrifaction of the reign of Felipe II.

The idea of their death, which had already haunted Mr. and Mrs. Little several times before my eyes since their arrival in Spain, took hold of them again in the crypt of the church of the Escurial, where Charles V and his successors, from Felipe

II to Ferdinand VII, are buried, as well as the Empresses and Queens of the houses of Austria and Bourbon.

After the warden had shown us by the light of his torch the name of Luisa, written on the tomb of Doña Maria Luisa of Savoy by that princess herself, with the point of her scissors, Mrs. Little said to her husband: "Tom, when we get back to Chester, I shall also write my name on my tomb with my scissors, so that one day, it can be shown to travelers, while saying to them: 'That's what Mrs. Little did.'"

Although Mrs. Little generally approved of what her husband said, except when he showed some benevolence for your maidservants, it was not the same for Mr. Little in her regard. He maintained a much greater independence with regard to his wife. So he had no hesitation in showing her what was strange in her project, and even slightly ridiculous.

"In truth, Betty," he said to her, "are you're losing your head, my dear love, in wanting to copy a Queen of Spain, being a simple cheese-maker's wife? Even if you did write your name on our tomb with your own scissors, Betty, no one among the tourists who come to Chester—and there are very few of them—would take any notice of it."

"But you, Tom, if you survive me, as I wish, would you not be touched, in coming to make your devotions at my tomb, to find the letters of my name traced in my own hand?"

"With the point of your scissors?"

"With the point of my scissors."

"Indeed, that would touch me," replied Mr. Little, after a few seconds of reflection. "You'd do it, then, with my intention?"

"Of course, Tom!" cried Mrs. Little. And she added: "For myself, I declare to you, nothing would soften my heart as much as to see on yours the name Tom, written by you with a pen-knife."

"Then I'll give my tomb a thrust with my pen-knife in order to be agreeable to you," replied Mr. Little, "since you'd experience as much pleasure in that as you would have had irritation I've delivered one in our contract."

It was scarcely habitual for Mr. Little, an earnest man, to joke in that fashion, so his unexpected pleasantry made me laugh heartily.

VII

On quitting Madrid we went to Aranjuez in order to visit the splendid palace constructed for Felipe II by the celebrated architect Herrera and where the abdication of Charles IV in favor of his son Ferdinand took place in 1808, following the so-called Aranjuez insurrection against Manuel Godoy, the Prince of the Peace.

As we were in the other little marble palace that stands in the depths of the gardens traversed by the Tage, the most grandiose and most marvelous gardens I had ever seen, and especially in Charles IV's billiard room, I noticed that an extreme disturbance had taken possession of Mr. Little. He had gone very pale, with a vague gaze and a sort of nervous tremor in his hands.

"What's the matter with you, Tom," Mrs. Little asked him. "You seem to be suffering."

"Suffering! Oh, yes!" replied Mr. Little, who could not suppress a sort of trepidation in his left leg. But he immediately pulled himself together. "That is to say...no...I'm not suffering at all. Pay no attention to me, I beg you, Betty, pay no attention to it."

However, Mrs. Little, who rendered to her husband all the affection that she received from him, took a small bottle of smelling salts out of her pocket and offered it to him to sniff.

"Here," she said, "breathe in, Tom, breathe in."

He pushed his wife's hand away gently. "It's useless; it doesn't do anything at all."

We had had lunch not long before. I approached Mr. Little and said: "Is your lunch giving you indigestion?"

"On the contrary," he replied. "But I beg you, occupy yourself with my wife rather than me; explain the curiosities to her, which I don't have the strength to explain to her at the moment."

In truth, it was the warden of the small palace who was furnishing us with all the desirable explanations, but, as Mrs. Little did not understand Spanish, I translated them for her.

After having traversed a series of little boudoirs, where I invited Mrs. Little to admire cushions embroidered by queens and musical clocks that had amused Infantas, we arrived in a certain cabinet of extraordinary magnificence, which Charles IV had had equipped for his personal use. The guardian described all the ornaments and did not fail to show us the essential piece, pronouncing with a smile what were perhaps the only two English words he knew: "Water closet."

I noticed, but without drawing the slightest conclusion from it, than on hearing those two words ringing in his ears and seeing the pierced throne on which Charles IV had sat at the commencement of the century, Mr. Little's face was suddenly illuminated, as if by a flash.

As we left that cabinet, the guardian was telling me some story about Charles IV and Godoy, a story that I was translating as he went along for Mrs. Little. Neither she nor I noticed, any more than he did, the sudden absence of Mr. Little. It was not until we were at the foot of a little staircase leading down to the gardens that we observed it.

"Tom, Tom, Tom!" cried Mrs. Little, in all the tones.

But Tom did not reply.

Knowing that he was indisposed, she was seized by a veritable anguish, which infected the warden and myself to some degree.

"The poor man," she said, "has perhaps fainted on the queens' cushions. Let's go back up, let's go back up."

Scarcely were we on the stairway again than we heard a noise of doors.

"That can't be anyone but him," I said to Mrs. Little. "You can see that no mishap has overtaken him."

It was, indeed him, his face as expansive now as it had been contracted a moment before.

"Oh, Tom!" cried Mrs. Little. "What a fright you gave me!"

"How the devil were you able to lose us, my dear Mr. Little?" I said in my turn.

"The essential thing is that I've found you again," he said, cheerfully.

"You look much better," said Mrs. Little.

"Ho yes, my dear Betty, much better. I no longer feel anything." And he added, addressing himself to me: "Ask the warden if we still have anything else to see."

Once again, in that regard, I served as the worthy Mr. Little's interpreter, and I learned that we had seen everything in Aranjuez except the vineyards, the plantations of fruit trees, and the meadows.

As we returned from the small palace toward the large one, along magnificent pathways bordered by trees several centuries old, I could not help looking at Mr. Little surreptitiously two or three times.

He eventually perceived that and ended up whispering mysteriously in my ear: "You've guessed, haven't you, what I've just done?"

"I suspect so. You've just sat down on Charles IV's favorite throne."

"Exactly—but not a word about it to my wife; she's capable of envying me."

"And you sat down there, like that for the pleasure of sitting down there?"

"Oh, no."

"I would have sworn it," I said, laughing. "There was a necessity..."

"Imperious." He added: "Never have I blessed a man as much as I blessed Charles IV for having that whim of a peerless water closet worthy of exhibition."

"Oh, if the warden knew what you had permitted yourself," I said, laughing harder. "It's much more serious, you know, than sitting down on the almost-millenarian stool of the judges of Castile, as Mrs. Little was tempted to do in Burgos."

Just as we had emerged from the small palace with our warden, two German men and three women had arrived, conducted by another warden. Suddenly remembering that circumstance, I said to Mr. Little: "You noticed those Germans; in a little while they'll be shows the mechanism in Charles IV's cabinet that you've profaned, and your profanation might not escape their sight and sense of smell."

"Don't say that," said Mr. Little. "You're giving me a cold sweat."

Buried as she was in her meditations, Mrs. Little was finally astonished by our prolonged conversation, and doubtless finding that her husband looked poorly for a second time, she said to him: "Is it getting worse again, my love?"

"Oh no, no, thank God," said Mr. Little.

In the meantime, and as we were walking slowly in the direction of the grand palace, we saw some kind of employee running toward us. He called to our warden: "Pedro! Pedro!"

As soon as he had reached him he spoke to him in a low voice.

Naturally, we had stopped to wait for our warden. Suddenly, the latter came back to us, without his comrade going away, and, addressing Mr. Little in a manner that seemed to me to be severe, he said to him in Spanish, with great volubility: "It appears that you dropped something in Charles IVs cabinet."

Without understanding what the warden had said, Mr. Little had no doubt that the relief that he had given himself was being reproached as illicit, so he protested in English that he had only yielded to an absolutely pressing, utterly irresistible need, and that he had certainly not intended to offend the memory of Charles IV.

As the warden, naturally, did not understand Mr. Little's excuses, I translated them into Spanish.

The warden then spread his arms wide and, bringing his hands together as if someone had given him frightful news, he cried: "Oh, that's too much! What! You have taken the liberty..."

"Say," I protested, "that he yielded to necessity, and you know very well that the *necesidad carece de ley*."[27]

"There must be a law, Monsieur, when one is in the palace of a king," replied the guardian Pedro with an entirely Castilian arrogance. Your friend had rendered himself guilty of a crime of *lèse-majesté* and it is incumbent on me to arrest him."

"Oh!" I cried. "You're going too far."

Meanwhile, Mrs. Little never ceased demanding of Mr. Little, who appeared utterly downcast, without obtaining a response: "What's going on, Tom? What's going on?"

"In the twenty years that I've been a warden at the palace of Aranjuez," Pedro went on, "I have never seen such a crime committed, never, never!"

"Perhaps you're exaggerating," I objected, "in calling it a crime..."

"No, Monsieur, and know that I'm risking, by not arresting your friend, losing my job."

"Just now, however," I said, "when you're colleague came to tell you about the little misfortune, you did not seem so affected."

"My colleague came to tell me that a wallet had been found in Charles IV's cabinet and he asked me whether it was anyone in the group I was leading who had lost it. He told me nothing about the other matter; it was your friend who revealed everything himself, through your intermediation"

Once more the spur of his conscience had driven a man to confess his guilt, and I had stupidly interpreted that inopportune admission.

No doubt Mr. Little had lost his wallet while lowering or pulling up what the English call their unmentionables, and which we in France designate in a less veiled fashion.

Having checked that I still had my wallet, I asked Mr. Little to see whether he still had his.

He no longer had it.

---

[27] "Necessity knows no law"—a Spanish proverb.

I informed the two wardens of that, who returned it to him, not without having made me understand that they expected from the owner a recompense all the more honest because the wallet had been lost in less admissible circumstances.

Mr. Little, whose wallet contained nearly five hundred francs, gave each of the two men a French louis, and the incident was closed, temporarily at least, for, when Pedro had brought us back to the outer gate of the grand palace, and I gave him three pesetas for the trouble he had taken in showing us the curiosities, he had the impudence to raise the question of Charles IV's cabinet again, which obliged the worthy Mr. Little to give him a duro as well.

And we left for Toledo.

VIII

Very bad news awaited Mr. Little there, in duplicate: at the telegraph office in the form of a dispatch, and at the post office in the form of a letter.

The foreman of his cheese-factory informed him that a fire had just broken out and destroyed it almost entirely.

Needless to say, Mr. Little's establishment was insured with one of the best companies in London. Mr. Little thus did not have to fear ruination, but it was a matter of determining the amount of the disaster with the company, of having the factory rebuilt, and coming to the aid of the workers who had no work to do. Thus, Mr. Little thought that he could not continue his voyage in Spain, but ought to return immediately to Chester. He discussed it in my presence to Mrs. Little, who responded in her plaintive tone, without emotion: "Ho yes, Tom."

It was truly cruel for them to leave Spain at the very moment of visiting Andalusia and its brilliant cities: Cordova, Seville, Cadiz, Granada and Valencia—which is to say, everything there is of the most curious in the Peninsula, to which they would never return.

At least they wanted to see a little of Toledo, since they were obliged to be there for a few hours, the train for Madrid not departing until the evening.

I accompanied them to the cathedral, the church of San Juan de los Rayos and the Alcazar, and after dinner I escorted them to the railway station.

It was not without a real sentiment of sadness that I separated from them. And when, by the gaslight in the waiting room of Toledo station, Mr. Little shook my right hand and said, emotionally: "*Au revoir*, Monsieur Le Bref," and Mrs. Little squeezed my left, saying: "Ho yes, Monsieur Le Bref," I felt my eyes mist over with tears.

There was not between me and the spouses Little one of those very rare sympathies that take possession of the entire being, but we already had the habit of living together, and, in the something like a month that we had been doing that, no coldness had come between us.

Mr. Little had promised to write to me when he returned to England. He kept his word. A week later I had a letter from him in Seville, and a very affectionate letter. He told me how much he and his wife regretted not having been able to go to Andalusia with me and he invited me in the most pressing manner to come and spend a month in his cottage the following spring, when the damage to the cheese-factory had been repaired.

With regard to that cheese-factory he lamented a great deal on the painful impression he had experienced on seeing it entirely in ruins, but he added that, after all, such a misfortune, reparable by insurance, was nothing compared to that other, ever-imminent misfortune, the death of his wife or his own: a misfortune against which, to tell the truth, he had tempted a kind of insurance, perishable itself, and which could easily have been the prey of flames.

In returning thus to an idea that he had already touched upon in conversation with me, he did not render it any clearer. I wondered what the devil he meant by the insurance of sorts that he had tempted against the misfortune of his death or that of his wife, and how that fantastic insurance was perishable, how it might have become the prey of flames.

I asked myself that in vain, and then the attraction of the voyage deflected me away from thinking about it, to such an extent that I said nothing about it in my reply to Mr. Little from Valencia, on the eve of the day when I was due to return to Paris.

After that we wrote to one another two or three times, at fairly long intervals, and then our friendship, like so many others, fell into desuetude.

PART TWO: IN ITALY

I

It had been four or five years since I had heard any mention of Mr. and Mrs. Little when I undertook my third voyage to Italy, from which I have just come back.

I have not been there once, and have never returned, without revisiting Pisa, the melancholy charm of which attracts me invincibly.

One day, I was in the dome of Pisa, and after having admired once again Il Sodoma's very curious *Sacrifice of Isaac*, I was watching the gentle sway of the monumental lamp—an oscillation that, three centuries earlier, had put Galileo on the path to the discovery of the pendulum, and by the force of my admiration I was, so to speak, communing with that sublime mind.

I had vaguely heard other visitors approaching behind me without having had any thought of turning round to cast a glance at them.

Three words, however, pronounced in a low voice: "Ho yes, Tom!" struck me singular, like a remembrance, at first ill-defined, but which I did not take long to specify.

I turned my head and was suddenly greeted by an exclamation pronounced in English: "Ah, Monsieur Le Bref, how nice it is to see you again!"

It was the good Mr. Little who spoke to me in that fashion, who had Mrs. Little on his arm, as before during our voyage in Spain. So far as I could judge through the thick veil that she was wearing over her face, the utility of which I could not explain then, she had not aged since I had last seen her. As for Mr. Little, on the contrary, I found him much changed, almost unrecognizable.

He had extended his hand to me; I shook it very affectionately.

"Be very sure," I said, "that I am equally glad to find myself with Mrs. Little and you."

So saying, I bowed to Mrs. Little and extended my hand toward her.

Mrs. Little, who seemed to me more fixed and stiffer than ever, responded to my inclination of the head, after a certain hesitation, it seemed to me, and only when her husband had touched her shoulder, but neither of her hands moved toward mine.

Mr. Little, thinking, rightly, that I was surprised by that said: "Don't be offended, my dear Monsieur Le Bref, if my wife doesn't give you her hand. She has something out of order in her arms."

"Oh, not at all, not at all!" I said.

And, bowing a second time to Mrs. Little, in order to show her that I did not hold it against her that she had only responded in part to my politeness, I said to her: "Fortunately, Madame, apart from your discomfort in the arms, you seem to be in good health."

"Very well," she replied, but only after Mr. Little had nudged her with his elbow.

That "very well" appeared to me to be a trifle cold and a trifle hard for the first words that she had addressed to me in so many years.

I knew full well that she was not loquacious, but after all, in our days in Spain, she would have added something to her "very well"—my name, for example, perhaps even modified by the epithet "dear": "My dear Monsieur Le Bref."

Nevertheless, I pretended to pay no attention to it. With my most smiling expression I said: "And how do you like Italy, Madame?"

"Very well."

Again!

"Have you seen Florence?" I added.

"Ho yes, Tom," she replied, not without hesitation and after her husband had squeezed her hand.

Why the devil was she replying to her husband when it was me who had spoken to her?

I could not help smiling at that. Mr. Little perceived it.

"Pay no attention," he whispered to me, mysteriously, "if my wife calls you Tom. She's unfortunately not equipped to pronounce any other name."

The expression "equipped" astonished me.

"Pardon?"

"I said," Mr. Little added, "that my forename, Tom, is absolutely linked to 'Ho yes,' in her organism, in such a way that she cannot say one without the other..."

"Oh!" I said, opening my eyes wide, for I understood less and less.

I repeated with Mr. and Mrs. Little the tour of the cathedral that I had already made. As I watched the woman walking on her husband's arm, I was astonished that her gait, which had already seemed a little stiff in the past, had become jerky. Her footfalls produced a very strange rhythmic click.

That poor woman, I said to myself, *definitely has something out of order, not only in her arms but also in her legs*— and I wondered whether she might have suffered an apoplexy or might be afflicted by a softening of the spinal marrow.

She walked, however, at a fairly brisk pace, and I heard her reply to her husband several times when he pointed out a silver altar, the mosaics in the choir and the marquetry stalls: "Ho yes, Tom."

When we emerged from the cathedral Mr. Little said to me: "Tell me, my dear Monsieur Le Bref, have you seen the baptistery and have you gone up the Leaning Tower?"

"Yes, this morning, again—for I've known them for a long time, having been to Pisa twice before. And you?"

"Not yet. It's worth the trouble, isn't it?"

"Yes, of course; it's necessary to see the pulpit sculpted by Nicola Pisano at the baptistery and go up the tower, from which the view extends over a part of Tuscany. In addition, you know, it's from the top of that tower that Galileo made his experiments with weight."

"I'd very much like to go up there," said Mr. Little.

"You'd do well...there's only one thing to fear, which is that it might be a little to tiring for Mrs. Little, who seems to me to be quite weary already, for the tower is fifty-nine meters high."

Mr. Little appeared to reflect momentarily, and then said: "Wait, I'll ask my wife what she wants to do."

On observing that Mrs. Little, who clearly must have heard her husband and me talking, had not yet emitted and personal thought and that Mr. Little had to ask her expressly what she wanted to do, I said to myself internally: *What a* sang-mort *that woman is!*

Meanwhile, the following little dialogue had taken place between her and her husband:

"Do you feel fatigued, my dear Betty?"

"Ho yes, Tom."

"You don't care about going up the Leaning Tower?"

"No."

"In that case, would you care to wait for me here momentarily with Monsieur Le Bref, who will be kind enough to offer you his arm?"

"Ho yes, Tom."

"As Mr. Little took his wife's arm from beneath his own, I extended mine to Mrs. Little as graciously as I could, but she did not take it, so Mr. Little was obliged to pass his wife's arm under mine himself. I was not overly astonished by that, however, already knowing that there was something hindering the movements of her arms.

Meanwhile, Mr. Little said to her: "In fact, my dear Betty, perhaps you'd be better in the carriage. What do you think?"

When he had touched her hand she replied: "Ho yes, Tom."

"In that case, Monsieur Le Bref will be kind enough to excuse you."

"Certainly," I said. "You have a carriage, then?"

"Always. I'm obliged to do that now. My wife can no longer make long journeys on foot."

"Really? She was such a good walker in Spain!"

"Oh, yes, yes," he said, with a sigh. "Unfortunately, it wasn't possible to restore all the qualities she had, and it's already a great deal for her to have conserved some of them."

What is he telling me? I thought, as I accompanied Mr. and Mrs. Little to their carriage, which was waiting for them on the piazza a short distance from the dome. There was such a great eccentricity in certain terms he used in speaking about his wife that I wondered whether I had unlearned the English language, or whether, he had always had that slightly over-imaginative fashion of talking.

When we were in the carriage I opened the door and attempted to assist Mrs. Little to climb the footstep.

"No, no!" exclaimed Mr. Little, abruptly. "Let me do it…you don't know how that's done."

At the same time, he took his wife by the waist from behind with both hands and pressed her until she flexed under his grip. Then he introduced Mrs. Little backwards into the vehicle where he sat her down comfortably on the cushions.

"Go and see the Leaning Tower now, then," I said to him. "I'll keep Mrs. Little company."

"Oh, you can leave her alone…that's unimportant. But I beg you not to lose sight of the coachman."

"Why is that?"

"I mean that, in the unlikely event that the coachman wants to make off, it will be necessary to prevent him doing so."

While Mr. Little drew away in the direction of the Leaning Tower, I approached the carriage door and leaned against it lightly in order to try to enter into conversation with Mrs. Little.

I asked her, in succession, several questions, of a perfect banality, undoubtedly, but nevertheless very gracious, and precisely those that good manners not only authorize but command. I asked her how long it was since she had left England, by what route she had traveled to Italy, what she thought of Pisa, etc., etc.

To my great surprise, she did not reply to any of my questions.

I concluded that her faculties were extraordinarily enfeebled.

Knowing that she was at least capable of answering yes or no, I asked her if she was suffering any pain, but she left that question unanswered like the preceding ones: not even a nod of the head, not the slightest movement of the hand; the coldest and bleakest immobility. I cursed the veil, which, by virtue of its unusual thickness, rendered impenetrable a physiognomy that might perhaps have spoken for Mrs. Little herself.

I could not, however, decently seek to lift that veil.

Having recalled the Mr. Little had only obtained reposes from his wife in my presence by touching her right hand, I tried to do likewise, with as much discretion as possible. Little by little, I had already kneaded almost all of the gloved hand with my fingertips without her appearing to feel it—at least, she had not made any movement. Finally, however, under a last pressure of my fingers, she said: "Ho yes, Tom."

I hoped that, in default of the clear sight of me that she appeared to lack, since she gave the impression of mistaking me for her husband, the faculty of speech had finally returned to her. Thus, I said to her, very gently: "It's me, Madame—you know, me, Monsieur Le Bref, who once traveled with you in Spain. As for your husband, look, here he is coming back from the Leaning Tower, and by putting your head through the carriage window you'll be able to see him…if you'd like to?"

But she did not say a word in reply, or budge in the slightest.

Utterly devastated to find the poor woman—who had always been somewhat taciturn, but whom it had once been possible to converse—in a state bordering on infancy, I judged it futile to persist further, and I turned toward the coachman, whose broad face was very open and sympathetic.

Like any good Italian, he liked nothing better than chatting, and we therefore conversed in his native tongue. In a quarter of an hour, in fact, he told me the things regarding the locale that one does not find in the Joanne guide or in Baedeker.

II

When he came back, Mr. Little said: "Have you visited the Campo Santo?"

"Of course; I've know it for a long time, and I saw it again yesterday, but I'd gladly return there with you if you haven't visited it, for I never weary of looking at *The Triumph of Death.*

"Let's go, then." Addressing the coachman, he said: "Driver, to the Campo Santo."

The coachman did not have far to go to ferry Mrs. Little, the three or four monuments that one has to see in Pisa all being close together.

On the way, Mr. Little said to me: "If I thought that one could have confidence in this coachman, we could leave Mrs. Little in the carriage and visit the Campo Santo without her…there would be much less inconvenience for us."

"Do you think," I objected, "that Mrs. Little that won't want to visit the Campo Santo, which is the greatest curiosity in Pisa?"

"What do you expect her to make of it? When I take her to visit something with me, it's in order not to be alone, to have someone to talk to who will reply to me. From the moment that you're with me, my dear Monsieur Le Bref, I no longer have the same reasons for having my wife on my arm."

"If that's the way it is, my dear Mr. Little, you can trust your coachman. No mishap will overtake Mrs. Little in his hands."

"You think he's honest?"

"As his horse, who, like him, gives the impression of being a very worthy animal, Mr. Little."

"In that case, I'll give him a good tip."

Then, passing his head through the window, he said to him wife, while taking her hand: "Until later, Betty."

And as he clasped her, she replied: "Ho yes, Tom."

Then we walked silently as far as the Campo Santo.

As we went in, Mr. Little said to me: "Isn't it horrible, my dear Monsieur Le Bref, to see my wife changed into that almost inert mass?"

"It's undoubtedly very sad," I remarked. And, without thinking in depth about the opinion I was uttering, I added, in order to console the worthy Mr. Little slightly: "But it's still better than having nothing of her at all."

"Oh, I'm very glad to hear you say that…it's so much better, my dear Monsieur Le Bref, that it was indispensable to my life. If my wife were entirely lacking to me, I wouldn't have survived for a month, not one month."

The custodian was waiting for us at the door, to which he had just brought four or five visitors back. A little chagrined, it seemed to me, that there were only two of us, he deigned nevertheless to propose to show us around the Campo Santo and give us the appropriate explanations.

The first thought that struck me at the door of the renowned cemetery was that Mrs. Little could not be long delayed in dying, given the deplorable state in which she found herself, and I wondered fearfully what would become of her unfortunate husband then—but it goes without saying that I made no mention of that painful reflection. Furthermore, my mind did not take long, like his, to be entirely captivated by *The Triumph of Death*, Orcagna's admirable fresco,[28] simultaneously so naïve and so profound.

To the right of the spectator, the group of lords and ladies sitting and chatting gallantly under the trees to the sound

---

[28] The fresco in question is now generally assumed to be the work of Buonamico Buffalmacco rather than Orcagna.

of sweet music; nearby, the angels and demons drawing the corporeal souls from the mouths of moribund men and women, or seeking to snatch them in mid-air; further away, the unfortunates vainly imploring Death; to the far left, other powerful lords and ladies on horseback are following a hunt, and suddenly, in the guise of game, finding at a bend in the path three open coffins, the first containing a fresh cadaver, the send a putrefied cadaver and the third a mere skeleton; on the nearby mountain, monks at the door of their chapel, one of whom is leading a hind while another accompanied by a hind and a rabbit are wandering together on a volcanic hillock into which culpable souls are being plunged by demons; the entire curious ensemble, strewn with steamers with inscriptions that, unfortunately, are scarcely distinguishable any longer, retained Mr. Little and myself for a long time.

Like any good Englishman worthy of the name, Mr. Little was equipped with marine binoculars, through which he looked at the various parts of the fresco successively.

"Do you see, my dear Monsieur Le Bref," he said to me suddenly, "that fat naked monk over whom an angel and a demon are fighting, the angel pulling him by the arms and the demon by the legs?"

"Yes, perfectly, and I even find the idea that Orcagna had there rather amusing."

"Well, now look slightly above and to your right, at that female angel clad in a robe with long creases, who is rising toward the sky with a man in her arms. Don't you think that the angel resembles Mrs. Little, and that the man in her arms is also a little like me?"

"Except for the costume," I said, smiling, the man in the fresco being as naked as a worm.

"The face...," said Mr. Little, very seriously. And he added: "May my dear Betty carry me thus in her arms, all the way to the throne of God!"

"As she certainly will, my dear Mr. Little," I replied, "when the moment comes...but it's premature, thank God, to think of your assumption."

Save for the magisterial sign of *The Triumph of Death*, which is developed on one of its interior walls and suits such a place so well, the Campo Santo is not at all lugubrious in itself. It is a pretty rectangular meadow surrounded by galleries. And yet, when the custodian explained the symbolism of the three coffins in the fresco to us, it seemed to us that we actually scented a cadaverous odor distributed around us. In order to escape it, I caught myself pinching my nose, as one of the riders on Orcagna's fresco is doing.

After checking, I realized that the odor in question was emanating from the custodian, as if his body were impregnated with the juice of a human putrescence several centuries old.

Fortunately, a clump of geraniums was emerging from the excavation of a ancient tomb. I detached two or three leaves, which Mr. Little and I crushed between our fingers in order to respire the perfume.

"At which hotel are you staying?" Mr. Little asked me, as we went back to the carriage where Mrs. Little was waiting for us.

"The Albergo Europa, on the Lugarno."

"We're neighbors," he said. "I'm at the Albergo Roma. When do you intend to leave Pisa?"

"Tomorrow morning."

"To go where?"

"To Siena."

"We'll leave with you. At what time?"

"Quarter past nine."

"That's agreed—but where shall we go now?"

"If you wish, we can go to see the fountain in the Piazza dei Cavalieri and the monument to the grand duke Leopold I on the Piazza Santa Catarina, after which you'll have seen everything that Pisa has of the most curious."

Mr. Little made me climb into the carriage, which had four seats, and I sat down opposite Mr. Little, still veiled, still motionless and still silent.

She seemed as indifferent to our return as she had been to our departure. Her attitude, more than starchy, chilled me. I wanted to say something gracious to her, but the words would not come to my lips. I contented myself with smiling at her and a slight inclination of the head.

The worthy Mr. Little took her hand and said: "You're very glad to find yourself with dear Monsieur Le Bref again, who has been such a good friend to us, aren't you, Betty?"

"Ho yes, Tom."

"How many times have you said to me: 'I'll never forget, Tom, that you owe your life to Monsieur Le Bref'?"

"Ho yes, Tom."

"Alas, I'll never forget either, that you owe your death to me, my dear Betty."

And as he said that, Mr. Little uttered a little sob, which he tried in vain to stifle, and which dissolved in a flood of tears.

I did not seek at first to explain the enigma contained in the words "you owe your death to me," spoken by a husband to a wife who, although enfeebled, especially intellectually, it seemed to me, was no less alive, it also seemed to me.

The fit of sincere dolor that had overtaken Mr. Little impressed me far more vividly than his wife, for the latter remained quite inert while I, by contrast, held out my hands to him—which he did not see, however, his face being plunged into his own.

Meanwhile, we had arrived at the Piazza dei Cavalieri, and the coachman, following the order he had received from me, had just stopped our vehicle near the fountain.

As the carriage stopped, Mr. Little hastily removed his hands from his face, held them out to me in his turn, damp with tears, and said: "Forgive me, Monsieur Le Bref, forgive my moment of weakness." Then he added, while wiping his hands and face with the aid of his handkerchief: "Where are we, if you please, Monsieur Le Bref?"

"We're at the fountain in the Piazza dei Cavalieri.

"Ah!"

"Do you see those women with their shawls knotted over their heads, in the process of catching the water-jet escaping from the mouth of that Amour in a little funnel? Notice the extremely graceful form of their buckets."

He leaned out of the window in order to see better. As for Mrs. Little, she had no more budged than a statue, and neither her husband nor I had troubled her meditation.

Suddenly, Mr. Little threw himself backwards as if seized by fear, and I saw surge forth at the carriage door a tall fellow clad in a black hooded cloak that only allowed his eyes, his teeth and his hands to show.

He extended a little alms-box toward us, saying: "*Pei poveri infirmi.*"

He was a member of the Brotherhood of Mercy, which collects for the sick. I told Mr. Little that in English, and he joined his offering with mine, Mrs. Little still remaining impassive.

After having seen the Piazza Santa Catarina and the monument to the grand duke Leopold I, we had ourselves taken back to the Lugarno, where I quit Mr. and Mrs. Little, reminding them that we were to meet at the railway station the following morning at nine o'clock.

III

They did not miss the rendezvous. Mrs. Little, still veiled, was clad for the circumstance in a large overcoat, as was Mr. Little. He gave his arm to his wife, whose jerky footsteps resounded on the external platform of the station.

"If you would care to climb up first," Mr. Little said to me, "you can take my wife, not by the hands but by the forearms, while I push her by the waist."

"Gladly," I replied. Unfortunately, however, I forgot the instruction to take Mrs. Little by the forearms. I grasped her hands, and as I lifted her up she voiced her eternal: "Ho yes, Tom."

Mr. Little and I sat her down in a corner, where she seemed to abandon herself to slumber.

I recalled then, by contrast with that dejection, the extreme animation that Mrs. Little had had five years earlier at the railway station in Bordeaux, when, blocking the carriage window, she had shouted in order to prevent me from climbing into her compartment; "Loa! Loa!"

The one in which we were now sitting was soon completed by a family composed of five individuals, all very becoming.

There was a professor from the University of Pisa, who was going to the vicinity of Siena with his wife and three daughters in order to attend a wedding celebration. Hazard had placed the gentleman in question beside me.

By way of a request for information that I made, and which he provided in the most affable manner, conversation was engaged between us and became quasi-general. Only Mrs. Little, in her corner, did not participate in it.

On seeing that dejected attitude, the professor's wife could not help asking: "*La signora è ammalata?*"

"*Un poco,*" I said.

As for Mr. Little, whether he understood the lady's question or not, he made no response. In fact, he had just asked the professor for information that, he said, he had not found in his guide, regarding the cheeses of Parma, and he was entirely intent on that matter, which interested him greatly, being, as they say, in the business.

"Are you very fond of cheeses?" asked the professor, in good English.

"I manufacture them in Chester."

"In Chester…oh, then I understand."

With that, Mr. Little and the professor exchanged cards. The latter, Signor Giammani, who taught chemistry at the University of Pisa, had written at one time, and even published, a comparative study of all known cheeses.

Mr. Little had had a stroke of luck. Signor Giammani gave us, in English, a veritable lecture on the similar or distinctive qualities of the various cheeses that shared the gastronomic favor of Europe. I confess that I was very interested in it on my own account, although I had never wanted to try any other cheese than cream cheese. It even made the journey from Pisa to Siena seem short. For his part, Mr. Little was delighted.

At one moment, taking Mrs. Little's hand, he exclaimed: "You hear, my dear Betty, the obliging things that this gentleman, who is one of the most competent men in Europe, is saying about our Cheshire cheeses?"

To which Mr. Little replied, as was her habit: "Ho yes, Tom." Then, Mr. Little having touched her shoulder, she bowed slightly.

She repeated her little salute in the same manner when, once we had arrived at Siena station, Signor Giammani and his family took their leave of us, very gracefully, and descended from the compartment.

When we had got down in our turn, I noticed that two of the professor's daughters turned round covertly to watch Mrs. Little walking, and that they were laughing at the poor woman's gait.

We arrived at lunch-time at the Aquila Nero inn, which had been recommended to us by Signor Giammani as one of the best in Siena. Our first concern, naturally, was to ask for rooms and have our baggage taken up. We were given two that were adjacent.

After a few minutes I heard Mr. Little close and lock the door of his room, and then knock on mine.

"Are you going down for lunch?"

"Very gladly…but isn't Mrs. Little coming down?"

"What would be the point?"

"To have lunch."

"You're wrong," he told me, "to joke in that fashion. You know full well that she can't eat."

"She's really so ill this morning?"

"Come on, my dear Monsieur Le Bref, you can't intend to mock our misfortune!"

"God preserve me! But what misfortune are you talking about?"

Instead of responding directly to my question he said, in a softer tone: "The most skillful mechanicians have not yet found a means of making artificial stomachs."

Thinking that Mrs. Little had been afflicted for some time with a serious gastritis, I did not persist.

Furthermore, I was so hungry myself that it scarcely left me the leisure to think about anything else.

When we went into the dining room there were four Germans there, a lady and three men, all four wearing spectacles on their noses and hats on their heads. They raised their spectacles when we entered, along with the noses they crowned, but not their hats—I'm referring to the men—although we saluted them very politely. Without taking any further notice of the Teutonic boors, who might have been the flower of Berlinese aristocracy, Mr. Little and I ate with all the appetite we had, no longer talking about Mrs. Little, for the subject seemed delicate to me, but about the curiosities we were going to see.

As the meal drew to its close, and I had just ordered coffee, Mr. Little said to me: "While you drink your coffee, my dear Monsieur Le Bref, I'll go take tea in the company of my wife in her room, and I'll come back without her shortly, in order for us to go out."

The waiter did not take long to appear, with a heavily laden tray in his hands, from which he removed, with my intention, a small cup, a small cafetière and a little sugar-bowl containing indecently tiny sugar-lumps, as large as sheep-droppings at the most.

What remained on the tray was the tea destined for Mr. and Mrs. Little. While I was putting something like half a dozen sugar lumps in my cup, admiring once again that singular Italian fashion, with which I was familiar, Mr. Little left the dining room, followed by the waiter.

After a quarter of an hour or thereabouts he reappeared, unaccompanied by Mrs. Little.

"I've just put my wife decisively to bed," he said. "Perhaps it's better thus. Having you with me, I'll perceive her absence much less."

"You're very good, and you honor me greatly."

We went to the cathedral, and along the way, our attention as particularly attracted by the round straw hats that the proletarian women were wearing, attached around the neck, falling back more often than not over their shoulders and palpitating gracefully above their foreheads, where they formed mobile aureoles of a sort. It was also attracted by a team of long-horned Tuscan oxen the color of white coffee, drawing a very narrow basket-cart.

The *sgraffiti*, or engravings, carved into the stones of the cathedral are a work unique in the world, but unfortunately badly damaged by the friction of the soles of numerous generations of boots. No trace of those *sgraffiti* would remain today if the precaution had not finally been taken of covering them with planks.

As the sacristan lifted up the planks to show us the work in question, my eyes chanced to fall on a strange little gnome of sorts, in the flesh and bone. With his very long nose and the almost black tint of his hair, crouched on his little legs, which rose up behind him in the manner of a tail, and his little crutches in his arms, he was strongly reminiscent of a crow.

That quasi-fantastic apparition troubled me so much that it did not cease to haunt my gaze even when I fixed it on the *sgraffiti*, and then on the white marble pulpit supported by four lions, magnificently sculpted by Nicola Pisano, on Bernini's Saint Jerome and the Magdalen, on the admirable frescoes of the Libreria, a highly original work by Pinturicchio in which the bits of the horses, the ornaments of the miters and the tiaras and the guards of the swords project in gilded nails, and finally, on the rich collection of old missals.

It seemed to me that the poor human crow personified the clerical spirit, as the dove does the Holy Spirit.

Next we visited the *Academia delle belle arti*, where one finds, among other works Caravaggio's *Hopscotch Players*,

Saint Catherine of Siena Receiving the Stigmata by Beccafumi, a Saint Paul by Rutilio Manetti and a Charles V by Holbein—after which we strolled until dinner through the city, paved, like Pisa, with large flagstones.

Mrs. Little did not come down for dinner any more than for lunch. I did not make any observation in that regard to Mr. Little, for fear of irritating him.

When he talked about leaving the next day for Orvieto, from which we were to go to Rome, however, I asked him whether he thought that Mrs. Little was in a state to support the fatigues of the voyage—to which he replied, without my understanding the meaning of what he said very clearly, that the poor woman was apparently no longer capable of fatigue.

Was she capable of refection? In any case, it was not the tea that her husband had sent up to her room in the evening that was of a nature to lend her much sustenance.

IV

At any rate, she was on her feet the following day at the same time as us, and ready to depart.

Naturally, I thought it my duty to salute her and enquire after her health, to which she replied to me in English: "Very well…thank you."

Immediately, however, Mr. Little said to me, still in English: "I'd be obliged to you henceforth, Monsieur Le Bref, not to address any speech to my wife, especially in public, in your interest as well as mine, for the difficulty I have in replying to you via her, as well as taking away all illusion from me, can only cause you a disagreeable sensation too."

"Oh!" I said, somewhat surprised.

"Well, yes, you understand that very well."

I did not understand at all, but I nevertheless replied: "Of course, of course."

And I promised myself no longer to address any remark to Mrs. Little, but to content myself with replying to her—and she never spoke to me.

I could not, however, prevent myself from exercising in her regard the small duties of politeness from which a gallant man cannot refrain—for example, helping hr to climb aboard the train to Orvieto at Siena railway station, as I had done at Pisa station for the train to Siena; but I did so mutely, for which Mr. Little thanked me warmly by means of a firm hand-shake.

Scarcely had we sat down when I saw two prelates coming toward us surrounded by priests and preceded by the station-master, holding his cap in his hand. The latter opened the door of our compartment and, perceiving the three of us, he jumped backwards, and then shouted: "Gorini, Gorini!"

Gorini, who as a subaltern employee, came as commanded.

"Have you lost your head," he cried then, "letting these passengers climb into a carriage reserved for Monsignor?"

The poor devil apologized to his chief as best he could and set about asking us to get out. But Mr. Little immediately refused, in English, while Mrs. Little, under the effect of her habitual prostration, did not seem to perceive anything.

It was the exact counterpart of the scene that the excellent couple had made in my regard at the station in Bordeaux when I had tried to climb on to the Bayonne train. While smiling at that idea, which gave me an amiable appearance, I got down rapidly from the carriage and, approaching the French bishop, I said to him: "Monseigneur, if Your Grace does not absolutely have need of all the places in the compartment, I would be infinitely grateful to you for leaving this worthy Englishman and his wife there, who are my friends. I permit myself to address this plea to Your Grace because the poor lady is not very steady on her feet, and it is not easy lift her up into a carriage or take her down from one. They are in any case, very discreet individuals incapable of inconveniencing Your Grace."

"I'm convinced, Monsieur," said the prelate, very amiably, "and may God preserve me from disturbing such worthy people, vouched for by you, who are my compatriot. Furthermore, we only need three places and will have plenty of room in your company."

"For myself, Monseigneur," I said, "I can easily go and sit elsewhere."

"Don't do anything of the sort, I beg you; I shall be only too glad to have you for a traveling companion."

While the French prelate and I were exchanging these courtesies, watched by all the travelers, Mr. Little and the station-master were arguing, without understanding very much, in English and Italian.

The station-master raised his voice, irritated by the passivity opposed to his injunctions to descend by the worthy Mr. Little, to such an extent that the Archbishop of Siena had to intervene to calm him down.

"*Piano, piano, signore...un pè piu di dolcezza.*"

The French prelate then put an end to the dispute, while taking his leave of the Italian prelate with a hand-kiss, which the latter returned, and an Episcopal blessing given to the Italian priests who were accompanying their archbishop, to the station-master, to the employees and to myself; then he climbed into our compartment, where, before sitting down, he also blessed Mr. and Mrs. Little.

He was followed by the two priests forming his little court, to whom I gave way in spite of their insistences that I board before them, and it was me who climbed up last of all.

The station-master closed the door and the train did not take long to pull away.

Then one of the priests took three breviaries out of a small bag he was crying, one bound in violet shagreen with Monseigneur's coat-of-arms, and the others in black shagreen, and each of them began to read his own, after making the sign of the cross.

Meanwhile, Mrs. Little still remained absorbed in her corner. Mr. Little and I consulted our guide-books, his in English and mine in French, without daring to speak for fear of troubling the pious meditation of Monseigneur and his followers.

Eventually, Monseigneur, having finished reading as much as he wanted in his breviary, drew closer to us—he was at the other extremity of the seat on which I was sitting—and, with a very good grace, he broke the silence.

"Is Madame suffering greatly?" she said, looking at Mrs. Little—without being able to see her profoundly-veiled face, naturally.

"Ho yes, milord," said Mr. Little, partly in good English and partly in bad French, "my poor wife had an unpardonable indisposition, she experienced...how do you say it?...a great chagrin to pearl."

"Monsieur means, Your Grace," I said, "that Madame is gravely indisposed and that she has difficulty speaking."

"Ho yes," said Mr. Little, "it was zagly that."

"And," said the archbishop, "you think that a voyage to Italy is doing Madame good?"

"Ho no, but it was me that this voyage did good, and my wife she accompanied me."

"Mr. Little, whom I have the honor of introducing to Your Grace," I said, "is never separated from his wife. It is the most united household that one can encounter."

"That does honor to both spouses," said the prelate, with a broad smile on his lips, inclining particularly toward Mrs. Little. Nor obtaining a word from her, or any sign of response, he turned to the two priests accompanying him, and remarked to then on the beauties of the countryside through which we were traversing.

The bishop had a god enough head, with colored cheeks, graying black hair, lively eyes peering through tortoiseshell spectacles, and fine fleshy lips. He appeared to be aged between fifty and fifty-five.

What diocese did he direct? I would have liked to know, and perhaps I would have asked one of the priests quietly if he had been my neighbor, but I dared not ask the question of him, and we arrived at Orvieto without my being able to enquire. I suspected, however, that it must be a diocese in the Midi, the two priests having pronounced southern accents.

The Monseigneur and I had still had an opportunity to chat, and he it was who drew my attention, at the station of Torrito, to a very gracious tableau, that of a young peasant woman with big dark eyes walking with a divine stride in the midst of green and bushy wheat-fields.

Orvieto station is some distance from the city. While the French bishop climbed into the Bishop of Orvieto's carriage with his two priests, Mr. Little and I installed Mrs. Little in an omnibus and when the fine carriage of the prince of the Church drew away at the rapid trot of its two spirited horses, we set off in quest of our luggage. While searching for it, we perceived the Monseigneur's, which were to be transported by the omnibus. A card pinned to two or three trunks informed us that they belonged to Monseigneur d'Agen, and thus my curiosity was satisfied by chance.[29]

As we arrived in the city, along the main street followed by our omnibus, we went past an entire band of guttersnipes, among whom were five or six adults of both sexes, who were bating cooking-pots, saucepans, buckets and watering-cans in the most incoherent fashion, and singing thirty-six interspersed songs at the same time as uttering shrill cries. It was a charivari...but who the devil was it for?

"I don't think that can be for the Bishop of Agen," I said to Mr. Little, laughing, "and much less for us."

"Doubtless much less for us," replied Mr. Little. And he added, palpating his wife's hand: "Isn't that so, Betty?"

"Ho yes, Tom."

Next to me in the omnibus were two Italians, who were laughing. They could have been from Orvieto. It transpired, in fact, that they were. I obtained an explanation for the charivari from them, which I gave to Mr. Little. The victims were a man and a woman who had married that very morning, although they were over sixty.

---

[29] The Bishop of Agen from 1874-1884, during which interval the present story appears to be set, was Jean-Emile Fonteneau.

In that regard, Mr. Little made a reflection that appeared to me very humane. "The children," he said, "are excusable. They only judge that senile marriage by appearances, which might seems somewhat grotesque, but it's an abomination that the men and women, who ought to know life, far from lending their shameful collaboration to the brats, are not dispersing them. They ought to comprehend that marriage is much more the satisfaction of a mental need than a physical need, and that, if there is an age when communal life is imposed as a necessity on a man and a woman, it is when they begin to grow old."

In speaking thus, Mr. Little could not help tears shining in the corners of his eyes, but, having wiped them way rapidly with his fingertips, he asked: "Isn't that so, Betty?"

Then, as he pressed his wife's hand, the latter replied, as was her habit: "Ho yes, Tom."

We stayed at the Locanda delle Belle Arti, which is, I believe, the only tolerate inn in Orvieto, which has been established in an incomplete palace,[30] of which there are so many in Italy. One might have inscribed above the door: Grandeur and Destitution.

The staircase was monumental, the corridors of unusual length and breadth, the rooms immense, but with nothing but stone floors, all the walls whitewashed, and planks closing unused porticoes here and there.

At Orvieto, as in Siena, Mrs. Little remained in her room while we had lunch, and after lunch, Mr. Little went up to take tea with her; then they both came down and we went in company to visit the cathedral, the façade of which, thanks to its foundations of black and white stone, is reminiscent of that of Siena cathedral.

When we went inside the priests of the chapter were singing vespers in the midst of complete solitude.

---

[30] The Locanda delle Belle Arti in Orvieto was in the Palazzo Ottaviani. It is no longer a guest-house.

What it is necessary to see in Orvieto is the cathedral, and there, it is, above all, the interpretation of two great artists, one made with the chisel and the other with the brush, of the same scene: the Resurrection, Paradise and the Inferno. I am referring to the sculptor Giovanni Pisano and the painter Luca Signorelli.

There is also the Christ and the Prophets of Fra Angelico, the Gothic Virgin with her cortege of angels of Lippo Memmi, the two great bas-reliefs of the two Moses, the one by the father representing the adoration of the Magi and the one by the son depicting the Visitation.

The work of Signorelli is particularly admirable. That alone is worth the journey to Orvieto. It is composed of four large angels and a ceiling, ornamenting an entire chapel. The four panels translate, in striking scenes that denote in Signorelli a profound thinker as well as a powerful artist, Paradise, the Inferno, the Advent of the Antichrist and the Resurrection.

As for the ceiling, it is the Last Judgment. Jesus appears there in the midst of his court of apostles, prophets, doctors, holy omen, patriarchs and martyrs, and, as is written in the scriptures, to his right are the just, extending their confident hands toward him, ad to is left he culpable, griped by fear.

On the former, a rain of stars is falling, and on the latter, a rain of fire.

Beneath the fresco of Paradise one sees the medallions of Dante and Virgil, and beneath the fresco of the Inferno, those of Horace and Ovid.

In the fresco of the Advent of the Antichrist, Signorelli has painted himself alongside Fra Angelico, but every other figure in that fresco is eclipsed by that of the Antichrist. The physiognomy that Signorelli has given him is the idea of a man of genius. He has succeeded in importing a Satanic expression into the classic features of Jesus.

I pointed out that Antichrist to Mr. Little, who pointed it out to Mrs. Little, who replied to him with her "Ho yes, Tom," but without raising her veil, or even the head beneath the veil.

There is a whole poem—and what a poem!—in the fresco of the Resurrection.

"You see that fresco of the Resurrection Mr. Little?" I said to my friend the cheese-merchant. "Can you guess why Signorelli has represented some of the dead for us in a skeletal state, while the majority are clad in their flesh?"

"It's probably," the worthy man replied, "to distinguish the recently-dead from the ancient dead."

"It's not that, Mr. Little." I said, "and for two reasons. Firstly, if your explanation were true, the skeletons would be more numerous than the fleshy bodies, and it's exactly the contrary; secondly, it has been prophesied for us that on the day of the Resurrection, the most ancient dead, even those whose bones are dust, will immediately resume their flesh."

"One can admit, however," said Mr. Little, "that there are successive degrees in reincarnation, and that, in consequence, at the appeal of the divine trumpet, some individuals will be reincarnated more rapidly than others."

"Yes, yes, but here's another explanation, that does much more honor to the genius of Signorelli, and which I think more likely. Notice that troop of skeletons arranged to the right of the fresco. To see them holding their sides like that, doesn't it seem to you that they're bursting into laughter at the singular idea that the Eternal has wanted to revive eternally those who have already had too much of their temporary life? Do you not think that the attitude implies a protest against the resurrection and a refusal to submit to it? Decidedly, Signorelli was a great mind."

But Mr. Little was scarcely paying attention to what I was saying; his mind was evidently elsewhere.

"What are you thinking about, Mr. Little?"

"I'm thinking that I might see my dear Betty again in the Valley of Jehoshaphat, in the flesh and bone, and that if, as I sincerely hope, we are both among the elect, it will be possible for us to embrace one another, before going to sit down side by side at the right hand of God.

I looked at Mr. Little with a certain astonishment, for it seemed to me to be rather premature on his part to aspire to the Last Judgment in order to see his wife again in the flesh and bone when he presently had her on his arm. I did not permit myself any allusion on that subject, however, while hoping privately that Mrs. Little, when she was resuscitated, would not be resuscitated as I saw her in Italy—which is to say, absolutely drab—nor even as I had seen her in Spain, when she was already passably dreary, but far more brilliant than she had ever been in this miserable life.

While one of the sacristans showed us that marvelous chapel, two emaciated black cats, which seemed to have been sent to us as a deputation by Signorelli's Antichrist rubbed against our legs and Mrs. Little's skirts, and then crouched down on the red steps of the altar, which they seemed to be guarding like two sentinels.

"Look," Mr. Little said to me. "Astaroth and Beelzebub!"

"Yes," I replied. And I added, laughing: "The chapter of priests, although the church is completely deserted at the moment when they are singing the glory of God with such lung-power, if not so much soul, cannot say that there was no so much as a cat here, since there are two of them, not to mention us."

On emerging from the cathedral we went to see the ruins of the amphitheater, today converted into a garden. What struck us most in those ruins—or rather, that garden—was a white marble statue, cruelly tested by time, of I know not what Pope, which seemed to personify the decadence of the papacy itself in our epoch. The two arms were broken, the nose flattened, the tiara broken—and to that broken tiara a washing-line was attached, laden with linen in the process of drying.

A remarkable detail: that statue of a vicar of Christ, thus reduced to the status of a drying machine, had its back turned to a splendid view.

"Decidedly," Mr. Little said to me, rather shrewdly, "that mutilated statue is a good emblem of the papacy, which has turned its back on the future, as the pope has turned his to one of the most beautiful panoramas one might see."

While our attention was, so to speak, shuttling between the statue and the landscape displayed behind it, the tenant of the garden, a laundress, I believe, was gathering a large bouquet of lilacs. As we were about to take our leave, she approached Mrs. Little very graciously to offer it to her, doubtless hoping that it might earn her a larger tip or, as the Italians say, a *buona mano*.

"*Signora, favorisca d'accettare questo massi di fiori.*"

But Mrs. Little made no movement of the hand to take it, and it was Mr. Little who refused the concierge's offer in English, under the pretext that Mrs. Little did not have the free use of her hands, and, being in addition very ill, she dreaded odorous flowers.

I took charge of translating Mr. Little's refusal into Italian, which I naturally did in such a manner as to render it less harsh, to the extent that that was possible. I softened it further by taking a spring of lilac from the bouquet and even further by giving the good woman a double lira—which is to say, two francs.

V

In the evening, shortly before midnight, we left Orvieto in a sort of down-at-heel post chaise, which was to take us to Rome in seventeen hours. We had been scalped at the Locanda delle Belle Arti, as witness the two cups of tea served in the morning and the evening to Mrs. Little, which had cost five francs apiece.

When Mr. Little, who had been kind enough to take charge of settling the bill, and to whom I reimbursed my proportionate contribution later, had told me about the exaggerated tariff for the cup of tea, adding: "If the tea had even been good—but I couldn't drink it," I thought it my duty to intervene with the proprietor. The latter, probably sniffing in me, with the finesse appropriate to an Italian, an authentic

Frenchman, even though he had only head me speak English with Mr. Little, replied to me *mezza voce*:

"Se fosse il tè per lei, l'avrebbe pagato due soltante lire e mezza, ma per inglesi...!"[31]

I admired the profound rascality of the hotelier all the more because what I had consumed myself had been charged appropriately; I admired it so much that I did not have the strength to insist.

In spite of the petty aggravation that resulted from that, which was further aggravated at the moment of our departure by the stable-hand, who asked us without rhyme or reason in English for a tip, which we did not owe him—he must have learned to ask for it in all languages, even Russian—and in spite of the jolts of the carriage, of which we felt the reverberations, and even in spite of the vague apprehension we had by night in the Roman countryside of being stopped and ransomed by bandits, we slept quite well, and Mr. Little and I scarcely exchanged three or four words before dawn.

At the relay in Viterbe, where we arrived after daybreak, I got down in order to stretch my legs, and Mr. Little did likewise, but his wife did not budge.

Seeing that she remained immobile, he said to her, taking her hand: "You want to rest, then, my dear Betty?"

And, the latter having replied to that: "Ho yes, Tom," he did not insist any further.

We were very desirous of breaking a crust, as they say, for we were beginning to feel hungry, but it was necessary for us to replace that exercise with another, less comforting one, which was putting a coin in the hand of a retired postillion with a wooden leg, who resembled Hyacinthe, the actor at the Palais-Royal, to such a degree, that one might have thought he was his twin brother, tested by the misfortunes of war.

Although, at Monterose we had again to grease the palm of an irreproachably-dressed, even well-to-do, gentleman who

---

[31] "If the tea had been for your excellency, he would only have paid two francs fifty, but for the English...!"

looked like a good bourgeois but who asked us or something *per il povero conduttore*, at least it was possible for us to have lunch.

While we were eating with a real appetite, sitting facing one another, while Mrs. Little remained in the vehicle, as at Viterbe, I said to Mr. Little: "Aren't you going to send the worthy Mrs. Little a bowl of soup?"

He immediately looked at me reproachfully, without replying to my question. Although I was a little troubled by that, I added: "You know that we'll arrive in Rome quite late, and that between now and then, Mrs. Little might suffer from hunger."

Again he shot me a glance that went straight to my heart, saying: "Come, come, Monsieur le Bref..."

I dared not persist, for I saw that, without meaning to, I had caused the excellent man pain, but in my conscience, it was impossible for me to comprehend how a man who showed so much solicitude for his wife in other regards could be so indifferent in that instance.

We returned silently to our vehicle, stopped outside the door of the inn, and at the doors of which three or four beggars where wailing in a lamentable fashion while the postillion attached fresh horses.

"*Signora, per l'amor d'Iddio, un poveretto balocco!*"[32]

They had sung that in every key, and other things appropriate to soften the most insensible heart, or at least to force the best barricaded purse, but Mrs. Little did not budge. Pitilessly, she let them warble.

Apparently indignant at such aridity of soul, the postillion, who might perhaps have suffered from it on his own account, cracked his whip over the ears of the rabble, saying: "*Andante via dunque...non si dona niente.*"[33]

Meanwhile, Mr. Little gave them an order in English to leave his wife alone, and they understood it because of his

---

[32] "For the love of God, Madame, a poor little coin!"

[33] "Get away...you won't be given anything."

tone and his gesture. But as he was an excellent man, easily moved, with a sincere pity even for a feigned poverty, he took a few sous out of his pocket, which he distributed to the beggars.

"Perhaps," I said, "Mrs. Little has already given something."

"No," said Mr. Little, impatiently. "How do you think she can have given anything?"

I understood that I had just committed another gaffe, and I climbed into the carriage in a crestfallen fashion, bowing to the perfectly immobile Mrs. Little.

Scarcely had we begun rolling along the road again, than Mr. Little said to me: "My dear Monsieur Le Bref, since I had the pleasure of encountering you in the cathedral at Pisa, I have had it on the tip of my tongue several times to ask you a question, but, fearing that you might see it as a sharp reproach, I have kept silent. I have not forgotten, in fact, that I owe you gratitude for having saved my life twice, and I do not believe I have the right to hold anything against you whatsoever."

"Eh! Good God, what could you possible hold against me, my dear Mr. Little?"

"I repeat to you that I don't recognize the right to hold anything whatsoever against you."

"But explain to me, I beg you, how I might have incurred your rancor."

Mr. Little then held out his hand to me, which I shook, and he said to me, with tears in his eyes and his voice: "How is it that you, such a worthy fellow, a man of so much heart, did not respond with a single sympathetic word to the letter in which I announced to you, three years ago, the death of my poor wife?"

"The death of your wife? Come, come, Mr. Little, is it really you who is joking in that fashion, and in front of Mrs. Little, whom your joke might shock, with just entitlement?"

"I'm not joking at all, for it's certainly not a joking matter. And since you mention joking, permit me to say that that is exactly what you have seemed to be doing, since we met in

Pisa, and you were still doing just now, notably in advising me to send a bowl of soup to Mrs. Little."

"Me, joking?"

"Of course."

"Oh, that's too much! You want to make me believe that it's me who is joking, when it's you! You're typical of our homeland, where that might pass as the last word in 'humor'!"

"I swear to you, Monsieur Le Bref, on everything I hold most sacred, that, unfortunately, I'm not joking."

"But then, that makes me dread, Mr. Little, that you are under the influence of...how shall I put it?...a temporary disturbance of your mental faculties."

"You didn't receive, then, the letter in which I informed you of the death of my wife?" said Mr. Little, fixing me with a stare that, in truth, had nothing distracted about it.

"No, truly, I didn't receive it, and I confess to you that I'm glad, since, definitively, here is Mrs. Little now, if not well, at least alive..."

As I said that I looked at Mrs. Little, expecting some acquiescence from her, or at least a burst of laughter—but there was nothing!

"You sincerely believe that my poor wife is alive?" said Mr. Little.

"Of course! Unless I'm seeing things."

"Oh my dear friend!" he cried, then, shaking my hands, "you can't imagine how much joy that causes me!"

I understood Mr. Little less and less, and, finding the joy he was manifesting because I considered Mrs. Little, who was sitting in front of me, to be alive, and his reproach for not having written to him on the occasion of her death, to be equally incoherent, I thought that he had definitely gone mad.

I no longer doubted that he had gone mad on seeing him immediately embrace Mrs. Little, something that he had never permit himself to do before in my presence, and hearing him repeat, in the midst of real tears: "Betty, my dear Betty...."

"Calm down, my dear friend," I said to him, very emotional myself. "Calm down." And I died, in a low voice: "You'll frighten your wife."

But he replied to me loudly: "Eh! How do you expect me to frighten her, poor woman, since she's been dead for three years?"

"That's true," I said, as if to agree with his mania. "But then, who is this lady, who resembles Mrs. Little so perfectly, so far as I can judge through her veil, and whom you just embraced, calling her Betty, and to whom, after all, I've spoken twenty times since the day we met in Pisa, calling her Mrs. Little, without you protesting once?"

Then, Mr. Little gently lifted the veil covering his companion's face, and said: "Look."

It really was his Betty, it really was Mrs. Little, with the face like a red ball, a Dutch cheese, as I had known, since our first encounter at the railway station in Bordeaux, but the prominent blue eyes which had never had much expression, had even less, and her parted lips, showing teeth almost as large as piano keys, maintained a complete immobility.

Meanwhile, Mr. Little, who was holding his wife's hand tenderly in his own, said with an emotion that was at first contained, but soon overabundant; "Betty, my dear Betty, answer me: Do you approve of my having lifted our veil, in order to show our friend Monsieur Le Bref your cherished and forever regretted features, such as he knew them?"

Without Mrs. Little's lips moving in the slightest, the customary little phrase emerged from that open mouth.

"Ho yes, Tom."

"Well," cried Mr. Little, in a voice blurred by tears, "do you understand now?"

Yes, yes, I understood, by dint of looking at Mrs. Little's inanimate face, what I had not understood at first. Mrs. Little was indeed dead, and the striking representation of her that I had before me was nothing but a mannequin, albeit executed with such artistry that it feigned life marvelously.

I shook Mr. Little's had, saying to him, profoundly moved myself: "My poor friend, be sure that I sympathize as much as is humanly possible with your just affliction, and that I deplore the false direction that your letter took, since my silence must have resulted for you in the thought that I might remain indifferent. Oh, you must have been deeply offended."

"I didn't know how to explain it," replied Mr. Little. And he added, wiping his eyes: "But now I can explain it very well, and I can also explain how, since our encounter in the cathedral in Pisa until just now, you have been able to believe that my poor Betty was alive. Has not the artist imitated her very well? And with the faculty that she has of moving and speaking, as long as her veil is lowered, the illusion is complete."

"Complete, indeed, Mr. Little, and I confess that if you had not lifted it for me, I would still have... But it's obviously not in order to give that illusion to the public that you're traveling thus with the mann...with the modeled image of Mrs. Little..."

"No. my ear friend, it's in order to have it myself."

"What! You can imagine that it's Mrs. Little, when you know the contrary full well, you who make that mechanism move and talk?"

"Yes and no...so little that if I reflect, the sad truth appears to me clearly, and then I'm gripped by a fit of despair, as you were able to judge just now, but more often than not, it isn't like that...I yield to the mirage, I imagine that my poor wife, even when I make her talk, even when I make her move, is still alive, and the horrible lacuna that her death has made in my existence is partly filled in."

"I understand, I understand—but perhaps, if you had done as so many others have done, if you had simply remarried, without absolutely forgetting the first Mrs. Little, you might have found almost the same rewards in the second."

"Never, never! Unless I had encountered a woman resembling my Betty in the most striking fashion...and how would I find her, even supposing that she exists? I had, therefore, to resign myself to the stratagem that you see, without which I would be dead of chagrin at present. And what is most horrible in the loss that I have suffered of my poor Betty, Monsieur Le Bref, is that it is, in a sense, imputable to me."

"How is that?"

"You know, for having been a witness to it in Burgos, what umbrage maidservants brought to Mrs. Little. I even told you about some of my difficulties in that regard."

"Yes, indeed."

"Well, it is in regard to a question that seemed quite innocent to me, but which had in my Betty's eyes the irremediable sin of being addressed by me to our maid...yes, it was because of that question that the poor woman fell unconscious in a transport of rage, and did not recover."

"A ruptured aneurism, no doubt?"

"Exactly."

"Poor woman! But what had you said to your maid, then Mr. Little?"

"Oh, something, I repeat to you, that seemed to me ought not to have disquieted Mrs. Little at all, umbrageous as I knew her to be—which seemed, on the contrary, only to be able to reassure her by her observation of my ignorance in certain regards... So, I asked the maid, in front of my wife, whether she had any night-chemises. That question did not, moreover, come out of the blue. It arrived at the very moment when my wife had just shown me some very sparse day-chemises that she had bought her, and some very high-necked night-chemises that she had bought for herself. And I reasoned internally that if the poor girl wore such sparse chemises in bed, she was in danger of catching cold, as is commonly said. Hence my question to the maid: 'Annie, have you any night-chemises?'

"'Annie, I forbid you to reply to Monsieur!' cried my unfortunate wife, turning purple. Then, turning to me and clapping her hands together, she cried: 'Oh! Oh! you have no shame! To ask such a question of a maid! What, then, do you suppose your maid to be, Monsieur? A maid who had night-chemises would be the worst of maids. Is it appropriate for a maid to have night-chemises…?'"

"'Perhaps, perhaps,'

"'What do you mean, perhaps?'

"'Well, propriety does not appear to me to raise an obstacle, my love, to a maid putting on night-chemises.'

"'Propriety, no, Monsieur, but decency.'

"'It seems to me, however, my love,' I said, 'with the greatest mildness in the world, that night-chemises that are high-necked protect decency more than day-chemises that are very low-necked, not to mentioned that they keep the torso warmer…and that is even, my dear Betty, what you understand for yourself.'

"With that, my unfortunate wife suffered a redoubling of frightful fury, vociferating inconsequential words, among which I distinguished the phrases: *vile debauchee, lubricious man* and *disgusting individual*, all epithets addressed to me, and finally, the word *camisole*, which I had the misfortune to emphasize by saying: 'As regards camisoles, it's you who need one at present, but a *camisole de force*.'[34]

"Immediately, I saw her eyes, her poor eyes, widen immeasurably, and I saw her fall down dead…dead, alas!"

Having spoken thus, the worthy Mr. Little burst into sobs. I tried to console him, by representing to him a host of god reasons why, after all, he had nothing for which to reproach himself, and I succeeded, albeit with great difficulty.

During Mr. Little's poignant story I continued looking at Mrs. Little, or at least her mannequin, whose veil was still lifted, and I admired the perfection of the stratagem. I admired it even more when, Mr. Little having asked me to touch his wife's wrist with my finger at the level of the good-luck bracelet that ornamented it, I felt skin as elastic as if it had been covered in veritable flesh. There was also no stiffness in the arm, the articulations operating with a perfect ease.

---

[34] A strait-jacket—the pun does not translate.

245

"Everything is becoming," Mr. Little told me, "and the mechanisms that make the body move allow it an almost natural flexibility...there's only the gait that is slightly jerky, as you've been able to see. The external organs are reproduced with an admirable fidelity. You only have to look at the ear, the cartilages of the nose, and the mouth, which is equipped with my wife's veritable teeth, perfectly enclosed in artificial sockets, just as the bare scalp is garnished with her own hair."

As he said that, Mr. Little used his thumb and index finger to agitate the cartilages of his wife's nose gently; he pinched the lobe of an ear; and, again gently, he opened the mouth, showing me a seemingly fleshy tongue, although naturally a trifle dry, and, pressing lightly on the tongue, she showed me a palate and an epiglottis, and even tonsils, the mucus of which was slightly better imitated.

"As for the internal organs," he added, "notably those of digestion and respiration, they don't exist, but are replaced by the automatic mechanism, which it was necessary to lodge somewhere; and there's still room in the abdomen for a small heating apparatus."

"A small heating apparatus?"

"Yes, it's necessary that by night, when she's lying next to me, I feel the gentle warmth of her body."

I admired that precaution, which was evidently not to be disdained. In addition to the fact that it added to the illusion for Mr. Little, Mrs. Little thus seemed much more alive to the touch; in winter, if she were armed by a few degrees more, it become an element of comfort.

"But it's very practical," the worthy Mr. Little told me, while agitating it in a manner that would have seemed absolutely insane to many people. "It is, in truth, very practical."

And, looking back on my condition of bachelorhood, which, if it has its good points, also—I don't hide it from myself—has as many bad ones, I thought that a marriage of Mr. Little's second fashion...for instance with a prettier mannequin that, instead of trailing it around with me from one railway carriage to the next, I could put in my trunk, only taking it out at bed-time…yes, I thought that a marriage of that sort would fill in the void in my soul somewhat, while being able to keep me warm on winter nights.

I even asked myself, although that became, involuntarily, somewhat extravagant, whether the artist who had fabricated Mrs. Little—the artificial one—might not, in fabricating a wife for me, arrange matters so that she had several exchangeable faces, in order that, although always having the same companion next to me in my bed, I could at least see her under different aspects.

I refrained from communicating that thought, which he would not have understood, to Mr. Little. He, the prototype of conjugal fidelity, wanted to show me, if not the mechanisms that made Mrs. Little move—he even made me understood that I kind of modesty would prevent him from ever showing me—at least the exterior switches that corresponded with them, and were found principally at the nape of his wife's neck, her waist and in the palm of her hand.

He explained to me how, once it was set up to work in the morning, Mrs. Little's automotive apparatus could be stopped at will by turning in one direction a simple button set in her belt, and restarted by turning it in the opposite direction; how, by touching Mr. Little lightly on the nape, at a point in the lace frill of her dress, he could make her nod her head; and finally, what was out of order in her arms, which had greatly intrigued me when I believed her to be alive.

On that subject, Mr. Little said to me: "The mechanician artist had found a means—which is truly admirable— according to whether I turned this little button on Mrs. Little's elbow one way or the other, of making her extend a hand and shake one that was offered to her, or raise to her nose a bouquet that she had in her left hand. Unfortunately, the mechanism of the right arm was disabled in Como, and the one in the left in Venice, and, when the latter misfortune occurred, it caused me such a great chagrin that I remained locked in my room for several days with my poor love, without wanting to go out any longer.

"Then the reflection came to me that, after all, as Mrs. Little did not know anyone in Italy—I had no idea then that we might encounter you—she would not have to shake anyone's hand, and that she could easily do without respiring a bouquet, whatever pleasure I would have had in seeing her do so, given that she no longer had the sense of smell, any more than the others. I therefore resumed going out with Mrs. Little, to see the curiosities of Venice with her and those of the other cities of our itinerary—and that is how we found ourselves together in the cathedral of Pisa.

"And now, you know, my dear friend, what frightens me is thinking that at any moment, another mechanism of locomotion in my wife's body might break down, which would result in a great embarrassment for me. That is why you see me making the slightest excursions with her in a carriage, for fear that too much exercise might fatigue her mechanisms. There is only one man in the world capable of repairing them, and that is the mechanician artist who designed them, who is in London."

"I'm astonished," I said, "That you have not brought him with you, for greater security."

"I thought of that momentarily, but one consideration caused me to renounce the idea."

"I understand...the annoyance of always having a third party between Mrs. Little and you...an annoyance that perhaps I am causing you myself."

"Which you are certainly not causing me, my dear Monsieur Le Bref. No, it wasn't that."

"Then too, the considerable augmentation of expense that would have resulted for you."

"Much less that, Monsieur Le Bref."

"Then I don't follow."

"It's quite simple. That mechanician knows my wife as well as, if not better than, I know her myself, since he's the one who made her. Well, just between ourselves, that doesn't please me—no, that doesn't please me. So it would require an absolute urgency for me to give him something to refit inside Mrs. Little's body."

As Mr. Little said that, his ordinarily ruddy face had become and even deeper shade of crimson. That excess of modesty, with regard to a simple mannequin representing his wife, demonstrated better than anything else the extent to which he identified it with her.

"And obstetric physicians," I objected, "would be even worse."

"Undoubtedly, undoubtedly," said Mr. Little, increasingly troubled.

VI

Like all Frenchmen who go to Rome I had the custom of lodging at the Hotel Minerva. But Mr. Little proposed to take us to the large Hotel di Spagna on the Piazza di Spagna, in memory of the voyage that we had made together on the Iberian peninsula, when poor Mrs. Little was still flesh and bone, and I hastened to consent to that.

It was, therefore, at the door of the Hotel di Spagna that we got down from the carriage, and as we descended, Mr. Little did not fail to show me the switch that he operated in Mrs. Little's belt in order to put her legs in movement.

As I followed Mr. Little, with his artificial wife on his arm, up the staircase of the hotel, I admired his ability to oblige himself to endure the embarrassment that such a comedy caused him to for the sake of the pleasure, so great it was, of having with him the consistent shadow of the person who had charmed him in life. I thought that in Mr. Little's place, I would at least have wanted to make other arrangements.

Why, I wondered, had that second Mrs. Little not been designed in such a way that she could be dismantled and reassembled, and consequently lodge in a trunk. She would have been infinitely more comfortable when traveling with her husband thaw he she was alive, whereas today, towed around all of a piece, she was infinitely less so.

As for me, a great traveler, always up and down mountains and valleys, it was thus that I would accommodate a wife, discreetly wrapped up with other luggage.

A declaration of principle subversive to that extent of the most elementary gallantry provoked in the feminine fraction of Monsieur Le Bref's audiences a series of exclamations, of which the charming Mina took charge of disengaging the disapproving character.

"I beg the pardon of the ladies who are listening to me, " Monsieur Le Bref said, but that is my opinion, and that opinion, let it be remarked, cannot be as shocking in a traveler as it would be in a sedentary man... Furthermore, let it be understood that I would unpack my wife every evening in order to give myself the nocturnal illusion of a companion, save for repacking her every morning, in order not to disillusion myself..."

That, therefore, is what I was thinking about on the staircase of the Hotel di Spagna in Rome, at the sight of the worthy Mr. Little guiding the hesitant steps of his artificial wife with a touching attention.

Suddenly, those reflections were interrupted by the passage of a maidservant of remarkable beauty, certainly one of the most beautiful women in Rome, where there are so many beauties.

She was coming down the stairs as we were going up. I could not help admiring her, and I saw clearly that Mr. Little was admiring her as much as me, and even more, for he turned round three times in order to look at her.

Oh, if he had acted in that fashion when Mrs. Little was on his arm in flesh and bone, what a quarter or an hour he would have spent! But, now that she was no longer anything but leather and sheet metal, there was not the slightest storm to endure. Mrs. Little seemed—and, in fact, was—absolutely indifferent to the incident.

The stairway of the Hotel di Spagna in Rome having reminded me of that of the hotel in Burgos, where poor Mrs. Little had made an abominable scene under the pretext that her husband had received in his arms the young Amparo, after she lost her equilibrium under a pile of white linen, I could not help congratulating Mr. Little on the amelioration that had occurred in the character of his wife, in that regard.

"That," he said to me very calmly, "is the sole superiority that my poor Betty's artificial personality has over her defunct personality, and yet...!"

There was in that exclamation a kind of implicit admission that the absence of the scenes of jealousy made to her husband by Mrs. Little relative to hotel maids—scenes from which I had seen him suffer a great deal in Burgos—did not leave him without a certain regret. What a strange thing human nature is!

I wanted to clarify that.

"Would it seem preferable to you if Mrs. Little still had the gift of making scenes?"

"Well...yes, my dear friend."

"I understand...you mean that if she made them, it would be because she was still alive."

"Undoubtedly, but in certain respects, I would not be annoyed if the mechanician had been able to give it to her automatically, with the faculty for me to accelerate or cut short the scenes."

"Really?"

"Yes—and that's perfectly explicable. My poor Betty was never as alive as when she was angry with me. It was only them that she seemed, as one might put it, to light up. The rest of the time she was, as you know, almost extinct. Thus, nothing could give me more fully the illusion that she is still alive that those sorts of tantrums, although so irrational, just as nothing takes away that illusion more completely than a calmness, so unnatural in her, when she sees me ogling as pretty maidservant, as I did just now."

During the first week that we spent in Rome, I obtained from Mr. Little, not without difficulty, that he sometimes spared himself, and spared me, the inconvenience of towing around his automation—which is to say, his wife; for, now that I was aware of the substance of which Mrs. Little was made, not having the same motives for illusion as Mr. Little, I found her constancy utterly tedious and our role somewhat ridiculous.

When he went out without her he had the custom of locking her in her room and putting the key in his pocket. And to the hotel staff who asked him whether Madame was ill and whether she might need something, he replied that she was indeed slightly indisposed, but only wanted one thing: not to be disturbed.

As, in addition, he brought her out from time to time, and had a cup of tea or brother sent up to her twice a day, which he absorbed secretly, suspicions were not awakened regarding his stratagem.

However, it was Mr. Little who could not resolve himself to a daily separation of several hours from his wife, whose company was evidently dearer to him than mine. Thus, it was necessary for me to endure his mania to take her almost everywhere. We returned with her to the Coliseum, the Capitol, the Vatican and the Pineto, the Borghese and Doria galleries, the Basilicas of St. Peter, St. John Lateran, Saint Mary Major and St. Paul outside the walls, to the Villa Madame, etc., etc.

Mr. Little even wanted to take her to Albano and the Tivoli, but I made him renounce that ludicrous project, by representing to him that such repeated excursions would end up causing Mr. Little's automotive mechanism to break down.

Events proved that I was right.

One evening, when the three of us were walking in St. Peter's, I suddenly heard something like the sound of a breaking spring, and I saw Mrs. Little fall down full length on the pavement. By a bizarre coincidence, Mrs. Little, although her husband was giving her his arm, collapsed abruptly without him having time to retain her, at the very moment when she had been touched by the rod of venial sins.

You know, of course, that in the confessionals of the basilica of St. Peter's, priests are on duty, holding a long flexible rod, with which they touch passers-by on the head or the shoulder in order to absolve them of the small fry of sins.

Alarmed by the result of the touch of his rod, not because he thought that it had done Mrs. Little any harm, but because imagined that she had fainted from fright, the absolver emerged precipitately from the confessional and came to help us lift her up, not without babbling apologies.

We tried to sit Mr. Little's artificial companion down, but were unable to succeed in doing so. Evidently, the mechanism that permitted sitting had broken, or at least gone awry. I gazed sadly at poor Mr. Little, whose expression was consternated. He doubtless feared that the accident would reveal Mrs. Little's automatism, and I confess that I dreaded that as much as he did.

Our anxieties increased further on seeing a young man approach who said that he was a physician, and who offered us his services. Without being authorized to do so, the young man even asked Mrs. Little where her pain was, but when she did not reply, as you can imagine, he must have assumed that it was out of modesty, the place where she was suffering probably being one of those that Englishwomen cannot name, even with the aid of circumlocutions, and he did not insist.

"*La signora non puo sedersi?*" he asked Mrs. Little.

As Mr. Little seemed not to understand, I said to him in English: "The doctor is asking Madame whether she doesn't want to sit down."

Mr. Little, whose presence of mind had returned, repeated the doctor's question to his wife, pressing her hand in such a fashion as to make her reply.

"No," she replied.

Mr. Little continued: "Are you in pain, my dear Betty?"

To which she replied: "Ho yes, Tom."

253

"In the region of the loins?"

"Ho yes, Tom."

When, translating Mr. Little's question for the physician, I had informed him of the affirmative response that Mrs. Little had made, he said that it was urgent to put the patient to bed and massage the region with an emollient. But how were we to get Mrs. Little back to the hotel?"

We could not take her there on foot, because it was impossible for her to walk, nor in a carriage, because it was impossible for her to sit down.

The physician thought that it was necessary to transport her on a stretcher and he left the basilica immediately in order to give the order one of the *facchini* who are always prowling around the doors of St. Peter's to bring one.

Then he came back.

"*Si tiene in piedi?*"[35] he asked me.

"Well," I said, "she wouldn't be if her husband and I weren't holding her up."

The man from the confessional, who thought himself partly responsible for the accident, then insisted that we take the victim into one of the sacristies until the stretcher arrived.

When we had laid her down on a bench therein, to the great curiosity of the priests who were there, and we had accommodated her head on a cushion, the doctor claimed that it was necessary for him to lift her veil in order for her to be able to breathe. Mr. Little opposed that energetically, as you might think, and even made his wife say, by mean of a clearly audible "no," that she did not want it.

Then the physician took it into his head to take her pulse, and naturally observed a complete lack of pulsations. Nevertheless, he did not want to believe that, and contented himself with saying that the pulse as very weak, almost imperceptible. Doubtless as a check, he applied his ear to the rib cage, where the heart ought to be, and could not hear it beating and more than the pulse. He raised his head, amazed, reapplied his ear,

---

[35] "Is she still on her feet?"

moving his head and if in search of the best place to ausculate, straightened up and took a few paces in the sacristy without saying anything.

Finally, he came back to us and said, in a doctoral fashion: "One can scarcely feel more heartbeat than pulse. If Madame hadn't spoken just now I'd be very anxious, but I assume that the near-annihilation of the pulse and the heartbeat is due to the fright that caused her fall. Soon we can put mustard-plasters on her legs, in order to obtain a good circulation of the blood."

I had a terrible desire to laugh at the diagnostic and therapeutic skills of a doctor who mistook a mannequin for a woman, but I pursed my lips and limited myself to replying: "*Va bene, va bene, si vedra, si vedra.*"[36]

"Perhaps," he went on, "a little bleeding will be necessary."

"*Si vedra, si vedra, Signor Dottore.*"

With his head in his hands, Mr. Little was walking back and forth in the sacristy repeating: "My dear Betty, my dear Betty."

"*Ché dice, il signor inglese?*" said one Monsignor who was in the sacristy, addressing me.

"He's saying: 'My dear Betty," Betty being the name of his wife...it's because he's very upset to see her in such a state."

"I understand," replied the Monsignor.

And the physician added: "The danger is certainly great, but believe me, I'll do everything possible to go get her out of it."

In the meantime, the stretcher arrived; we lay Mrs. Little down on it and we set off for the Hotel di Spagna, unfortunately followed by the Italian doctor, who, doubtless seeing in the English couple clients capable of paying well, was hanging on to his prey, no matter what we tried to do to get rid of him.

---

[36] "That's all right, that's all right, we'll see, we'll see."

For a moment he disappeared, and we thought he had finally yielded to our objurgations, which were conceived in the most gracious terms, but not at all. He had simply gone into the premises of a pharmacist, from which he did not take long to emerge with a box of mustard plasters.

When we arrived at the Littles' room, he went in behind the porters, while I remained discreetly on the threshold.

Having placed Mrs. Little on a divan, the porters left again, but the doctor was still there.

"*Signor dottore*," I called to him.

He approached, and I invited him to go with me, insisting that the invalid needed rest above all, but he did not want to listen to reason, saying and repeating that his professional duty obliged him to remain.

He even engaged Mr. Little, offering to help him undress Mrs. Little and put her to bed, so that he could examine her, palpate her at his ease, discover the internal or external lesions that must have been produced by the fall, and apply the appropriate treatments to them.

You will understand the worthy Mr. Little's embarrassment. He asked me in English by what means it would be possible for him to get rid of that diabolical doctor, and I replied that there was only one that could not fail, which was to pay him to go away.

In an Italian as bizarre as his French, he therefore offered to pay the importunate fellow, and, with that intention, took his purse out of his pocket, but the fellow protested in a dignified manner that they would discuss that later that he would doubtless have to visit Madame several times before she had recovered, and that, in any case, the initial consultation was not concluded, since he had not yet examined the patient.

"No, no," said Mr. Little, with an entirely British sangfroid. "*Andate vin.*" And at the same time, he handed the physician two five-franc pieces—but the latter refused very energetically to take them, still in the name of professional duty.

Thinking that it was perhaps too little, Mr. Little offered twenty francs—further refusal—and then forty francs.

"Soon, if you wish," said the physician, "but once again, allow me to accomplish my professional duty. It is necessary that I first place mustard plasters on your wife, and perhaps draw a little blood."

"Offer him sixty francs," I said to Mr. Little, and perhaps he'll consent to leave us alone."

And, indeed, as Mr. Little took another twenty francs out of his purse. I said to the physician in a confidential tone, as if I wanted to espouse his cause: "Signor, here's a fine sum of sixty francs; believe me, take it, since he absolutely doesn't want to put your science to contribution."

"Monsieur," he replied, haughtily, "I would never accept money that I haven't earned."

"You have earned it, Signor, you have earned it by proceeding with the examination in the sacristy of St. Peter's sending for a stretcher and accompanying us here."

The physician shook his head negatively, and I whispered to Mr. Little to raise the sum to eighty francs. He resigned himself to doing so, but in vain. The physician claimed that we were insulting his professional dignity.

That crampon-physician was beginning to irritate me furiously, so I said to Mr. Little: "Right…offer him a hundred francs, and if he still doesn't make himself scarce, throw him out, and even down the stairs, without giving him anything."

Mr. Little having offered the hundred francs, on my advice, he neither accepted them nor refused them, but represented to us so mildly and so modestly the humiliation to which we were subjecting him, by preferring to pay him for not giving his cares to a patient rather than giving him, that there was some scruple on my part about leaving him in error relative to Mrs. Little's condition.

"What if, in order to get rid of him, while saving his self-respect," I said to Mr. Little, "you were to confess to him that it is not within the competence of a physician but that of a mechanician to treat your poor wife?"

Mr. Little did not reply at first, but he started reflecting on the case. After a few seconds, though, he said to me: "No, no—it's something that no one other than you must know."

"But it must be known in Chester!"

"In Chester, yes, and in a part of England, but I want at least that it should not be so in Italy."

"I won't hide it from you," the physician said to me, "that Madame's condition appears to me to be very grave, to such an extent that it is not impossible that she might die for want of sufficiently prompt treatment while you are deliberating. It seems, in truth, that you have sworn the death of the patent, since you're preventing her from receiving my cares."

Molière, in my place, would certainly have responded to the Italian physician that it was, on the contrary, because we had sworn to preserve the life of the patient that we were preventing her from receiving medical treatment, but I contented myself with smiling and, turning to Mr. Little I said to him in English: "The very persistence that he puts into wanting to employ his art in spite of us shows that he's a idiot. He's so myopic that one might believe that he can see very little. Believe me, to get rid of him, allow him to continue his medical examination, and even allow him to apply the remedies he judges appropriate.

Mr. Little yielded to my arguments. He agreed that he would undress Mrs. Little and put her to bed, after which the physician could do what was necessary.

That was, in effect, how things went.

Before anything else, the doctor examine Mr. Little's face, from which Mr. Little had been obliged to remove the veil, and he soon declared doctorally that the parted lips and the fixed eyes indicated that the poor woman had not recovered the usage of her senses. He went so far as to place his cheek in proximity with Mrs. Little's lips, as if he wanted her to kiss him, which made Mr. Little so indignant that he nearly flew off the handle. But he only did that, in reality, as you will understand, in order to feel the invalid's breath, for, after having said to us fearfully: "*Non sento lo spirito*," he hastened to ask us, for a decisive proof, for a mirror—"*un specchio*"—which we gave him.

Having observed, naturally, that the mirror was untarnished, he remarked, not without naivety, that the signora nevertheless had the complexion of a healthy individual.

All things considered, he judged that nothing was more urgent than to place the mustard plasters, and with that intention, he uncovered the patient's legs—which, in truth were entirely natural, and if nature had not equipped the right foot with a little toe with a nail there was as good an imitation as the one must have ornamented the original.

While the mustard plasters were taking effect—or, rather, not taking effect—Mr. Little made me party to the apprehension he had that they might spoil his wife's artificial skin.

Meanwhile, the doctor was making every effort to ausculate the heart, with his ear applied to Madame's embroidered chemise—without perceiving anything at all, naturally.

After twenty minutes, the mustard plasters having not modified Mrs. Little's condition, he became very anxious. After pacing back and forth in the room several times, silently, with his chin in his hand, he came to where I was sitting, some distance from the bed, and confided to me that the situation was definitely very grave, that the signora might already be dead, that that was in any case greatly to be feared, and that I ought to do my best to prepare the husband for such a cruel event, while he, although there was scarcely any doubt about the circumstance, in order to acquit his conscience would attempt a bleeding, in order to have the proof of it.

I had a mad desire to laugh, but I could not in all decency satisfy it.

Mr. Little, naturally very afflicted by the accident that had overtaken the locomotive apparatus of his pseudo-wife in the basilica of St. Peter, and also bewildered by the truly unexpected behavior of that fool of a physician, was leaning on the night table next to the bed and seemed plunged in an immense chagrin.

Having tapped him gently on the shoulder, I confided to him what the astonishing disciple of Aesculapius had just told me, and I added: "I understand all the pain that this accident to Mrs. Little must have caused you, since, until the mechanician has repaired her, it will be impossible or you to take her on your excursions, but, on the other hand, you ought to be glad to see a physician deceived by her and believing her to be flesh and bone. So much stupidity on his part might even be advantageous to you, by permitting you, when he has certified the death, which cannot be long delayed, to take the body back to Chester in a coffin."

"Yes, but once arrived in Chester I would find myself in a great embarrassment, for everyone knows back there that my Betty is dead and buried. What would they say on seeing the arrival of that coffin, which would not be followed by an inhumation?"

"You'll reveal the matter to the authorities and a few friends, since they already know of the existence of your artificial wife, and they'll admire even more the skill of the mechanician and the good fortune that you have had in still being able to possesses an animated and lifelike image of your wife."

While we were conversing thus, the physician had taken a lancet-case from his pocket and a rolled-up strip of cloth, which he placed on the table, and he brought a bowl from the bathroom, apparently destined to receive Mrs. Little's blood, in the event that any gushed forth.

"It's definitely necessary to carry out a bleeding," he said to Mr. Little. "Allow me to do it."

"But he's going to cut into my poor wife's arm," replied the worthy Englishman, "And there's no longer any means for that wound to form a scar."

"Yes, yes! When the mechanician repairs Mrs. Little, he'll be able to design at the place of the wound a little white line, like those appearing on the arms of people who have been bled. That will add further to the illusion of life. In the meantime, the death will be certified by this skillful doctor;

the blood won't flow, and that's what we need. So let him do it."

Meanwhile, the doctor asked me to hold the bowl under Mrs. Little's arm, which he had laid bare, and which was, believe me, marvelously modeled, with discreetly blue subcutaneous veins in places.

He cut, and, as you might think, not a single drop of blood emerged from the incision.

"I had, in truth, retained some hope," he said, "however faint, because of the appearance of the visage, still colored, but this is the proof that none can remain. The poor woman is really dead. See for yourself. All the blood is in the heart. You will have to prepare your friend for the sad reality. I can't say precisely that it was his fault, but perhaps, without the delays that he brought to the acceptance of my help, we would not have to deplore this misfortune."

"Alas, Signor," I exclaimed, "What must be must be; but since you had the extreme goodness to come to our aid with a zeal that I am pleased to recognize, when the poor woman was still alive..."

"No, no," the doctor interrupted, "she was already dead."

"Yes, but in sum, we hoped that she was still alive. Now she is dead and we know that she is dead, can you not continue your good offices?"

"How?"

"Well, by making the arrangements necessary after a decease, and which our quality as foreigners, only knowing Rome as foreigners know it, does not allow us to make ourselves. I'm convinced that Mr. Little would testify his gratitude broadly."

"But it's not customary," he said, resuming a smile more acute than might have been expected of him, "for physicians to occupy themselves with such things. They can do so less than anyone else, in order not to give purchase to the slander that, after losing the dying, they hang on to them even after death. I can only speak to the owner of the hotel, who will take all the necessary measures diligently. Firstly, is the inhumation to take place at the Campo Santo of Rome or should the body be transported to England."

"It must be transported to England."

"Immediately, or after a sojourn in a temporary crypt?"

I extracted Mr. Little from the dolor in which he appeared to have plunged—and had, in fact—in order to report that further conversation to him and ask him whether he wanted provisional obsequies in Rome for Mrs. Little, in order to remain in the eternal city for a few more days, or whether he preferred to depart the following day or the day after for England, with the apocryphal body of his wife.

He decided on the second alternative, as being more appropriate in two ways, firstly because it avoided the comedy of fictitious obsequies, and secondly because he would be able to replace the once-more-inert body of Mrs. Little in the hands of the mechanician more rapidly.

All the dispositions having been made in concert between the physician and the hotelier, who were remunerated generously, Mr. Little quit Rome the following evening—which is to say, last Saturday—and I believed it to be my duty to accompany him, even though he insisted that I stay, not wanting, he said, to hasten my departure. It was not important to me whether I departed a little sooner or later, for I had known Rome for a long time, and I hope to return there several more times before dying.

On arriving at the railway station in Rome, in the waiting room, I started. The first person who struck my eyes was our physician, whose name as Signor Minelli. I knew his name because I was in possession of his card, and the name was easy to retain, as that of a doctor even more astonishing than Diaforus.

Had he sworn to follow us to England and had he promised to carry out an autopsy of Mrs. Little once removed from her box?

I was afraid of that, but I soon observed that I was mistaken. He was simply going to Civitavecchia, doubtless to give his aid to a moribund.

He darted a slightly inquisitive glance at Mr. Little, whose physiognomy was by then quite plaid, and then asked me in confidence a most unexpected question.

"*Il suo amico voleva molto bene alla moglie?*"[37]

"Very much," I told him. "Never was any woman more loved by her husband. One sometimes speaks of 'loving madly,' and it's almost always an exaggeration, but in this case it's quite literal, I assure you."

"Truly?" he said. "I wouldn't have thought so."

"No similar love has ever been seen," I said, except that of Orpheus for Eurydice, at it's even stronger than that."

Our journey from Rome to Paris went much more agreeably, for me at least, without Mrs. Little than it would have done with her, and although I deplored her first death in Chester, I secretly rejoiced in her second one in Rome.

We are contenting ourselves with passing through Paris; I'm leaving again with Mr. Little for Chester, where the mechanician, alerted by telegram, will in us and determine the repairs to be made to the defunct wife.

If, as is to be feared, they will be considerable, they might last for some time, during which poor Mr. Little is counting on my presence to help him avoid the chagrins that might perhaps be rendered more painful by Mrs. Little's second, entirely artificial, death than by her first, natural one.

At the same time, I shall see his own automaton, of which he had promised to show me its most hidden workings, not having, so far as that one is concerned, the modest reservations that the automaton of his wife inspires in him.

I know already that the automaton in question, which still lacks teeth and hair, since it will inherit the model's, is destined, like that of Mrs. Little, after the death of the proprietor, for Madame Tussaud's. Mr. Little hopes to eternalize in that fashion the memory of a faithful amour that death, thanks to an ingenious subterfuge, was unable to succeed in breaking.

---

[37] "Did your friend love his wife very much?"